Right All Along

Right All Along

A Willamette Valley Romance

HEATHER HEYFORD

LYRICAL PRESS
Kensington Publishing Corp.
www.kensingtonbooks.com

All Kensington titles, imprints, and distributed lines are available at special quantity discounts for bulk purchases for sales promotion, premiums, fund-raising, educational, or institutional use.

Special book excerpts or customized printings can also be created to fit specific needs. For details, write or phone the office of the Kensington Sales Manager: Attn.: Sales Department. Kensington Publishing Corp., 119 West 40th Street, New York, NY 10018. Phone: 1-800-221-2647.

Lyrical and the L logo Reg. U.S. Pat. & TM Off.

First Printing: October 2018
ISBN-13: 978-1-5161-0258-7
ISBN-10: 1-5161-0258-4

eISBN-13: 978-1-5161-0261-7
eISBN-10: 1-5161-0261-4

10 9 8 7 6 5 4 3 2 1

Printed in the United States of America

Acknowledgments

What do you get when you play a country song backwards? You get your house back, you get your wife back, your dog back, your truck back . . .

Joking aside, writing books has given me enormous admiration and respect for songwriters. Ironically, it can be harder to write something short than something long. Every word has to pull its own weight. That's true of all kinds of music, but I'm particularly in tune with country music's midland roots and wordplay that can be funny and thought provoking at the same time.

Often in my books, the hero is the one who needs to learn something. It's been my experience that if men would just open their eyes, things would fall neatly into place! Right, ladies? Then again, if not for that blind spot, we might not need soul-searing love songs and romance novels.

And so I'd like to acknowledge Pat Terry and Travis Tritt for inspiring *Right All Along* with their ballad "Help Me Hold On" about a guy who finally recognizes that his best friend is the love of his life, and who tries to mend the damage he's done while there's still time. I hope you love it as much as I loved writing it.

Chapter One

One of Jack Friestatt's twins ran up to him, rust-colored braids flying out behind her.

Jack's hand went to her upper back in response to her side hug. "Where's Frankie?" he asked, scanning the soccer field. Where there was one twin, the other was usually close by.

"She sprained her ankle," Freddie puffed, pointing to a bench where her sister sat, holding an ice pack on her ankle.

Jack jogged over to Frankie with Freddie on his heels.

Sister Mary Margaret—guidance counselor, French teacher, and girls' soccer coach—excused herself from another parent and came over to where Jack knelt before his daughter.

"What happened?" he asked.

"Bit of a sprain," said the nun in her heavy Kiwi accent. "Might want to wrap it when you ge' home, just ta keep down the swellin'."

"Let me see."

Gingerly, Frankie peeled back the ice pack. Jack saw nothing out of the ordinary, other than that the skin was pink with cold.

"Does it hurt?"

"A little."

"You'll live," he said, giving her a grin and tugging her braid.

"How do you know what it feels like?" spat Frankie, scowling.

What had happened to his sweet little girls over the past several months? One minute they were perfectly complacent, the next they'd started arguing with him and their grandmother over everything.

"Do you 'ave a minute?" asked Sister.

"Hang tight," Jack said to the girls. "I'll be right back."

He and the coach meandered away from the shouting children and the other parents who were arriving to pick up their kids.

"How's the harvest coming along, then?"

May was autumn in New Zealand. "The new vines are finally producing. We're in the midst of our first crush." Speaking of which, there was plenty of work that needed doing. Jack was impatient to get back to it. He glanced behind him at his girls.

"And the twins?"

"Excuse me?"

"Your daughters?"

Why was Sister asking him? She saw the twins every day at school.

"Fine. Why?"

"Their grades might be slipping a bit."

"Maybe a little. But they're not failing anything—are they?"

"I still 'ave their French finals to grade. Tell me . . . is Frances still *enjoying* playing soccer?"

"She's whined a little." *Actually, a lot.* "Don't all kids complain when it comes to doing what they're supposed to do?"

"Middle school can be a difficult time. Children are experiencing change on a daily basis, simply through the process of growing. There are the awkward, physical manifestations. The emotional and hormonal changes that make them that much more vulnerable . . ."

Jack watched his girls from a distance. "What exactly are you trying to say?"

"I wonder if her injury isn't more psychological than physical."

"You think Frankie's faking?" he asked, incredulous.

"Faking's too strong a word. It could be that an injured ankle is an expression of pain she's feeling inside. Is there anyone the girls can talk with about these confusing changes they're experiencing?"

"They can always talk to me," said Jack, becoming a little miffed.

"Of course. They're blessed to have you. Never underestimate the role of a father. But there comes a time in a young girl's life when she might prefer to talk to . . . someone who has been through what she's experiencing. In other words, a maternal figure. Someone consistent, who can ground her when she's feeling unsure. Establish predictable routines."

Jack's mother, the undisputed family matriarch, immediately leaped to mind. Just as quickly, he dismissed her. As much as he respected her and appreciated the help she'd given him since Emily died, Melinda Friestatt was CEO of the family vineyards and winery. Even though they all occupied the same house, she was often busy working. Not only that, he sensed a growing gulf between her and the twins.

Maybe he was spending too much time in the vineyards himself. That's why he'd come to New Zealand from his home in Oregon five years ago, to add sauvignon blanc to his family's growing list of wines. Mother said if he was successful, she would consider granting him a bigger role in running the company.

Or maybe he just hadn't wanted to see it. But now that he thought about it, Sister was right. The twins had begun pushing the envelope.

"I don't want to overstep. St. Catherine's has grown extremely fond of the girls, and we'll miss them when they're gone. But we always knew the day would come when you would take them back home, to America, where they belong. The school year is winding down. Factoring in the state of your business, of course, perhaps now might be a good time."

From the beginning, the plan had been to stay in New Zealand until the new vines produced fruit and then reevaluate.

"Whatever your decision, I know you'll do what's best for your girls." Sister enfolded his hands between hers and patted them. "God bless you."

Chapter Two

Ribbon Ridge, Oregon

Harley Miller-Jones drove through the flat swath of the Chehalem Valley, past modest family farmsteads with ambitious vegetable gardens until she came to rolling hills combed with grapevines.

Slowing, she peered through the windshield up at the grand Victorian mansion crowning the ridge right before she pulled into the driveway of the little concrete-block house she'd grown up in, built during the Depression with economy in mind.

Neither Dad's truck nor Mom's SUV were there. Letting herself in using the key from under the hollowed-out fake rock on the stoop, she set her backpack on a kitchen chair and looked around in the quiet. There was the same shabby-chic living room furniture that had been there forever. She fingered new, printed cotton curtains. Recognized Mom's chicken scratch on a scrap of paper: *detergent—toilet paper—garden center: impatiens.*

For years, Harley had been waiting tables to make ends meet. Finally, her hard work and dedication to her craft were finally paying off. When she'd decided on the spur of the moment to make the three-hour drive from Seattle to tell her folks the news, she should have realized there was a chance they might not be home. Now she'd just have to wait.

Restless, she opened the fridge. Score! Dad's epic lobster mac and cheese . . . his specialty. Dad had always been the cook in the family.

She sat down with a bowl and a spoon and thought about how she used to boost herself up on a cushion at this very kitchen table with her tongue curled over her lip, frowning over her beginner attempts at copying pictures out of library books.

In high school, Harley took every art elective she could, even staying after school sometimes to wash paintbrushes and scrub sinks. Junior year, Mrs. Rhoades entered one of her drawings in a contest. Harley was thrilled when she won. Senior year, she won again. Mrs. Rhoades told her that she had been born with a gift that, with practice and dedication, might be honed into a useful skill. She encouraged her to apply for a scholarship. But Harley had no specific vision for her future. All she knew was that she liked to draw. Not only that, there was no extra money for college tuition. And even if there was, where did you even begin to pick a college? Then there were all those applications and financial aid forms to fill out. Harley's parents had never gone beyond high school, so she knew they couldn't be of much help.

When Mrs. Rhoades realized there wasn't much chance of her continuing her education, she took Harley under her wing. She explained that to understand how shapes work in three dimensions, it was better to draw from life than pictures. The Victorian was the ideal subject. It dominated the view from Harley's bedroom window. In the summer, the sun etched the shadows of the surrounding oaks onto its pale yellow façade. In fall, the turrets peeked through the autumn mists like a castle in a fairy tale. Winter revealed its sharper angles. Harley had drawn it in every season and from every perspective.

By the time she graduated, her house drawings had become her signature. She started selling prints on a popular arts and crafts website, investing her meager profits in higher-quality art supplies: sable brushes, handmade Japanese papers with deckle edges. Having found some success with that, she developed her own website and began selling directly from there.

Bit by bit, her sales grew. Not satisfied with designs on paper, she conceptualized them on dinner plates and researched ways of making that happen. After a few false starts and wrong turns, a dinnerware manufacturer agreed to collaborate with her on a small collection of china. A branding guy came up with the name Honeymoon Haven. While family was of utmost importance to Harley, she'd never been seduced by the idea of the white lace gown or having cake smashed in her face. But she had to admit, the name had a ring to it. Consumers thought so, too. The first and now the second run of Honeymoon Haven dishware had sold out.

An hour later, when neither of her parents had shown up yet, she decided to hell with the surprise and called her mom's cell.

"Hello?" Mom's voice was all but drowned out by jangly music, loud beeps, and chimes.

Harley winced and held the phone away from her ear. "Mom? Where are you?"

"At Dotty's. Where are *you*?"

"I'm here. At home, in Newberry."

In the phone, she heard the telltale metallic ratchet of a handle being yanked.

"Talk louder. These slot machines are so loud I can't hear a thing you're saying."

"I said, I'm *here*. At *your* house."

"Why didn't you tell me you were coming? I'd have stayed home."

"I wanted to surprise you—" she adjusted a light blue iris in a vase, "—and Dad. I'm taking a couple of days off."

"Well, I'm here now, and I just won a hundred dollars on this nickel machine. Whoa!" *Ding-ding-ding-ding.* "Make that a hundred and fifty! Mama's on a roll, baby girl!"

Harley sighed. "Where's Dad?"

"What's that?"

"I said, *where's Dad?*"

"Tillamook. He'll be back early tomorrow morning."

How could she have forgotten? April was spring Chinook season. Dad always took a few days off his job fixing and selling used motorcycles for Joe Bear to go to the cabin. He even let Harley cut school and go with him, before she started high school and got so in to her artwork she didn't want to miss classes.

"Figured it'd be just me tonight, so I headed up here to Dotty's."

"We probably passed each other on the road. How late do they stay open?"

"Two thirty."

If Mom kept winning, they'd have to sweep her out of the casino with a broom.

"I'll wait up for you."

"Oh, honey, don't do that. You know what they say: when you're hot, you're hot. No telling how late I'll be."

Mom might like her slots, but she didn't touch so much as a drop of alcohol. She said she'd seen more than her share of drunks in her dancing days, and she wouldn't be caught dead looking like that. Besides, though she'd given up dancing long ago, she had filled the void with hard-core hiking and yoga. Downward dogs and hangovers didn't mix.

"See you in the morning, then. Be careful driving."

Chapter Three

Harley got up early to catch her parents before Dad had to go to work.

"I have something to tell you," she said as she stirred her coffee. It's about my dinnerware with the Honeymoon Haven motif."

"Cin?" said Dad, hopping on one foot on the backdoor mat, pulling on his work boots. "Throw some of that macaroni and cheese in my lunch bucket, will ya?"

Mom opened the fridge and peered inside. "It's gone."

"Whaddaya mean, gone? There was just some of it left in there yesterday. Who ate it?"

"I did," said Harley. "Last night, for supper." She took a deep breath. "Dad. Mom. The china company wants to expand our brand partnership. Starting next year, my Honeymoon Haven designs are going to be on serveware and table linens . . ."

"Really!" Mom smiled. "Hear that, Tuck? Tucker Jones! How many times do I have to tell you not to wear those boots in the house? I just cleaned the floor."

"Three steps," he said, edging past Mom to get to the freezer. "Just want to show Harley my catch and then I'll be out of your hair." He reached into a plastic bag and carefully withdrew a firm length of silver iridescence with a bright black pupil and a hint of pink along its belly. Dad cradled the fish with hands like meat hooks at the ends of beefy forearms covered in tattoos of cancan girls and mermaids. "How do you like that?"

Harley talked and texted with her parents regularly. Sometimes they even video chatted, though that usually ended with them suddenly remembering something urgent they had forgotten they had to do and had to go without delay. But Dad had an intense physicality that could only be truly appreciated in the flesh. Even if he would never understand the first thing about her work, she adored him. She grinned up at him. "Nice."

"I'll leave 'er out on the counter to thaw and tonight when I get home, I'll clean 'er. You'll be here for supper?"

"I wouldn't miss it."

Dad slid the salmon back into the bag and laid it on a plastic tray on the counter and headed toward the door.

"They also want me to come up with designs for a holiday tabletop line for both china and paper . . ."

"It's trash day," Mom hollered to Dad's back as she cranked on the water in the sink full blast to wash the breakfast dishes. "Don't forget to put the cans out."

"I been taking the trash out for twenty-nine years," said Dad. "I don't think I need instructions."

"That's not all," said Harley, still trying to get their attention. "I'm in talks with a furniture company about doing a full line of home décor, lighting, and bedding."

"How about that? Won't Louise be psyched," said Mom, plunging her yellow rubber gloves into the soapsuds.

Louise and her husband, Abe, owned the Victorian on the ridge. Mom had been making good money as an exotic dancer, but she gave that up when she got pregnant with Harley and started cleaning houses for Newberry's upper crust, of whom Louise was one.

"Louise always got a kick out of hearing me talk about your little drawings. Oh, Tuck? Take the lid off the can. Last time they threw it onto the flowerbed."

"Have you seen the guys that lift them cans? They're kids. What do they care about a few flowers? Few lids won't hurt 'em anyway."

". . . And so, now that I can afford it, I've decided to adopt a baby."

The faucet shut off with a *thunk* and a shudder of the old pipes.

Dad spun around on the threshold and stared at Harley, his forehead furrowed.

For a long moment, the only sound in the kitchen was the muted voice of the local newscaster on the kitchen TV, reporting on the effect of the recent weather on the county's wine grape crop.

"What's this?" Dad walked back to the table like wading through wet cement.

This time, Mom didn't say a word about his boots.

"You heard. I'm going to adopt."

Mom came over to the table, drying her hands on her dish towel, and lowered herself into the chair across from Harley's. "It's hard raising a baby by yourself. Don't you want to wait till you find Mr. Right?"

Mom was a good one to talk; she and Dad had never officially tied the knot. Yet their relationship seemed to grow stronger with time until now, despite their separate interests—or maybe because of them—they were solid as a rock. But apparently, when it came to their only daughter, they had a different set of standards.

"I've given up on finding a man."

"What about one of those dating apps? I thought you said you were on one of them."

"I am. And you're right; it's almost too easy. I can have five guys a night, if I want—"

Dad clapped his hands over his ears and screwed his eyes shut. "Do me a favor, wouldja? Save that kind of talk for after I go to work."

"—but no one I want to have a baby with. My clock is ticking. I'm almost thirty years old. You know how much I've always wanted children. If I can't have any of my own, I'm just going to do it."

"Thirty's nothing. You got plenty of time. Doesn't she, Tuck?"

"You always said how glad you two were to have had me so young," said Harley. "You said you loved growing up along with me."

"Well, sure, but . . ." Dad frowned, while Mom twisted the large turquoise stone Dad bought from a Navajo artisan on a road trip to New Mexico that took the place of a traditional wedding ring.

"Didn't I always say you was artistic?" said Mom finally.

"That's true, Mom. You always did."

Harley's heart warmed. Mom never failed to look on the bright side. People like the Miller-Joneses, who lived paycheck to paycheck, couldn't afford to buy their kids electronic tablets or ski weekends at Mt. Hood. Slim as her pocketbook was, though, somehow Mom had always found money for art supplies. Once, clutching a set of Electro Pop Sharpies Mom had waited a half hour for her to pick out, Harley had peered up at her from where they waited in the line for her weekly lottery tickets and asked, "*Are you sure?*" "*Don't worry about it,*" Mom had barked. And whenever Harley's sketchpads ran out, a ream of snow-white copier paper would mysteriously appear after her next cleaning job.

Dad folded his lower lip between his thumb and forefinger. "How far along are you with this idea of yours? Hell, I don't even know the right questions to ask. What do you do, call up and place your order, like for takeout? Do you get to pick what color eyes it has and if it's gonna be good with its hands?" His eyes widened. "Do you already got one in mind?"

Harley laughed. "As a matter of fact . . . I was having coffee last week with Kelly. She's a web developer who lives in my building. Her husband's a doctor in the Reserves. At the time I moved in, he was deployed. Kelly and I were both new in town and looking for a friend.

"I confided in her about wanting to adopt, and she burst out bawling. Turns out, she just found out she's pregnant."

Dad and Mom exchanged glances.

"She already has two toddlers, born in the same year. They don't want another baby. At least, not right now."

"That's what they say now. What if they change their minds?" asked Mom.

"They'd already talked it through. Even contacted an adoption agency. Anyway, Kelly squeezed my hand so hard I thought it would break, and she was shaking, and we just looked at each other and then *I* started crying and—"*sniff*"—well, to make a long story short, we knew it was a sign." *Sniff.* She snatched a napkin from the basket in the middle of the kitchen table and honked into it.

Mom came over and hugged Harley's head into her pillowy breasts, smothering her in a cloud of patchouli. "Awww, honey. Don't cry. So, they canceled the agency?"

"I found a family lawyer online, and she told me that it can take years to get a baby through an agency, and I should seriously consider what Kelly had to say."

"When is it—" Mom started. "Is it a he or a she?"

"Around Christmas. We won't know the gender until eighteen weeks."

"Long as you can take care of it," said Dad, now somewhat recovered. "The only ones who say money's not everything is the ones who've got it." He kissed the top of Harley's head. "Now I got to go before I fool around and get my ass fired. How long till you go back up north?"

"I thought I'd head back Friday afternoon. I have an appointment Saturday morning with a Realtor."

"Guess you'll be needing some more room, now that there'll be two of you."

"Kelly wants the baby to be raised in a house, not an apartment. That's where she hopes to raise their other kids, and she doesn't want anything less for this one."

"Your first real house!" exclaimed Mom.

"Actually—" she had one more piece of news, "I'm starting a bed-and-breakfast."

"A B and B!?" Mom exclaimed. For the second time, she and Dad exchanged looks. "Don't think we don't go along with your fancy. We're always there for you . . ."

Except when you're off playing the slots or hiking the Appalachian Trail for months on end, thought Harley, bemused. Her parents had always been adventurous types.

". . . but running a bed-and-breakfast won't be easy. The place always has to be neat as a pin."

"I can do it. I have a successful business, remember?"

"No offense, but you were never that big on housecleaning."

So maybe Harley never made her bed when she was still living at home. Come to think of it, she still didn't. It didn't seem important. But she would if she had to.

"I'll be making decent money on my franchise deals, but I'm far from rich. And I'll be raising the baby on my own, so the extra income will come in handy. Because I already work from home, it seems like the perfect solution."

"If that's what you want." Mom lit up. "Why, you ought to come back home here, to Yamhill County! They're slapping up hotels as fast as they can to take advantage of the wine boom, but there aren't enough quaint little places where you can get the real feel of the area. All you got is that swanky resort on the other side of town where a salad'll set you back fifty bucks, or one of those chains on 99, where you need earplugs to drown out the traffic noise so you can sleep at night. Nothing much in between."

Return to Ribbon Ridge? Harley might be a born risk-taker, but that was one risk she would never take. For her, Ribbon Ridge would always be synonymous with Jack Friestatt.

From the day eight-year-old Harley came across Jack in the hedgerow surrounding his family vineyards, they became inseparable. Playing hide and seek between the rows . . . stooping to examine rocks. And especially Jack's favorite thing to play—pirates. Harley drew the maps and Jack swiped his mother's silver spoons to dig for buried treasure.

If not for Emily Redmond, they might still be together today.

The Redmonds, like the Friestatts, had lived on Ribbon Ridge for generations. The two families were twisted together like a grapevine on a wire. Emily and Jack had been born in the same hospital, baptized in the same church, and attended the same parochial school. They went to all each other's birthday parties. The Redmonds and Freistatts even vacationed together, in exotic places like Hawaii and Alaska.

To a kid like Harley, it might as well have been Mars and Jupiter.

There was an unspoken expectation that Jack and Emily were destined for each other. They even had their own nickname—Jemily. Harley shouldn't have been surprised when Jack suddenly married Emily when they were eighteen.

But Harley *was* surprised. More than surprised.

She was devastated. She couldn't bear to stick around and watch Jemily live out their fairy-tale existence. She had left Ribbon Ridge for good.

But once again, fate proved it had no respect for fairy tales. Jack's family moved to the wine country of New Zealand to expand their business. There, five years later, Emily was killed in a car crash.

Yet for Harley, Ribbon Ridge was still steeped in Jack's presence. Every time she came home to visit, in her fertile imagination she still saw him everywhere she looked. His red truck haunted the back roads, his rangy gait stalked down Main Street.

"Mom, aren't you forgetting something? You'll be gone around the time the baby comes. You're going to Spain to hike that Camino-whatever trail."

Mom and her longtime hiking buddy, Blain, had already conquered the triple crown of hiking: the Pacific Crest, the Appalachian Trail, and the Continental Divide. Now they were ready to hike in Europe. Back when Harley was in high school, Mom's unconventional ways raised more than few eyebrows, but Dad didn't seem to mind. Then again, her parents had never believed in sacrificing their individuality to their partnership.

"Camino de Santiago de Compostela."

From the sound of it, Mom had been practicing her Spanish accent. "Right. That one."

"I'll only be gone a month."

"I was going to start looking around the Seattle suburbs. Maybe the Bainbridge Island area."

Mom swallowed back any misgivings she might have had. "Just think. You're going to be famous for your art—"

"That's kind of a stretch." Harley laughed.

"—you're going to buy your first house, and you're having a baby, all at the same time! It's all so exciting, I can't stand it!" She raised her coffee mug in a salute. "Here's to you, baby girl. I can't wait to tell everyone!"

"Hold on. Dad, you too. You can't tell anyone. Not a soul. I don't want to jinx this. Kelly isn't even past her first trimester yet."

"Then when? How long do you expect me to hold on to news this juicy? I don't know if I can stand it."

"I don't know yet. It's all still brand-new. Now, listen. I wanted you to be the first to know. But you're going to have to play along with me, do it my way until I give you the word. Do you promise?"

"My lips are sealed," said Dad. "See you tonight."

Across the table, Mom looked doubtful. "I'll try, but I still don't know why—"

"Mom! Promise."

She sighed. "If you say so. I'll do my damnedest."

Harley poured herself another cup of coffee while Mom moved efficiently around the kitchen, putting her own house in order before going off to straighten someone else's.

Harley knew she could trust Dad. Mom, she wasn't so sure.

Chapter Four

A week later, Harley was walking to her neighborhood coffeehouse in the rain when Mom called.

"How's the house-hunting going? Find anything that strikes your fancy?"

"Not yet—" Crap! She hopped out of the puddle she'd stepped in, cold water dripping from her sandal. "—but we've just started looking."

That wasn't completely true. She'd looked at no fewer than a dozen properties, but all of them were either laid-out wrong or on a busy street where a child couldn't safely ride a bike or too far from the main tourist sites. She was merely aping what the Realtor had told her Saturday after a long day of looking. But she wasn't quite as impulsive as she used to be. She'd done a bit of her own research. Every place remaining on her list was a compromise. Then again, maybe she was setting her sights too high.

"What's new with you?"

"I was just talking to Louise . . ."

An Asian woman sporting blue hair and fishnets tipped her head sideways to avoid Harley's umbrella.

"Anyways, the Grimskys are taking their dream trip to Italy, and then they're retiring to Arizona. They already picked out a place down there. I've started helping them pack up their stuff."

"Wait." Harley's feet froze on the sidewalk. "What?"

"They're taking a long vacation—"

"No. Go back. The Grimskys are moving? They're putting the Victorian up for sale?"

"Didn't I tell you? Louise is getting her hip replaced. She won't be able to do stairs for a while, so instead of waiting, they're going to move first and have the surgery down there so she can recover in her new home. She made me be sure to pack the framed print you gave her—you know which one, that best seller—so she can hang it on her wall down in Arizona. It's one of those fifty-five-and-over places that's all on one—"

"The Grimskys are selling, and you waited until today to tell me?"

There was a pause on the phone. "When was I supposed to tell you?"

"Yesterday. Before that. The very second you found out."

"How was I supposed to know that? Listen. You remember the Grimskys couldn't have kids. When I told them you're adopting a baby, Louise told me to invite you up to see the house."

"I told you not to tell anyone about the baby!"

"It's just the Grimskys."

"Mom!"

A lumbersexual in a plaid shirt whose grooming

was better than hers dodged her, and she realized she was standing in the center of the busy sidewalk. Her feet began moving again.

"Do you really think the people down in Tucson are going to give two hoots about what Miss Harley Miller-Jones from Newberry is up to?"

"Seattle. I've been in Seattle for ten years." By now, she was practically a native. The barista at the coffee-house brought her usual without being asked. She could point out Kurt Cobain's house to tourists, and she knew never to visit Pike Place Market on a Saturday.

"Once word gets out, it's just a matter of time before other people find out."

"I don't get what the big deal is. In today's world, people *need* good news. Matter of fact, they crave it. Is this because of Jack?"

Harley tensed. Mom knew how badly Jack had hurt her. If it hadn't been for him, she never would have left Newberry.

"Because Jack's been gone going on five years now. He's a whole hemisphere away—as far from Ribbon Ridge as you can get. You don't have to worry about running into him anymore."

She stooped to deposit her usual folded bill into the hat of the homeless guy who lived at the corner. "I could never afford the Victorian anyway."

Mom sighed. "You'll never know if you don't ask. We can go up and see it when you're here Saturday for my birthday. What have you got to lose?"

No fair pulling out the birthday card. "I'll think about it."

"Oh, good. Louise will be thrilled."

"I didn't promise anything . . ."

"You can go to my goat yoga class with me, too."

She groaned inwardly. Harley and yoga had an on-again, off-again relationship. She only went back when enough time had passed between classes for her to forget how grueling it was.

"It *is* my birthday."

Harley sighed heavily. "Okay." After they said good-bye she dropped her phone into her bag. But a door she had slammed shut all those years ago had cracked open, and a sliver of light shone through.

Chapter Five

The following Saturday

Harley stared at a spot on the wall, hands in prayer position, trying to balance on one foot.

"Breathe . . ." said the instructor.

Easy for you to say. Sweat trickled down between her shoulder blades. She bet not even B.K.S. Iyengar could hold tree pose for long with a goat licking the sensitive spot behind his knee. The barely stifled giggles of the other yogis didn't help matters any.

Whoa . . . *oof.* The straw beneath her mat rustled as the kid skipped blithely away.

Time crawled while she tried to maintain the pose. She looked around for a clock to watch, but barns didn't typically have clocks, and this one was no exception. Note to self: *Yet another reason not to do goat yoga.* They were piling up. She wrinkled her nose. *Piling up . . . literally.*

The instructor was speaking again. "Lying on our

backs, we're going to go into bridge. So, bending our knees, placing our feet close to our sit bones. And now, class, if your body wants to—"

My body definitely does not *want to.* But she refused to admit defeat. Mom was twice Harley's age, and her body was as supple as a seal's.

"—*press* your feet and arms actively into the floor, *lift* your heels, and *push* your tailbone toward your pubis. Annnnnd *breathe . . .*"

Pubis? Carefully, so as not to snap a neck vertebra, Harley turned her head to where Mom was rocking an awesome bridge. On her stomach stood a darling brown goat with a pink nose. Harley had to admit, his practice had done wonders for his balance.

"Whew! That was amazing," said Mom afterward, her mat bag slung over her shoulder, hydrating herself as they walked to the car. "Hey! I have an idea. You should offer goat yoga at your B and B."

Harley couldn't speak. She was still trying to catch her breath.

"What's going on with the little one? Fill me in."

Amazing how the slightest mention of her baby helped her recover. "I brought something to show you," she panted.

The moment they were seated in her car, she pulled her phone from her bag and pulled up the photo.

Mom gasped. "There he—she—?" she looked questioningly at Harley.

"It's a boy." Harley beamed. "I'm going to have a son!"

"A son!"

"There's his little, you know." She pointed to a pin-dot on the sonogram. "See?"

Mom held the photo closer to her face and squinted. "I'm not sure."

"Right there," said Harley, trying not to take offense. "Look closer."

"Hm." Mom shook her head and handed it back to Harley. "I'll try looking at it with my readers when we get home. Meantime, Louise'll be expecting us."

Minutes later, Harley and her mom walked slowly up the stone walkway leading to the Victorian, admiring the colorful annuals coming into bloom. Gazing around at the broad porch and up at the aqua-painted ceiling, she grew excited despite herself. As many times as she'd drawn this house . . . fantasized about living in it . . . she'd never dreamed that one day she'd actually be standing on its threshold.

The carved wood door opened to an elegant woman with close-cropped silver hair, hooded blue eyes, and a hint of an overbite. Fine chains of platinum and diamonds encircled the crepey skin on her neck. "Cindy, come in. Harley. I've heard so much about you, I feel like I already know you. I'm sorry it's taken this long for us to meet." She stepped aside with a sway of her caftan, revealing a cream-colored foyer, high ceilings, and a parquet floor.

Mom had always been easily impressed by the places she cleaned. She talked about them so much, they all started to sound the same. Now it was Harley's turn to be impressed. She handed her hostess the present she'd brought.

"What's this?"

Following the success of her debut collection, Harley had come up with a set of related drawings

depicting the house in all four seasons. "A little me-
mento to remind you of your Ribbon Ridge house,
after you move."

Louise leaned her cane against the wall. With a
vein-roped hand she accepted the package, peeled
back the wrapping paper, and shifted through the
dessert plates with open admiration. "Cindy. Why
didn't you tell me the new designs were out?"

"You can't buy them in any store," Harley interjected. "These are one-of-a-kind digital proofs given
to me by the manufacturer."

"For me? How thoughtful. I can't wait to show
Abe." She carefully set the stacked dishes on a table
in the foyer and retrieved her cane. "How would you
like a tour?"

Harley and Mom exchanged glances. "Only if it's
no trouble."

"We're trying to sell, remember? The more people
who go through it, the better. Follow me."

Louise led them to an airy sitting room with a marble fireplace and floor-to-ceiling windows.

"As you can see, we've already gotten rid of a lot of
things. Our place in Arizona is much smaller, so no
sense taking them with us. What's left either doesn't
fit in the southwest or just seems to belong here. I
thought I would leave them and see if the new owner
wanted them." She turned to the pile of moving
boxes in the corner. "Your mother has been an enormous help. I don't know how I could have done it
without her."

"I didn't see a For Sale sign in the yard," said
Harley.

"Abe and I have been going back and forth about
which Realtor to use. We each have a close friend in

the business. But I think we've finally made a decision. The sign will be going up tomorrow."

Harley drifted across the parquet floor to the dining room, pared down to a crimson-colored chair and an antique sideboard in a honey-colored wood. Above it hung two modern prints of poppies.

Next, they came into a cozy parlor with a simple, matte-black fireplace surround topped by a large round mirror. An oversize ottoman, like a giant's pincushion in yellow tufted velvet dominated the center of the room, beneath a chandelier of multicolored glass teardrops.

Behind Louise, Harley rolled her eyes and mouthed, *oh my gosh* to her mom. In return Mom lifted a brow, as if to say, *didn't I tell you?*

Louise gestured to the room at large. "I have so many fond memories of this room." She sighed. "The whole house, really. It's a good house. Abe and I spent many happy years here. He'll be back in a bit. He's out taking Fancy for a walk."

Louise approached the staircase, caftan flowing out behind her. "Would you like to see the upstairs?"

"Are you sure?" asked Harley, with a glance at Louise's cane.

"Oh, this pesky thing." She smiled. "Despite what it looks like, I'm not an invalid." She was already dragging herself up the staircase with the aid of the handrail.

The second floor continued the theme of ivory walls, parquet floors, and chandeliers.

The first room they came to had a wall consisting entirely of bookshelves. A ladder to reach the uppermost shelves leaned against it.

"The study, obviously." Louise strolled over to the

tall window and opened it to the warm summer day. A breeze sent the sheer white curtains billowing. "As you can see, it gets full afternoon sun. I always thought it would make a wonderful artist's studio."

Chills went down Harley's spine. As an only child, she had imagined the Victorian's interior hundreds of times, filled with laughing children. But the reality far surpassed anything she could have dreamed up.

The house had an airy ambience. Harley followed Louise through arched double doorways, across marble bathroom floors.

"The nursery," said Louise. A wrought-iron bassinette of painted wood stood against a wall, and a matching crib stood in the center of the room. "We won't be needing this furniture either, where we're going. This room has the best view. Come over here and look out. You can see all the way across the valley."

Mom elbowed Harley, bringing her out of her reverie of tickling little toes and bedtime stories; first days of school and blowing out birthday candles. She drifted toward the window where she closed her eyes, placed her hands on the frame, and then opened them. Spread out before her lay the Chehalem Valley as she had never seen it before. Long seconds passed as her eye traveled over familiar vineyards and meadows and farmettes, but from a fresh perspective. And then, she looked straight down and saw the house she'd grown up in. From here, it seemed infinitesimally small and insignificant.

Her heart thumped wildly. As familiar as she was with the Victorian, never until this moment had she ever fathomed the possibility of owning it. But now that she was here, she couldn't bear the thought of letting it go.

"We went so far as to convert its bathroom into a laundry room." Louise smiled wistfully. "We never did manage to fill the nursery. But this saved me many a trip up and down the stairs lugging a heaping laundry basket over the years."

Possibilities filled Harley's head to overflowing. *Why couldn't she have felt like this about any of the houses her Realtor had shown her?* "How many bedrooms are there?"

"Six, each with its own bath. The mattresses might be old, but they're in great condition. None has been slept on more than a few times."

Perfect for a B and B.

Downstairs, a door opened and closed. "Louise?" shouted a man's voice.

"Up here. I'm showing Harley the house."

Footsteps plodded up the steps and across the floorboards.

Louise turned sideways.

"So," said a voice behind Harley, "this is the artist I've heard so much about."

Harley turned to see a man with a determined face wearing an Argyle-patterned sweater vest. "I'm more of a designer," she replied.

"Now her designs are going to be on linens, too," gushed Louise. "Can you imagine? Our house is going to be famous."

"Do you have a card?" asked Abe.

Outside of the business, it was the first time anyone had asked for one. By the look on her face, Harley thought Mom might burst with pride. "What's the asking price?" she blurted.

"Mom—" Like there was even an outside chance Harley could afford this.

"It's a perfectly reasonable question," replied Louise. "We thought—"

At the number Louise quoted, Harley's balloon of excitement burst and sank slowly to the floor.

Fifteen minutes later, she and Mom were headed back to the car. "What did you think?" asked Mom in a voice filled with maternal hope.

Harley forced her gaze away from the house and onto the brick walk. "There's no way, even with my advance. My merchandise is still in the production phase."

"But once it's out there in the stores . . ."

"Seriously, Mom," said Harley, her frustration finding its way into her voice, making her sound impatient. Didn't Mom realize she wanted the Victorian every bit as much as Mom wanted her to have it? "That house is way beyond my reach. But thanks for bringing me here. It was really nice of the Grimskys to show me around."

When Harley got a call from an unknown number on her drive back to Seattle, she almost didn't answer, thinking it was a sales call. But something told her she should.

"Miss Miller-Jones? Abe Grimsky. After you left, Louise and I had a little talk."

Harley's ears perked up.

"I'm retired now, but I was in business for a half century. Started out with nothing, ended up not so bad. I did it all for Louise. My wife is everything to me. As time went on, there wasn't much I couldn't give her. Not many places I couldn't take her to. The one thing she wanted that I could never give her was a child."

It was a lovely sentiment. But why—?

"I saw you today, looking at the nursery."

A jumble of emotions went through Harley. Surprise at Abe's phone call. Compassion for the Grimskys, who had everything except what they wanted most. And a budding anticipation.

"Louise saw you, too. I watched her, looking at you. As I said, there's nothing I wouldn't do to make her happy. And nothing would make her happier than to know the little one of the designer of those dishes was growing up in that nursery. That's why I'd like to give you the chance to offer on the house before we sign the Realtor contract tomorrow."

"Excuse me?"

"What was the point of working so hard all those years if I can't indulge myself in the end?"

"Mr. Grimsky, I know what the asking price is. It's way out of my price range."

"Listen to me, young lady. I built that house with my own two hands, back before you were a light in your mother's eye. Before anyone around here even heard of pinot noir, when the Chehalem was nothing but a forest of filbert orchards. Practically every dollar I get back will be pure profit."

"But still . . ."

"Want some free advice from a successful businessman? Don't look a gift horse in the mouth. Hang up the phone, sit down tonight when you get home, and take a look at your finances, then call me in the morning and let me know your decision."

Chapter Six

September, three months later

Jack's mother arched her lower back as far as she could within the confines of her safety belt. "I just got an email from my cousin Judith, the Realtor," she said, looking at her phone. "The property on the corner of Ribbon Ridge Road is for sale."

"The Victorian?"

Squeezed next to each other on the plane, they spoke quietly.

"Judith was angling to get the listing. It was as good as hers until out of the blue, the Grimskys found a buyer on their own on the very day they were to have signed the listing agreement. They're set to finalize the deal tomorrow morning."

Jack turned from his window view of the rocky Oregon coastline. "And?"

"Jack. Isn't it obvious? That land should be ours."

"It can't be, what? Two, three acres?" The Grimskys' small parcel of ground was undeniably valuable, but acquiring it wouldn't make a huge difference in the company's bottom line.

"That's a thousand cases of wine."

"A drop in the bucket, considering we're yielding a quarter million cases a year." He tipped his head sideways to stretch out the kink in his neck.

"It's the most southeastern slope on Ribbon Ridge. There's no better aspect for growing wine grapes."

"Seems to me it'd be the house you'd be after. You always talked about what a great B and B the Victorian would make."

Melinda had been hoping her son hadn't been paying attention or wouldn't remember all the times she'd mentioned converting the Victorian herself. But it was true. The house had charm galore and was in the ideal setting for tourists to the wine country.

She knew more about the sale than she let on. According to Judith, the prospective buyer was none other than Harley Miller-Jones. Harley had always had an artist's eye. No doubt she had seen the Victorian's potential, too.

Melinda had been steering her son away from Harley all his life. Now, if it looked like she was competing with her for a vanity project, she would seem like Goliath to Harley's David. Jack would be sure to take Harley's side.

"The timing's pure luck. The second we land you need to figure out how you can snatch it up. Ryan's handling the transaction on the Grimskys' behalf."

Jack glanced at his wrist. "Mother," he said, his head falling back onto the headrest, his eyes closing. "It's already after five. Ryan's office will be closed."

"It seems like days since we boarded in Auckland," sighed Mother. "I've lost all sense of time."

What Jack wouldn't do for his Dad's input at times like these, to balance out his mother's strong opinions. But though Dad was long gone, Jack was still struggling to stand up to Mother. He often thought it would be far easier if she were working against him. Yet, deep down he knew that everything Mother did, she did with what she firmly believed were his best interests at heart.

When Jack was thirteen, he and Mother accompanied Dad to Portland, where he was running a marathon. Their job as cheering committee was to hoot and holler when the starter shot his pistol, then scurry down side streets to a predetermined mile marker. Easier said than done in an unfamiliar town of steep hills, even with a map on Jack's phone. GPS wasn't always reliable. Sometimes they got lost and had to backtrack, forcing them to jog if they were going to reach their destination in time to wave Dad on.

When they finally got to 13.1, the popular halfway point swarmed with other supporters, they found a spot and waited, craning their necks and panting as if they were running the race themselves. Jack tried to maneuver his hand-lettered sign reading *It's a hill—get over it*, in front of all the other ones, checking the time every thirty seconds.

Dad's ETA came and went. Another five minutes went by. Ten. Dad was young and fit. *Maybe he stepped on a rock and twisted his ankle*, said Mother.

After twenty minutes they started walking against

the flow of oncoming runners. They hadn't walked far when they saw a small huddle of people hunched over something on the ground and heard the siren.

Some Good Samaritan offered them a ride and they followed the ambulance to the hospital, but despite repeated, frantic attempts with the defibrillator, Dad never regained consciousness. Hours passed in a slow blur until Alfred, the Friestatts' vineyard manager, arrived and Mother fell into his arms. Finally, they all drove back home in stunned silence.

Don Friestatt had been the scion of one of Ribbon Ridge's founding families. In a heartbeat, Jack became the sole heir to vast acres of vineyards and a thriving wine business.

When they pulled up to the estate, there were already lots of vehicles spilling out of the driveway. Inside, relatives, friends and strangers alike rambled through the spacious house, swirling their drinks, telling Jack that now he was the man of the family and it was up to him to take care of his mother and the business.

But Jack wasn't a man. He was a boy. The reality was that from that time on, his mother had set the pace, made all the important decisions. Not just for the family wine business, but for everything.

"First thing tomorrow morning, then," said Mother. "Head over to Ryan's office. Find out what the buyer is offering and top it. Make the Grimskys an offer they can't refuse."

She sighed confidently. "What with managing estates in both Marlborough and Oregon, plus the winery, you're going to be busier than ever. The next order of business is finding you a new wife. There'll never be another Emily, but you can look for someone as much like her as possible. Someone biddable and reliable. A wife, a mother, and an advocate."

Jack stretched his legs as far as the seatback in front of him would allow. "You're a businesswoman yourself. Hasn't the idea of the traditional, corporate wife become somewhat of an anachronism?"

"Wife—or husband, for that matter—the spouse of a high-profile business owner provides an essential support role. There's no shame in that. It's a unique and specialized job. Few people are cut out for it."

His and Emily's relationship might never have been white-hot, but in the five years they were man and wife, they'd settled into a cooperative existence. Emily had taken on the lion's share of raising the twins and managing their social life. Not that Jack wanted to avoid parenting and spending time with friends. But as Arabella Cellars' estate manager, he was his mother's second in command in charge of production, hiring and firing, infrastructure, and R&D. He spent long days on the phone, in the fields, and in his office.

"I've been doing a little research, and I already have a promising candidate in mind," said Mother. "Judge Mitchell's daughter, Prudence. Gustave has invested wisely over the years."

"Prudence?" Jack pictured one of the stars of his girl's high school soccer team. She was known for wearing a tracksuit, both on the field and off. "Pru never married?"

"No. And—she's an only child."

Emily had died before inheriting her family's land. That left Jack back at square one, as far as Mother was concerned.

"What's Pru been doing with her life?"

"After earning her master's and her CPA, she started her own accounting firm. If she's anything like our accountant, she's organized, trustworthy, and has excellent time management skills. That, plus her obvious appreciation of athletics was what caught my eye."

A distant view of snow-capped Mt. Hood appeared through Jack's window, a sign that they were almost home. As much weight as Mother put on Judge Mitchell's wealth, Jack had his own reasons for seeking a new partner. Sister Mary Margaret's advice stuck in his head. Maybe she was right. Maybe a new mother was exactly what the twins needed to turn them back into the sweet little girls they'd been until puberty hit.

And while Pru was more likely to make the cover of *Sports Illustrated* than its swimsuit issue, that was precisely the point. He wasn't looking for love. What he was looking for was a sensible, steady, and practical mother to help him keep a tight rein on two high-strung adolescents.

"You talked to the judge?"

"I took pains to maintain ties with all my influential friends in Oregon while we were overseas. I'll text you Prudence's cell phone number. She's expecting to hear from you as soon as we get settled in."

Chapter Seven

Ribbon Ridge
The next day

Harley skipped up the steps to the law offices of Ryan O'Hearn Associates, scarlet leaves crunching beneath the soles of her buttery leather boots. Her mood matched the spring in her step. A decade ago she'd left Newberry for the big city with nothing but her portfolio full of drawings and a broken heart. Now she was coming home, a strong, self-made woman.

Home . . . endless, rolling vineyards. Wildflower meadows to roam in place of crowded sidewalks. Goat yoga. Deep down, Harley's heart had never left wine country.

But she wasn't coming home to the little block house. She was about to purchase the home of her dreams. And what better time than harvest? The air hung with the heady scent of ripening grapes while the vineyards swarmed with pickers' brightly colored jackets.

A glass door opened silently to a sleek reception area. Her eye skimmed over the quality chrome and glass furnishings, and she shrank a little. Then she squared her shoulders and smoothed down her new, watered silk kimono. Her outfit was as far as you could get from the days when she'd excused away her thrift shop wardrobe by claiming to have a thing for vintage.

"Harley Miller-Jones. I have a nine o'clock appointment," she said, her breathlessness giving away the butterflies in her stomach.

"Have a seat," said the receptionist, rising. "I'll tell Ryan you're here."

Ryan, not Mr. O'Hearn. That casual attitude was what distinguished towns like Newberry from their more cosmopolitan neighbors. Harley noticed details like that. Little things, like the black silhouette of tree branches against an autumn sunset, the endless variation of green in a summer landscape, the textural contrast between pinecones, rough in her palm, and fat, purple grapes, threatening to burst with the slightest pressure.

Forget sitting. She snatched the latest issue of *Wine Spectator* from the coffee table and flipped through it as she paced impatiently before the masculine gray sofa.

Ryan O'Hearn materialized with a smooth smile and an outstretched hand. "Harley."

One glimpse at his well-cut suit and crisp white shirt, combined with the cold, hard press of his gold signet ring against her skin, brought the past rushing back to her—the chasm that existed between the haves and the have-nots, back when she was growing up in this town. Harley's mom was once a stripper. Her dad had ridden with an outlaw motorcycle gang. To this day, they had never seen fit to make their union legal. But after the check she'd just deposited into her bank account at the signing of her latest design contract, there was no longer a reason for Harley to feel inferior . . . less than.

"Hi."

There was surprised approval in Ryan's eyes as they flickered over her. "Last time I saw you—" He bit his tongue.

"The country club." She'd waited regularly on Ryan and his extended family at the big table outside, under the pergola.

"Still ordering your steak medium rare?"

He was too well-bred to take the bait. He smiled thinly. "How've you been?"

"Fine," she said automatically.

"I seem to recall you liked to draw, back in the day."

At the implication that she couldn't possibly be making a living from her art, she cringed. But there was a reason for the term *starving artist*. And expecting noncreatives to understand the innate drive to paint or write or sculpt was like some jock expecting Harley to one day work up to a seven-minute mile. Wasn't going to happen.

She'd come a long way since then. She lifted her chin and looked Ryan in the eye. "More than fine."

"Let's head over to the conference room, shall we?" Ryan extended his arm toward a hallway.

The thick carpeting absorbed their footsteps. *Pretty sure I'll never be using words like* shall, *even if I get as big as Kate Spade,* she thought. In that instant, it registered: The difference between old money and new.

Abe Grimsky had prepared Harley not to expect him or Louise to be present today. He'd hired Ryan to represent them. Abe had said he didn't anticipate any glitches. It was a simple matter of signing the papers. One stroke of her pen and the Victorian would be hers.

Ryan opened the door and stood aside, revealing a long, polished wood table surrounded by leather swivel chairs. At the opposite end, a man with a head of wavy hair that touched his collar rose to his feet and adjusted a silver cuff link. His artfully rumpled shirt, jeans, and tweed jacket with the collar popped up exuded the certainty of a man who labored for pleasure rather than profit. The quintessential gentleman farmer.

Harley's breath caught. A deliciously familiar masculine scent stirred a thousand memories. Her heart slammed against her ribs. It's him. *It's him it's him it's him.* Her eyes flew to his, and a shared flash of recognition bound them together. Would the day ever come when she could run into Jack Friestatt without her pulse going haywire?

In a dither she whirled around to Ryan. "What's *he* doing here?"

The three of them had gone to Newberry High—although Ryan had graduated before they'd started. Sat in the same classrooms, studied the same subjects. Ate lunch in the same cafeteria. But outside the chain-link fence surrounding the athletic fields, their lives couldn't have been more different.

The O'Hearns and the Friestatts were as entangled as the vines covering Ribbon Ridge, planted generations before by descendants of the first Henry Friestatt. Jack's winery, Arabella Cellars, was named for Henry's wife.

And then there was regular, middle-class Harley.

Dazed and desperately outnumbered, she returned her gaze to Jack.

"Harley!" *God almighty,* thought Jack. "It's been ten years . . ." Ten years, and he still couldn't look at her without seeing drops of wine spilling onto her tied-up T-shirt, the night of his bachelor party.

He remembered her like it was yesterday. Untamed waves of curly chestnut hair caressed the shoulders of her denim jacket. He used to tell her it would be a crime to get it cut. It was insane, but now he wanted desperately to believe the fact that she hadn't was, in some small part, in deference to him. After all these years, she made him believe there might still be a tiny part of him that hadn't been bridled, cinched, and buttoned-down.

The years had been kind to her. Her skin glowed with health and the way the fabric of her dress draped her curves was indicative of its quality. But her chestnut hair still billowed out around her head, as out of control as ever. He shifted his gaze above her neck, hoping that would slow the blood rushing through his veins like whitewater. Hard as he'd tried—and he'd tried plenty hard—he'd never been able to forget her. As the years had gone by, he'd conveniently put out of his mind the sour note on which they had ended. But judging from the fire in her eyes, *she* hadn't.

"The question is, what are *you* doing here?"

Ryan stepped toward them, ready to intervene if need be. "I would have notified you sooner," he said to Harley, "but I'm as surprised as you are."

Jack's eyes glittered, as if nothing were amiss. As if the transgression that had come between them could be brushed away as easily as the piece of lint on his shoulder.

"You left the day I got married."

Of course. Jack couldn't forget his anniversary, even if he wanted to, and why would he want to—even if he'd been a widower for half the time they'd been apart?

A slow burn crept up her neck. *And she'd told herself she was over him.*

He didn't seem to notice. Why should she be surprised? That was the infuriating thing about Jack . . . the thing that had always driven her crazy. As close as they'd been, Jack had never made Harley any promises. They were nothing but live and let live. One minute they were making out in the bed of his truck and the next he was walking another woman down the aisle without a backward glance. They might have been casual, but she was human. Her feelings had been crushed.

Now, here she was again, like Pavlov's dog, salivating when he deigned to pay her attention.

The room swirled. Harley's hands grew clammy and her tongue felt thick. She grabbed the back of the nearest chair. When she could trust herself to walk, she aimed her body in his direction. Then she put every ounce of concentration on placing one foot in front of the other, hoping her knees wouldn't fail her. She didn't stop until she was frowning straight up at Jack, and his chin backed into his neck a centimeter. "What's going on?"

Jack pulled out a chair for her and waited, aristocratically shaped hands, roughened by hard work, curved over its back. "You're looking well."

It struck Harley that Jack would be polite even if bombs were falling around them. But his forced smile gave away a rare inner hesitancy. He failed to meet her glare. For once in his charmed, storybook life, he looked out of place.

"Let's sit down, shall we?"

"Again with the *shalls*," she muttered under her breath, lowering herself into the chair.

"So, what's up with the house?" Jack asked Harley. If anyone knew how much that house meant to her, Jack did. At what he was about to do, his stomach felt queasy. But if Mother thought they should have it . . .

Harley huffed with indignation. "I'm buying it. That's what's up. The question is, why are you here? You're supposed to be in New Zealand."

There was a bitter taste in Jack's mouth as he slid a map out of a leather folder. With the Friestatt buying power, snatching it from Harley's grasp was going to be a cinch. "The Grimsky property is adjacent to my vineyards."

"So?"

"It's the only parcel on that side of the ridge I don't own. It only makes sense for me to acquire it."

"What do you need another house for?"

What, indeed. The entire Friestatt estate would one day be his, including the rambling farmhouse to which he, his daughters, and his mother had just returned the night before.

Her eyes widened in realization. "You're planning on tearing the Victorian *down*?"

He winced inside. "Now, Harley. Calm down. Everyone knows you had a special . . . attachment to the Victorian. But time moves on. This is business. You understand."

"That stunning example of architecture—razed, for the sake of a few more vines? Are you insane? Have you been inside it?"

"There's a real estate term—highest and best use. Ribbon Ridge is one of the most coveted viticultural areas in Yamhill County. The best use of that slope is for growing grapes. It's a fact. Ask anyone."

"Tsk. Well, that's too bad. I beat you to it. The Grimsky place is mine."

"Not until the paperwork's signed."

"That's why I'm here." She clicked her plastic pen advertising the Turning Point Tavern. "Ryan? The papers?"

"Not so fast," said Jack.

She looked at Ryan incredulously. "Can he do this?"

Ryan's hands fell open in helplessness. "We don't have anything in writing yet."

"But you said—"

"I wasn't present during your impromptu chat with the Grimskys before they left. I haven't made you any personal guarantees."

"That's not fair and you both know it." Her cheeks felt hot, and her chest was rising and falling rapidly.

"No offense, Harley, but Abe Grimsky is my client, and I have to do what's in his best interest. I owe it to him to hear Jack out . . . to obtain the best possible deal for him."

"Does Mr. Grimsky know about this?"

"Don't blame Ryan," said Jack. "Like he said, I didn't tell him I was coming. I just showed up five minutes before you. We only found out the property was for sale last night."

"We?"

"My mother and I."

"How did—"

"Her cousin Judith is a Realtor."

Harley's shoulders slumped. "Is there anyone in this town you're not related to? Sure puts those few of us whose last name isn't Friestatt or O'Hearn at a disadvantage."

"Harley. I'm all my mother has. I have a responsibility to her and to the estate."

Harley's eyes pleaded first with Ryan, then Jack. "What do you expect me to do—just hand it over?"

"It's not yours to hand over," said Ryan with maddening calm.

"It will be, as soon as I sign those papers."

The tension expanded to fill the room.

"I'm calling Mr. Grimsky," she said finally.

Harley punched in Abe Grimsky's number and put her phone on speaker so there would be no further misunderstandings.

> *You've reached Abe.*
> *Ciao! Louise, here.*
> *We can't come to the phone right now. We're probably chowing down on some good pappa al pomodoro as we make our way through Tuscany. If it can't*

*wait until Thanksgiving, you can call my lawyer,
Ryan O'Hearn. We'll try to leave some room for
turkey.*

   Ciao!

As Harley's phone clattered to the table, her elbows came down on the conference table and she
sank her forehead into her hands. *Seriously? Thanksgiving?*

Jack was right—she *was* sentimental about the
house. But her need for it was very real. She had a baby
on the way. She pictured the curled-up fetus, snug inside the safety of the birth mother's belly. Right now,
he was only about the size of an orange, but he was
growing bigger and stronger every day. Harley already loved him almost beyond endurance.

She'd gone to great lengths to describe to Kelly
the spacious house on the hill where her child could
run barefoot through the meadow and sleep with the
windows open to the summer breezes that blew in
from the Gorge. By Thanksgiving he would be fully
viable, able to survive outside the womb should Kelly
happen to go into early labor. Everything had to be
in place.

She couldn't bear to think about what might tran-
spire if the worst happened and he arrived early and
she didn't have her house in order. Her stomach
roiled, and she tasted her breakfast for a second
time, imagining the horror of it spread out in a half-
digested heap on Ryan O'Hearn's gleaming wood
conference table.

"I have an idea." Ryan ripped two sheets of paper
off his yellow legal pad and slid one toward each of

them. "Why don't you each bid, and we'll let the Grimskys decide?" At Harley's look of skepticism, he added, "No tricks. You have my word."

A bidding war seemed like a hole-in-one for Jack, with his unlimited resources. Both men assumed Harley only wanted the Victorian on a whim. Aside from her parents and the Grimskys, no one in Newberry knew about her arrangement with the china company, let alone her multiple other franchise deals in the works. Even for Harley, it wouldn't fully sink in until the royalty checks started arriving.

It would be months before she would see any revenues . . . *years* until she started earning the kind of consistent income she needed to support herself and her child. She'd already resolved to take another day job until word got out about the B and B paying guests started showing up regularly.

Think fast. She pictured the hill where the Victorian now stood, flattened. Once the house was gone, it was gone.

Her heart pounded. She was already taking a huge gamble with the adoption. Kelly and her husband had the right to back out at any point throughout the pregnancy. Their consent wouldn't become irrevocable until a few days following the birth. If the unthinkable happened, did she really want to be stuck running a B and B with a big mortgage?

As deeply as she still cared—would always care— for Jack, she was no longer that naïve, disadvantaged teenager whose heart he had toyed with. Biting her lip, she scribbled a number, folded the paper in half, and slid it across the table to Ryan, hoping neither he nor Jack noticed how her hand shook. Then she held her breath and waited.

Jack pressed his thumb to his lip and thought for a moment.

Please, Harley prayed. *I need this house.*

Slipping a monogrammed gold pen from inside his sport coat, Jack jotted down a figure, creased the note shut, and handed it to his cousin. "Whatever happens, happens."

Ryan unfolded Harley's note and smoothed it open, exposing her dollar amount for all to see.

Her face burned. Too late, she realized that what was an exorbitant figure in terms of her modest bank account was a joke when it came to wine country real estate. Even with the amount she'd tacked onto her original offer, the number was obviously far below the property's market value. She nibbled the side of her thumb, imagining the laugh Jack and Ryan would share at her expense after she left. Newberry was a small town, but Jack was one of its biggest fish. How had she ever let herself believe she could compete? Her merchandise was still in the production phase, and already she'd let a little success go to her head. It was on the tip of her tongue to say, *Never mind, don't even open Jack's note.*

Too late. With agonizing slowness, Ryan was already unfolding Jack's offer.

She counted the seconds until she could slink out of Newberry and never show her face again. Surely another suitable house would turn up in the Seattle area. It *had* to.

Ryan frowned down at Jack's offer, as if perplexed. Then he placed it on the table side by side next to Harley's.

There had to be some mistake. Jack had underbid her. Her eyes sought his, but they remained focused on the papers he was returning to his folder. Rising and tucking it beneath his arm, he said, "Congratulations, Har. I wish you all the best. Now, I have other things to do today." He reached across the table to give her hand a curt shake, and then he was out the door.

Chills shot through Harley. Somehow, she had won. The Victorian was hers.

Chapter Eight

"Jack," Harley called, jogging after him as he strode through the parking lot of the law office toward a faded red truck that had seen better days. "What happened back there?"

He glanced backward without breaking his gait. "You got the house, fair and square."

She caught his sleeve, forcing him to turn around. "You practically *gave* it to me. So why did you even bother coming to the meeting?"

"I didn't know Ryan was going to pit us against each other." He shrugged. "Win a few, lose a few."

"You're taking this very calmly. What about the land? It's perfect for growing grapes. Even I know that."

"There are growers who would kill for it. But it's better that you have it. It just feels right." He paused. "Besides, I owed you."

Now, he thought, they were even.

* * *

Jack's hands were sweaty on the steering wheel of the old Ford V-10. The tissue-paper flowers made by the student council during countless study halls that covered the windshield made it almost impossible to see out.

"I can't see a thing through that peephole they left me," he complained to the band director, who was about to shut him inside the truck for the duration of Newberry High's annual Homecoming Parade, the fall's premier event.

"Did you go to the lav?" asked Mr. Desatento. "Because once it starts, you can't stop, no matter what."

Jack nodded solemnly.

"Remember, keep it in second gear," Mr. Desatento said. "That way you'll be less likely to jolt someone overboard." Someone being a member of the homecoming court, riding in the pickup's bed. No pressure.

Despite the balmy fall weather and the fact that it was ten a.m., it was dark as Hades inside the cab, and just as hot.

"The air conditioning doesn't work," said Jack, punching futilely at the controls.

"Beggars can't be choosers. When's the last time you heard of a Maserati being donated to the booster club?"

"Seriously, Mr. D, how am I supposed to see where I'm going?"

"It's two miles. What can happen in the space of two miles when you're going four miles per hour?"

Jack had had his license for a grand total of a month, and unlike many of his newly legal friends, so far, he hadn't hit a thing. So far. And it was a good thing, because his mother didn't have the patience for slipups, especially public ones. Now he was about to blind-drive a three-thousand-pound vehicle with passengers, standing up and waving. And Mr. D was supposed to be the responsible one.

"What happens if I miss a turn?"

"I picked you out of the entire student council because I thought you could handle it. But if you can't . . ."

Jack had been raised to believe there was nothing worse than shirking responsibility. "I can handle it."

"Good, because—" The teacher's head turned to look at something out of Jack's limited range of vision. "Harley! I need you."

"What, Mr. Desatento?"

At the sound of Harley's voice, Jack struggled between elation and panic. The two of them had spent their early years playing pirates. Jack's parents weren't like Harley's, who gave her free rein to roam. He was restricted to the vineyards and the meadow. But Harley kept coming back. Their raft was a fallen tree, their swords the long, pointed leaves torn from her mother's irises, with her permission. He thought life would always be like that—epic and free and amazing.

But all that ended abruptly the day his father died. Jack had put his childhood behind him and gone to work learning how the vineyards and winery operated.

He still hung out with Harley once in a while. But now he had grown-up responsibilities. Mother had gone from taking care of the house to spending her days learning the business so one day it would be there for him. He could hardly let her go it alone.

His life was neatly laid out for him. One day he would take over the family business and settle down with a compatible woman. A woman with a good head for business, who would be a sensible mother to his children, not the artsy-fartsy daughter of hippies.

"You designed this thing—" The art department had built the float, but everyone knew Harley had come up with the cool jungle design, in keeping with the tiger mascot. "—and now the driver can't see out the window," continued Mr. Desantento. "I need you to be Jack's eyes." He turned back to Jack. "Get out and let Harley in. There's a bigger hole over on the passenger side of the windshield. She can look out of that and help you steer."

"Naw," said Jack. "It's okay, Mr. D. I got this."

"You still have that truck."

Jack's face got a puzzled look, as if Harley had remarked that he still had the same arms and legs. "She's been in a garage all this time I've been Down Under. She's a part of me. Still runs like a charm. No sense getting rid of 'er."

She bit back a smile. They'd made more than a few memories in the back of that truck.

He kept walking, but she wasn't finished. She followed him, talking to his back. "You have no idea what this means to me."

When he nodded mutely without turning around, it was almost enough to make her change her mind about thinking him polite.

She stopped then and called to his back. "I truly am sorry about Emily. I know she's been gone a while now. But on the off chance I ever saw you again, I planned on telling you that."

She would never forget reading about Emily's death in the local news, only five years after she and Jack were married.

> *Last night, a late-model Volvo slammed into a*
> *bridge abutment on a narrow New Zealand road . . .*
> *The deceased was Emily Redmond, daughter of*
> *Dawson and Cordelia Redmond, formerly of this*
> *county and now of Riverside, California. Emily*
> *leaves behind twin daughters, Frances and Frederica,*
> *her husband, Jack Friestatt, and a sister, Cait, now*
> *of Portland.*

Impossible. Harley pictured Emily the way she'd known her. Aside from being born into an important family, Emily was remarkable for her ordinariness. She was pretty without being beautiful. Earned Bs in school, not As. Friendly, but not vivacious.

Jack halted and turned around slowly, a muscle twitching in his jaw, as if he had a lifetime of things to say but didn't have the faintest idea where to start.

She almost liked it better when he was cold and hard. When his vulnerability showed, she was too tempted to throw herself at him and forgive him for everything. "Well," she said, walking backward toward her own car, parked on the street. "See you. Er, on second thought, I guess I won't. Be seeing you, that is." She waved her fingers. "Bye."

He hesitated. "You have a time when you have to be back at work?"

"I'm my own boss. I decide when I work. Nobody tells me what to do."

"Nobody ever did." He snorted softly. "What the hell. Let me buy you a cup of coffee."

Half of her couldn't wait to get away from him. After all this time, he still made her palms sweaty and her mouth dry. Too late, she wished she had simply let him go instead of running after him. But questions rooted deep in their shared past, questions that had robbed her of uncounted nights' sleep, sprang to her mind. She shrugged. "I guess I could use some caffeine."

Chapter Nine

It was a short walk to the coffee shop just around
the corner.

"There's one." Jack pointed with his chin toward
an empty table at the back of the cafe.

Weaving between the tightly wedged tables, Harley
lost count of all the people who said hello to him.

"You look exactly the same," said Harley when
they had finally squeezed into their chairs across
from each other. Which was a lie. He'd gotten even
better looking.

"So do you."

"No, I don't." It wasn't fair. Being a working artist
meant hours sitting in a chair. She had packed on
ten pounds in as many years. Then again, if experience had taught her anything, it was that life itself
wasn't fair.

"So. You tired of Seattle?" He made a self-disparaging
face. "Stupid question. You must be, or you wouldn't be
moving back here."

That was the other thing about Jack. Even though

he was born wine country royalty, he had this humble, self-effacing side.

"I liked Seattle. Except that lately, when those hackers in their power hoodies strode past me on the city sidewalks with their cell phones glued to their ears, I wondered if I would ever truly be one of them, no matter how successful I became."

He laughed.

She stiffened. "What's so funny?" Was it so farfetched to think she could be successful?

"Power hoodies."

She relaxed again, as the server arrived already holding a coffee pot and poured them each a cup.

Jack glanced around. "All these people, pretending not to stare. Don't tell me you didn't notice."

"I was thinking it was my outfit. It's the only spot of neon in a sea of earth tones."

"That's not it. Today might be the first time in decades they've seen me with a woman that wasn't my mother or my wife. To top it off, that woman happens to be none other than Harley Miller-Jones."

"The Great Newberry Parade Disaster," drawled Harley, remembering along with him.

"Do what I say!" Mr. Desatento glanced down at his watch. A lock of hair slid out of his thin ponytail. "The parade's about to start. Don't argue with me. I'm assigning Harley to help you."

Jack looked at Harley and swallowed. Even with her hair recently dyed a very non-traditional purple, she still held some magical power over him.

After he'd snuck out of the house for Harley and wrecked his minibike, and been caught kissing her in the same month, Mother had strictly forbidden him to be anywhere near her. She'd even threatened to send him away to military school, triggering nightmares of marching in lockstep in a uniform. Now Mr. D was talking about wedging Harley and him together inside the tight space of the float?

"But I was going to walk along outside in case there's a decoration malfunction," said Harley.

"Decoration malfunction? You're worried about a flower falling off. I hate to tell you this, snowflake, but when you forgot to leave room to see out, that right there's a major design defect. Do you two want to be the ones to tell the parents of the homecoming court that they might as well go home? Good luck with that."

Mr. Desatento had a point. Making homecoming court was a bigger deal to the parents than to the kids themselves. Fathers dug wrinkled suit jackets out from the backs of their closets. Mothers had carnations pinned onto their breasts for their picture to be taken with their children, down on the field before the game.

One of the candidates for king was Jimmy Polanski. But Harley didn't know what Jack knew, which was that Jimmy was the son of the president of Newberry Bank—the bank that held their mortgage. Dad's death, Mother's learning curve, and some bouts of crippling cold weather had resulted in some late payments. Mrs. Polanski had the power to take everything from them. They had to stay on her good side.

The passenger-side door was already duct-taped shut. Mr. D held the driver's side door open *as far as he dared to allow Jack to squeeze out so that Harley could get in. "Careful!"*

In climbed Harley, dressed for the weather in a skimpy tank top and short shorts.

Once Jack and Harley were crammed in next to each other, their teacher talked to them through the crack in the window. "I'll be walking backward next to the float, spotting you. I'll stick out my left arm to indicate a right turn and my right for a left. Got that? And remember, do not exceed four miles per hour. All I need is Sylvie Collins screaming bloody murder should she get the slightest bump."

Sylvie had acted in all the school plays. She was never happy unless the spotlight was shining on her . . . no matter how much turmoil it caused.

"But how am I supposed to tell how fast I'm going? The speedometer's broken!"

"Four miles an hour. Do the best you can. And if you see me cross my forearms, stop."

"I can't even see the road, let alone you walking next to me."

"Keep your ears open. I'll yell the instructions to you."

"I feel like we should have rehearsed this."

"And rehearse the band and teach my classes and do report cards on time? Plus, this year I've been blessed with three freshmen whose names are all 'Heaven' spelled backward, and each one pronounces it differently. Nevee'ah, Nevi'ah, and Nev'eah . . . by the time I get them all straight, they'll have graduated. I don't get paid enough for this as it is."

"I don't suppose you're holding back and you

have some sort of remote-control emergency stop button."

Mr. Desatento tsked and rolled his eyes. "What do you think this is, Friestatt? The Rose Bowl?" With that, he slammed the door, making Harley jump.

Parades were designed to be fun, lighthearted events. But Jack, typically, had done his homework. There had been a surprising number of scary incidents. Any number of things could go wrong. People had gotten wedged between floats or parts of them, fallen beneath the wheels, and even been electrocuted when floats ran into overhead power lines.

Jack blinked in the semidarkness. "He's only doing the teacher gig until he can get his hobby winery up and running."

"Same as Mr. Langhorne and Ms. Chang. Come to think of it, they only lasted, what, a couple of years? What is it with everyone and his brother starting a winery?"

"They all want a piece of the action."

Harley looked around at the drab interior. "Turns out, floats aren't nearly as festive on the inside."

"I'll just be glad if they don't have to pry us out of here with the jaws of life after I crash into the bank on the corner."

Harley giggled as she fanned herself. "I thought guys loved stuff like this."

He felt for the gearshift, his hand accidentally brushing against her thigh. "Yeah, I love driving in the dark in a potentially lethal death trap while innocent people are dancing out there in the bed." He was student council president. If something happened, what would people say?

*From somewhere in front of them came the sound
of the band playing the Newberry High alma mater.*

"Ten seconds!" came the teacher's muffled voice.

Jack shifted into drive. "Can you see anything?"

*Harley craned her neck. "The band's still march-
ing in place. There. Now. They're moving forward."*

*"Here goes nothing." Sweat beading on his fore-
head, he frowned in concentration and, with a jolt,
shifted into drive.*

The truck crept forward at a snail's pace.

Beside him, Harley burst out laughing.

"What?"

*"Kind of anticlimactic, that's all. I mean, after all
that hoopla with Mr. Desatento."*

*"Laugh. Go ahead. It's not your ass in a sling if I
wreck this thing."*

*"Why are you so worried? I mean, aside from
someone getting hurt. Seems like your whole identity is wrapped up in this sucky little high school parade."*

*"Because it is! I can just hear my mother if I
mess up. Everything's such a big production with
her. She'll say I humiliated her in front of the whole
town."*

*Harley made a sympathetic face. "Stinks to be
you."*

*Harley didn't see him through the filter of his
family. She wasn't envious of him, like the kids who
didn't even know him who invited him to their parties, or resentful of his being born a Friestatt, like
the anonymous jerk who vandalized his locker with
spray paint. She saw through the bullcrap to who
he was inside, just a regular person.*

"Watch for the bank on the corner and give me

plenty of time to make the turn. That's going to be the hairiest part."

"Aye, aye, Captain."

At the throwback to her childhood nickname for him, their eyes met in the dimness. Memories of their pirate days in the vineyards danced between them. A lot had happened since then. Slowly but surely, the forces of fate and family were pulling them apart.

But he couldn't think about that. Right now, he had a float to drive.

After he successfully navigated the first turn and the bank, his shoulders relaxed a bit. To think he'd been worried about this. Piece of cake.

Now came the longest stretch, the main route.

It actually got a little boring. Going slow was exactly what seventeen-year-olds with a massive crush on each other didn't want to do. They wanted to floor it, go full speed ahead.

Jack could feel Harley's body heat, inches away. He thought of those first exploratory kisses behind the garage. Those kisses had starting something, something fascinating and powerful that couldn't be undone.

"Tongues'll be wagging around dinner tables tonight," said Jack.

Harley's head spun in a tangle of emotions. She was relieved and grateful at getting the Victorian, yet confused and suspicious over the way it had come about. Now, this. How could she have forgotten? To her hometown, she was still just a waitress with an art hobby.

She picked up her bag from its spot at her feet and half rose to leave. "If you've changed your mind about the coffee—"

Like a shot, Jack leaned across the table and dropped his voice to an octave she'd never heard from his mouth when he was a boy—a man's voice that brooked no argument and had her sinking back into her seat. "I spent the past ten years getting up before dawn and working till I couldn't see my hand in front of my face. Then I sat down with my kids for dinner, fell into bed, and did it all over again the next day. Seven days a week, fifty weeks a year. Only break was at Christmas, when the wine's finally resting on its lees and the vines are dormant." He sat back then, eyes determined, muscles in his face still taut, nostrils flaring as his breath rushed in and out. "Let 'em stare."

Harley's bag dropped to the floor. She realized she knew nothing about this new, grown-up Jack. She'd only been thinking about everything that had happened to *her* in the interval they'd been apart. Now it occurred to her that just as much had happened to *him*.

She folded her hands on the table. "Tell me how you're really doing."

Jack ripped open a packet of sugar, stirred it into his coffee, and fought for calm.

"Are you still grieving?" she prompted him.

"It's never easy losing someone. But it's the girls I'm worried about. Tell me something. Is it normal for eleven-year-old girls to be so—bonkers? Then again, you were—"

Harley elevated a brow almost imperceptibly.

"No offense. Especially Freddie. She's driving me up a wall. I wish I knew what to do for her."

"I remember that age. That's when the girl wars start. The teasing, the gossip . . . and your girls are navigating it without a mother. Maybe that's why they're a little bonkers, as you call it. But then, when it comes to losing a parent, you're the expert."

The minute he could following his dad's funeral services, Jack had snuck out of the house and run the three miles down Ribbon Ridge Road to Harley's house. When he saw her face behind the screen door, the dam of emotion he'd been holding back broke. He didn't have to act like a man around Harley. He could be himself, a thirteen-year-old boy.

"I was gutted when my dad died. But I got past it. Had to. As for the twins, their grades have been slipping. They've been trying to get out of things they never balked at before, like sports. Refusing to eat right."

"I can't say I ever went through that."

"No. I guess not." Harley had been raised in a world of her own design, unencumbered by rules. A world without uniforms and structured play dates and expectations to be followed without question. Even when she was a teenager, she still sang to herself and hung upside down on the monkey bars like a little kid, not caring if her hair got woodchips in it. Behind her back people called her a flower child.

With not a penny to her name, no legacy to uphold, she made life up as she went. She hadn't thought twice about throwing everything she owned into a backpack and taking off for Seattle. In essence, she was everything Jack wasn't.

"What's your mother say about it?"

"You know my mother. She always did have lofty expectations."

Harley cradled her mug between her hands. "The tree that won't bend doesn't last with the storm."

He chuckled humorlessly. "Then again, how could I complain about my life? Ski vacations. A new truck when I turned sixteen. Me moaning about my childhood would be like someone complaining the AC was too cold in their beach house in Cabo."

Harley smiled. "That truck—someone sure got their money's worth there."

"Whereas you . . . you followed your own drummer. Hanging out after school in the art room, just you and the teacher. Climbing up the hill to draw that Victorian. Even cutting school if you felt like it."

For the first time that day, she laughed, too. "Thing is, I hardly ever felt like it."

"What I'm trying to say is, you were free to do whatever you wanted with your life. No one had any preconceived ideas of how you'd turn out."

"It's not like my parents didn't take care of me. They had steady jobs and a house, and they were involved in my life, but as a support system. They didn't believe in orchestrating my every move."

Jack took a slug of his coffee.

"It wasn't like I had total carte blanche, you know," said Harley, going back to that time when their futures still dangled before them, full of potential, like a wrapped gift. "There *was* that one time I crossed the line."

Jack pictured that summer evening when her dad caught them kissing behind the garage and he laughed. "I had just finished asking you what you would do if your dad came out there, and you said you'd tell him to mind his own business. And then he did come around the corner and told you to get in the house, and you took off like a shot."

Harley laughed again, eliciting a wry smile from Jack and nosy stares from those nearby. "I think it was the first time I'd ever been reprimanded."

"It was far from funny when he narced to my mother."

"He wouldn't have said a thing to this day if not for us having tipped over your minibike a couple of weeks earlier. He just saw her at the market and asked her how your knee was doing."

Later, Mother had railed at Jack, berating Harley in the process.

> "What are you doing, spending time with that girl?
>
> "Nothing! We're just friends."
>
> "She got you to sneak out of the house in the middle of the night!"
>
> Harley didn't have to sneak to do anything. Sneaking out was all Jack's idea. But it was embarrassing enough at that age that his mother had found out he'd kissed someone . . . anyone.
>
> "Harley isn't the right young lady for you. She has nothing to offer you."
>
> "I told you, we're just friends!" Guilt stung him for his betrayal of Harley, but his true feelings for her were powerful and dangerously delicious, and even if he could have described them, he was too immature to stand up to Mother.
>
> "That's how it all starts. What would your father say? It would kill him to see you throw your life away with a girl like her. With privilege comes responsibil-

ity. You can't see it now, but our actions have far-reaching effects. You're special. You have to think about the future."

Jack had never told Harley all the hurtful things Mother said. But it got to him.

"At least my dad didn't threaten me with military school," said Harley. When Dad told her he didn't approve of her sneaking around, making out behind buildings, they'd had their one and only fight. Harley told him if he and her mother weren't so weird, maybe Melinda would be more accepting of her. Dad might be tough, but he was sensitive. She could tell that demeaning his lifestyle had hurt his feelings.

But even that wasn't enough to keep Harley and Jack apart.

"Your mother never thought I was good enough for you."

Jack ducked his head and scratched the nape of his neck. "Let's not go there. Not today." His hand returned to his coffee cup, and he lifted his eyes to meet hers. "In any event, I don't blame your old man, now that I have girls of my own. I catch one of them swapping saliva with some little twerp, I'll probably do the exact same thing. Wait till you have kids." He looked up with a start. "Or maybe you already do."

Now Harley was the one who looked away. It was a logical question. She used to talk about having children all the time.

"Not yet."

His eyes flew to Harley's left hand.

"Still Miller-Jones," she sang, slipping her hand into her lap. God forbid she give him the impression she was lonesome. The last thing she wanted was his pity.

"Not that I haven't dated . . ." She tilted her head as she fingered the edge of her napkin. "It's just that . . . well. You know.

"How about you? Do you have a girlfriend Down Under?"

He shook his head.

A tiny, foolish spark ignited inside her.

"So," said Jack. "Tell me what you've been up to. Whatever it is, it's working for you."

"I've been doing a little designing."

"It's cool that you kept up with your hobby."

"My designs have kind of taken off." She pulled out her phone, scrolled, then handed it to him.

"That's—" Speechless, Jack pointed to the screen and then looked up at her in a new light.

Harley smiled proudly. "My dishware, on my website. Go ahead. Keep scrolling through."

"Your drawings, on dishes? I remember looking over your shoulder in art class. Everyone thought you were talented, but . . ." No one ever thought that funky, free-spirited Harley would one day turn her doodles into something viable, something concrete.

"The china's just the beginning. I'm branching out into other forms of home décor. Bed linens. Ceramics. Who knows? Maybe even furniture."

"Props to you." That explained the down payment on the Victorian. But he still couldn't believe she'd have an easy time making the mortgage payments. Oh well. None of his business.

She slipped her phone back into her bag. "I'm still going to need other sources of income until the new merch starts selling. That's why I wanted the house. I've decided to open a bed-and-breakfast."

Jack bit his tongue. He could almost accept Harley's drawings finding a market. What did he know about art? But the Harley he knew was a stargazer. Not a businesswoman.

"How long are you here?" she asked.

"Here?" The jet lag had started to kick in.

"Here. In Newberry."

"I'm staying."

She frowned. "What do you mean? You live in New Zealand now. Everyone knows that."

"Not as of yesterday. I accomplished what I went there to do. The new vineyard's up and running. We're back."

She froze, her eyes round. "But—" She set down her cup and reached for her bag. "I should be going."

"Where're you off to?"

She dumped a few crumpled bills onto the table and rose. "Just . . . *going*."

Some ideas for cross-promotion had already popped into his head. His winery, her B and B. But she was already headed toward the door.

He rose, reaching for his wallet. "Harley, wait."

By the time he made it outside she was skipping down the sidewalk, climbing into her old car, parked nearby.

Jack stood there on Main Street and watched Harley drive away, feeling inexplicably as if his heart was attached to it by a rubber band. The farther she got, the tauter it stretched, until he was sure it would snap.

Talking with her was so easy . . . like picking up the thread of a conversation from yesterday instead of ten years ago. She still had that natural ease about her. Just sitting next to her today at the café, he'd felt himself begin to thaw from the outside in.

Chapter Ten

Harley's knuckles were white on the steering wheel. If only she hadn't made such a snap decision to buy the Victorian! But she'd always had an impulsive streak. She should have taken the time to find out about Jack's situation. Now she was stuck here with him again. How was she going to handle that?

As kids, they'd been the proverbial peas in a pod. Growing up, there were the inevitable hurdles to climb. Each found new friends and discovered new interests. But they couldn't stay away from each other.

Teenage Harley had nurtured a pipe dream that one day Jack would take care of his winery and she would do her art and have a passel of kids. And then came the day right before graduation, when Jack came to her gray-faced and blurted out that Emily Redmond was pregnant, and that the baby was his.

The next time she saw Jack was also the last time.

It was late that June night. Harley was slumped in

the backseat of a car full of chattering kids on their way to a party. Whose party and where it was, she couldn't care less—as long as it was as far away from Jack Friestatt as possible.

When the car stopped and she realized that they were at the Friestatt estate, it took her friends forever to coax her to go in. No one knew what she knew— that Emily was pregnant, and that her pregnancy had shattered whatever dreams she'd had for Jack and her. To think that Jack Friestatt could ever really care for her! She'd been so naïve.

But what else could she do? It was one a.m. and she was three miles up Ribbon Ridge. Her options were to sit in the car and wait, walk home in the pitch black—there were no streetlights on the ridge—or wake her hardworking parents needlessly for a ride.

The party was in full swing. Harley tried her best to blend into the crowd. She didn't see Jack sitting at the bar until his arm shot out and caught hers. Judging by how he swayed on his barstool, his grooms-men had done a commendable job of getting him wasted.

"All I ever wanted was you."

Alcohol goes in, truth comes out. Wasn't that the old adage? Adage or not, no sense trying to figure out a drunken groom at his bachelor party. She slipped through Jack's fingers and into the crowd, frantically searching for the nearest exit. When she finally made it outside, she ran the three miles across the ridge in the dark, cougars and coyotes be damned. As she ran, the cold night air-dried the hot tears streaming down her face. When she reached her little house, she tiptoed inside and collapsed, covered in sweat, onto her narrow bed.

The next morning was Jack's wedding day. Harley packed up her old hooptie, leaving her tearful parents standing in the driveway, Mom's head leaning on Dad's shoulder, her hand clenching a balled-up Kleenex, and headed north in a cloud of exhaust fumes until she ran out of gas. She swore she was never coming back.

If only Jack's mother hadn't had so many expectations. If only Jack had loved Harley more than Emily. But you couldn't turn back time. Jack had made his choice, and Harley had learned that giving away your heart only leads to it getting broken.

She grabbed her sketchbook and an old beach towel from the stack in the mudroom of her parents' house, went outside, and crossed the street to where Ribbon Ridge Road rose abruptly, wound along the backbone of the long hill, then fell and ended a few miles beyond. The road was narrow, without much of a shoulder. While traffic was sparse, curves and blind spots made walking along it risky. It made sense to walk the paths between the vines up the hill to where the Victorian sat. Back when she was little, the people who lived and worked on Ribbon Ridge got used to seeing her up there.

The early fall afternoon was pleasantly warm. A kestrel flew overhead. She strode between rows of vines studded with amethyst clusters and then cut into the meadow through knee-high fescue and oat grass. Come spring, this would be dotted with blue lupine and orange poppies. And she would be here to witness it! The thought gave her energy to push on.

When she got to her favorite spot, the sun was already behind the Victorian's roofline. She spread her towel on the grass, crushing it and releasing an herbal scent.

Out here in the fields, without the constant distraction of airliners taking off and landing nearby at Sea-Tac or the pungent cooking odors from the apartment next door, Harley became engrossed in her work.

"Is that who I think it is?"

A wiry man in a driving cap came panting up the hill toward her. He had a silver mustache and wore his shirtsleeves rolled up.

Harley set her tablet aside and scrambled to her feet. "Alfred!"

"Don't get up," Alfred scolded in a voice that sounded like gargling gravel.

Too late. Harley threw herself at him. "It's so good to see you again." Her eyes squeezed shut, taking in the comforting scent of pipe smoke and leather.

Withdrawing from her, he held her at arm's length, examining her like a favorite niece.

"Still acting like 'No Trespassing' signs don't apply to you. I swear, if a fence had a 'Wet Paint' sign, you'd be the first one to touch it."

Too bad Jack wasn't more like Harley, thought Alfred. But it wasn't Jack's fault he'd grown up with a father kicking his rear-end to get out there and take chances, experience what life had to offer, instead of just his mother conditioning him to believe that appearances and propriety trumped everything else.

Losing his father had been Jack's second stroke of bad luck. The first was being born in an era when kids started having their lives planned down to the microsecond. Jack was a prime example of that. Melinda immersed herself in every hour of the boy's day. She had him taking every possible lesson you could take. Golf . . . saxophone . . . martial arts. There was nothing wrong with music lessons or organized sports, except that all Jack ever wanted to do was follow Alfred around and play outside.

Back when Alfred was a kid, your mother swooped your bowl of Frosted Flakes out of your hands while you were still slurping down the milk, hollered at you not to slam the screen door on your way out, and that she didn't want to see you again until dinner, and don't be late.

Alfred and his friends spent their summers covering every inch of the development on their bikes. They built forts out of the mountain of fill displaced by the building of their own houses, keeping a sharp eye out for muskrats after one ran right over Alfred's foot one winter when he'd stomped through the thin ice of the drainage ditch. Later when they got their licenses, they would drive to Lake Berryessa and dare each other to jump off the bridge.

He could just imagine Jack at that age, standing along the railing, peering off the bridge into the murky water twenty-five feet below. Jack never would have had the nerve to jump.

But Harley would have. She was a throwback to simpler times. Whatever Cindy Miller and Tucker Jones's rumored shortcomings, they had let her be a kid, and Alfred approved wholeheartedly.

"Are you going to throw me out?"

"Why start now?" Alfred grinned and looked around at the sea of unruly native plants swaying around their legs. "It's that time of year. Meadow needs mowed."

"I like it like this."

He grinned. "You would."

In the slanting rays of the late afternoon sun, Harley studied him with her artist's eye and realized he wasn't as ancient as she'd once thought. Could be his lines and spots were the result of working outside. Or maybe it was because *she* was older.

"It'll be time to pick soon."

Harley noted the instrument in Alfred's hand, used to measure the amount of sugar in the grapes. You couldn't grow up in the Willamette Valley and not know about the crush. Even for those not directly involved in the wine grape business, the crush was everything. The grapes were the reason for the new jobs springing up in support of the wine industry, jobs in tasting rooms and bottling plants and restaurants, bringing with them a healthy injection of tax dollars. If not for the crush, the new bypass would never have been built, and Newberry would still be a sleepy, little off-the-grid farm town.

Deciding when to harvest the grapes was crucial. Harley didn't fully understand it, but Jack used to say it happened when the sugar, the acid, the pH—and, some said, the phase of the moon—precisely aligned. At that moment, it was like throwing a switch. Night or day, everything else was put on hold. The call would go out for the pickers, fingers crossed that they were waiting on standby for the phone to ring and another vineyard hadn't beaten you to the punch.

Alfred tilted his head sideways to look at her sketchbook, lying on the towel. "Still at it, I see. You've more than done it justice."

"I've drawn this house so many times I can do it with my eyes closed. But there's nothing like drawing from observation. There's always a fresh angle I didn't see before."

"Tending grapes is a lot like drawing. It's more than a job. It's a way of life. Hear you're up in Seattle now. Ever think about your old stomping grounds?"

"More than you know. As a matter of fact, I'm back. I just bought the Victorian."

Alfred's eyes widened. "Well I'll be. The Grimskys weren't the most social, but they'd wave when they saw me. Heard they were moving to Arizona."

"They're already gone. They took a side trip to Italy, but the point is, they won't be coming back."

"Never even noticed the 'For Sale' sign."

"It never went on the market. I put my drawings of the house on a set of dishes. That pleased Mrs. Grimsky. So much so that Mr. Grimsky gave me the chance to offer on the house before they signed with a Realtor."

"I'll bet your parents are tickled pink."

"Actually, it was all my mom's idea. She worked for the Grimskys. I have her to thank."

"Did you know Jack's back, too?"

Harley nodded. "We just ran into each other in town."

"Timing's uncanny."

"I didn't come back because of Jack. I have lots of plans in the works. My fall is going to be as busy as yours," she said, nodding to his refractometer.

"That's right." He'd been so startled by the irony of Harley and Jack returning at the same time, he'd almost forgotten what he was out there to do. "Time to get to it." He turned to go. "Good to have you back."

But as Alfred walked down the hill, a foreboding crept over him. He wondered if Melinda had heard that Harley was back on Ribbon Ridge.

Chapter Eleven

Mother would be waiting for Jack's report. He dreaded telling her he hadn't gotten the Grimsky property. He'd been conditioned to back her up at every turn, not go against her wishes.

Seeing Harley again had dredged up so many memories. He wondered how things would have turned out if he hadn't gotten Emily Redmond pregnant on their joint family vacation the Easter before graduation.

When Emily came to him in tears and told him she was late, Jack held her and tried to console her, grateful she couldn't see the panic in his face as he struggled to come to grips with the consequences of her bolt from the blue. For despite the fact that he'd known her forever, Emily's body felt foreign in his arms. Yet Emily wouldn't lie about something like that. In any event, a man took responsibility for his mistakes.

"What about college?" Emily cried. She was undecided as to what she wanted to do with her life, but he'd been accepted into Portland State. Mother thought he should study business, if only to have the sheepskin to show for it. He gazed blindly over Emily's shoulder. "It's a given that one day I'll take over the winery. I don't need college for that. And soon," he gulped, "you're going to be a mother."

He went to Emily's parents and asked for her hand, as if it were understood that marriage had always been in the cards and the only effect of the pregnancy was to move up the date. It was the honorable thing to do. Besides, the fault was at least half his. And if he hadn't manned up on his own, his mother would have grabbed him by his ear and marched him over to the Redmonds' house herself.

The next eight months went by in a haze. Jack embraced the Full Nuptial. Bought life insurance. Accompanied Emily to her prenatal appointments, where they soon discovered they were expecting not just one child, but two.

In her second trimester, she complained that as soon as she found a comfortable position his snoring woke her up. Her getting up to pee every hour didn't do much for his sleep either. He started sleeping on the couch, believing it was only temporary.

When the doctor vetoed sex until after the births, he breathed a secret sigh of relief. He wanted to feel physical attraction for his wife, but there wasn't a hint of it to be found. And it had nothing to do with the size of her belly. He consoled himself with the thought that maybe, later, they would bond over parenthood.

But raising twins proved to be no aphrodisiac. That first, grindingly hard year, they alternated night-shift duty so that at least one of them always woke fully rested. The strategy worked best when the off-duty parent could sleep uninterrupted. It only seemed logical that Jack move into one of the guest rooms.

In time, Jack learned that babies didn't flip a switch from bawling to be fed or changed a few times a night to sleeping straight through. Instead, it was a herky-jerky process. Only in hindsight did you notice you'd made it to the light at the end of the tunnel. One day, it dawned on him that he was no longer dog-tired. He counted back to the last time the sound of crying had dragged him out of bed and realized the worst just might be over. By then, he had already reverted back to his comfortable, single guy routine of falling asleep sprawled out spread-eagle by himself and not budging until the alarm went off.

Then Emily started getting migraines, and the gulf between them only widened.

On the surface, Emily was everything a man could want. Attractive, agreeable, a doting mother.

What the outside world never saw were Emily's crushing headaches, her vague sense of malaise that neither he nor the posse of specialists he consulted could figure out how to remedy.

> *"My life has no meaning" was her constant re-frain.*
>
> *Jack came to dread hearing that phrase. "How could you think that? You have everything a woman could want. A husband who'd do anything to make you happy. Healthy children. A life of ease."*
>
> *"I don't know."*
>
> *"Is there some kind of work you want to do? Do it.*

Do you feel like you missed out by not going to college? Go. There's nothing holding you back. I'll be your biggest cheerleader."

Emily wasn't lacking intellect, nor clinically depressed. She simply had no dreams. No hobbies. And with Jack always working and no interests of her own, it was no wonder she felt neglected.

Without the glue of romantic love to hold them together, they each sought solace elsewhere, Emily with her family and the cave-like darkness of her room, and Jack in his work. And his studies. His mother had urged him to commute to the local college in his spare time.

Sometimes, when the loneliness threatened to gnaw a hole in his gut, Jack would go for a ride in his truck and think about how different things would be if he had a chance at a do-over. But not often, because it only led to beating himself up yet again. If only he hadn't given in to an impulse that, looking back, he couldn't even recall.

Yet in all that time, he *never* wished Harley would come back to Newberry. On the contrary. After the initial shock of her leaving, he was glad she was gone. Living in the same town with her . . . being forced to watch her fall in love with someone else . . . that would have been more than he could have borne. Still, he'd taken some secret solace in knowing she was only a three-and-a-half-hour-drive away.

Then Mother and Alfred started talking about expanding into sauvignon blanc. Mother said moving to the heart of the sauv blanc market would be educational for the girls, expand their horizons. When they finally moved, it felt like Harley was gone from his life forever.

At the intersection of Valley and Ribbon Ridge Roads, Jack leaned into the windshield, peering up the hill at the Victorian's asymmetrical shape, the unusual aqua color of the porch ceiling visible from the road below. It was a local treasure, and yet such an integral part of the landscape that he'd long ago stopped noticing it. Now he saw that Harley was right. Without the Victorian standing guard, Ribbon Ridge wouldn't be the same.

Jack closed the front door to the estate and tossed his jacket across a chair, bracing himself for the confrontation he knew was coming.

"When are you going to stop flinging your clothing onto the nearest piece of furniture?"

He looked up to see Mother behind the railing on the second-floor landing, her mouth set in a line of disapproval, and he plowed both hands through his hair.

He waited with a sinking feeling for her to descend the stairs, knowing that each step was a step closer to his fate.

"Well?"

Jack hesitated, his heart thudding against his ribs. His mother was a formidable woman. Rarely had he openly defied her.

"Tell me. How much?"

"I didn't get it." Adrenaline surged through his veins. His pulse raced.

"What?"

"I got outbid."

"What do you mean? I told you to do whatever it took, no matter how much it cost."

Somehow, he found the courage to face her head-on. "Did you know who the Grimskys' buyer was?"

Her eyes flickered around the room in search of something to land on. "Does it matter?"

That's when it dawned on him—somehow, she knew it was Harley. "Yes, it matters. It matters a lot." Righteous anger crept over him. "What is it with you and Harley?"

She looked him full in the face. "Harley Miller-Jones was an aimless wild child who grew up without a guiding hand. She was always a negative influence on you."

"So she's a little quirky. What else do you have against her?"

"A little? Hah! Quirky with a capital Q."

"Did you really want that land so badly? Or did you just not want Harley to have it?"

Mother pressed her lips together. But the look in her eyes confirmed that was exactly what she had wanted.

"Tell me what happened with the house. Is it too late to repair the damage?"

"I let Harley have it."

Mother dropped her hand from the newel post. She slinked toward him. "You what?"

"I gave her the Victorian."

Given what she'd done for him after the parade, it seemed like the right thing to do.

* * *

"How have you been?" asked Harley, still craning her neck to see. "I never see you anymore."

"I know." He should say something more, something to let her know he hadn't forgotten her during their forced separation following the kissing incident, but he had to focus all his concentration on keeping the float on the road, not staring at her small but perfectly shaped breasts.

"I miss you." She tore her eyes from the little opening in the windshield to gaze at his face. She licked her lips. "Do you miss me?"

Feelings he'd been denying rekindled inside Jack. He could smell her strawberry lip-gloss. He swallowed. His pants felt too tight. His shirt was a straitjacket.

"Do you?" she asked softly, inching closer, ever closer.

Jack's breathing grew fast and hard.

And then, lightly, Harley kissed his cheek.

Jack turned his head so their mouths met. As he did, he slid his arm around her waist and pulled her body against his damp T-shirt.

She was so lithe . . . so luscious . . . so willing. A teenage boy's dream.

The float edged forward at a snail's pace. He was used to it now. All he had to do was keep the wheel straight. That was all.

He pulled her close until he could reach around her back and fondle one of those tempting breasts.

She was halfway on his lap. Her head fell back onto his shoulder and she let out a moan.

A crash split their eardrums and their heads snapped forward on their necks, hitting the windshield.

People were screaming.

Jack jammed on the brakes, sending Harley to the floor in a heap. The truck lurched and swayed, and he heard cursing from the bed. Then, in slow motion, they began to fall sideways.

"Hold on!" he yelled to Harley. "We're tipping over!" As their little world continued to fall, their arms flew out in search of purchase. And then there was an awful crunch of metal and the shattering of glass.

Among the spectators who'd pulled them from the wreckage was none other than Mother and the bank president.

"What happened?" asked Mrs. Polanski.

"It's all my fault," said Harley. "I was supposed to be telling Jack where to go, and I wasn't paying attention."

As Harley's stretcher was being loaded into the ambulance, Jack heard Sylvie Collins yelling, "My leg hurts! Can't you see that? I'm bleeding!"

"It doesn't look serious," said the EMT. "I'll get you a Band-Aid."

After the parade float incident, Harley's spontaneous admission of guilt had let Jack save face, and at the same time kept Mother in the bank president's good graces. All this time, he had let the whole town go on believing that the wreck was her fault.

Mother's hand flew to her mouth and she began to pace the foyer, racking her brain. "This is awful. What are we going to do?"

"Do? Nothing. It's done. Like I said before, the lot isn't that big. Besides, Harley said the house is a landmark, and I realized she's right. It's been there ever since I can remember. It'd be a shame to tear it down."

"And you wonder why I'm not willing to give you greater responsibility."

Shame and anger washed over Jack.

"It's time!" Alfred stuck his head in the door, his usually placid face transformed with excitement. He held his refractometer high. "The Brix is at twenty-four. I'm calling time to pick."

The name Alfred Ricasoli was synonymous with Arabella Cellars. Nobody knew the vineyards better than he did. Even their winemaker deferred to Alfred's opinion.

"No!" shouted Jack, halting Alfred in midstep. "I'll call the picking crew." He snatched his jacket from his mother's fingertips.

Rather than taking offense, a surprised grin broke over Alfred's face.

"What are you doing?" Mother asked Jack. "You can't worry about the crush. You just flew halfway around the world. You need to get to bed and get some sleep."

But Jack was already scrolling through his list of contacts.

"Alfred," said Mother. "Say something."

"He's got a point," mumbled Alfred, earning him dagger eyes.

"Jack." Mother lowered her voice and touched his arm. "You're exhausted. What with the girls acting out, keeping tabs on both sides of the business . . . Let me pour you a drink. Debora will have dinner on the table soon, and after that you can get a good night's—"

But Jack was suddenly tired of being treated like an incompetent child. He jerked his arm away. "I'm a grown man. I think I know when I'm tired."

"I'll spread the word to our people," said Alfred.

"Be there as soon as I get everything set up," said Jack.

Melinda flew after Alfred, glancing over her shoulder to make sure Jack wasn't following. But he was still inside, on the phone with his picking-crew chief.

She caught up with him in the lab off the barrel room. "Alfred. There you are."

"Calm down. What's gotten into you?"

When Don Friestatt was alive, Melinda scarcely acknowledged Alfred's existence. After Don died, she was totally unequipped to take over the business, but she was bound and determined to learn every detail, with one purpose in mind: so that one day, it would be there for her son. Alfred couldn't help but respect that. Jack was a good kid, and it was only right that the operation be preserved to pass on to him.

As no one had been at Arabella Cellars longer than he had, the job of teaching Melinda the ropes fell to him.

One day, a year or so after Don's death, when they had their heads together over a spreadsheet, she kissed him.

Their occasional affair had been going on ever since. Even while Melinda was in New Zealand, Alfred had continued to handle the viticulture side of the business while Melinda took care of the financial end.

A less-pragmatic man might have taken offense,

refused to put up with Melinda. But any illusions Alfred had had of romantic love had been wiped out when his first wife left him for his best friend. That had taught him to live in the moment, because the moment was all anyone really had.

It wasn't just that. He saw beyond Melinda's haughty, imperious exterior to the intelligent, sensual yet fearful woman inside. He gentled her with the patience of a trainer conditioning a Thoroughbred filly. He might have to walk on eggshells around her, but he'd made a conscious decision that she was worth it.

He also genuinely enjoyed her company. As long as he was willing to see her on her terms, his reward was occasionally being able to caress her creamed and perfumed skin with his workingman's hands.

He'd missed her when she was gone.

"What am I going to do?" Melinda moaned. "I thought all my problems with Harley were over. I still shudder to think of how close Jack came to ruining his life with her." Now all her anguish came surging back. "Do you know what Jack did this morning? He let Harley get her hands on the Grimsky property."

Alfred set down his refractometer and picked up his clipboard. "Melinda. Now is not the time. Can't you see—"

She dug her fingers into his arm. "What's gotten into him? Please. Talk to him. For me."

Alfred scribbled a notation on his clipboard and tossed it onto the counter. "It's long past time you faced it, Melinda. Your son's a grown man. He can make his own decisions."

"Now that girl's going to be living just over the ridge again!"

"*Woman.* Harley is a woman, and Jack's a man.

Wonder if he got through to the crew chief?" Alfred muttered, heading toward the door, Melinda on his heels.

Outside, the estate was coming to life. The atmosphere fairly hummed in anticipation. In the corner of his eye, a cellar rat—one of the smart but restless youngsters on a break from college, or a recent grad, not yet ready to settle down to a job in accounting or pharmaceutical sales—clapped on his ball cap, straightening its bill with a seriousness of purpose. Another worker strode rapidly toward the vineyard from the employee parking lot, cupping his phone to his cheek as he warned whoever was on the other end not to wait up for him tonight—or tomorrow night either, for that matter.

This was the crush. Christmas morning was nothing in comparison. This was what wine people lived for.

"Don't you see?" Melinda cried, jogging to keep up. "That's exactly the problem! Without Emily, there's nothing keeping them apart."

"It's been years," said Alfred without breaking stride. "You got your way. Jack married Emily. You got two beautiful granddaughters to show for it. Jack's young. If it turns out he and Harley still have feelings for each other, why stand in their way?"

Chapter Twelve

The pickers swarmed into the fields clad in fluo-
rescent orange, headlamps strapped on over
their bandannas. Often, they picked at night, when it
was cooler for the pickers and the grapes. Each one
jumped off the truck, grabbed a plastic bin, and
headed out to the middle of a row. At the end of
each row sat a flatbed hooked to a tractor that pulled
it along, stopping every few rows to be filled with bins
until it was stacked to the top. It dropped off the
bounty at the crush pad to be crushed, stemmed,
and sent into vats, then motored back out to the
fields for the next load.

The crush, with all its sweaty labor and the urgent
need to get the fruit picked at its absolute optimum,
had always been Jack's favorite time of year. He loved
the sight of hundreds of lights bobbing and dipping
across the dark valley like fireflies . . . the heady
aroma of bruised, ripened fruit filling the air . . . the
reassuring *thunk* of bin being stacked upon bin.

Three days of working shoulder to shoulder with

the pickers, hefting countless bins of grapes onto the crush pad had tamed the initial excitement. He and Alfred had settled into their former, easy give-and-take, as if his five-year absence had never happened. He was dumping yet another bin into the crusher when Alfred said, "Something I been meaning to ask you. Are Kiwi women as friendly as they say?"

A grin split Jack's face. "That's a fishing expedition if I ever heard one. If there's something you want to know, why don't you just come out and ask?"

"It's been five years you've been a widower."

There was a pause as Jack tossed the empty bin onto a stack of them. "The answer is no. I haven't found anyone yet."

Alfred propped one foot on the concrete pad and crossed his arms on his knee. "Catch like you? You must not have been trying hard enough."

"Nothing against the Kiwis. But it wouldn't be practical for the girls to get attached to a stepmother with family in New Zealand, now would it?"

Alfred raised a brow. "Your mother's influence is showing. Melinda's nothing if not practical."

"Picking a wife isn't something to experiment with. Especially now that I have the girls. It's got to be someone who shares our values. Our vision."

Alfred wiped his brow with his sleeve. "I ran into Harley."

At the mere mention of her name, Jack felt the usual confusing mix of feelings. He was grateful for the distraction of the truck pulling in with a fresh load of grapes. "Harley's the exact opposite of what I'm looking for."

"I was always fond of her. Must be doing something right if she can afford to buy the Victorian."

"I'm happy she sold some artwork. But the girls are going to be teenagers. I need someone who's going to guide them with a firm hand. Harley never had that kind of guidance herself. How can she be expected to give it?"

Alfred grinned. "What's the matter? Scared of what's going to happen when your girls start having the same kind of feelings you had when you were that age?"

Jack felt himself redden. "Right now, all I know is that time's running out. The girls are what brought us back to Ribbon Ridge now, aside from the fact that the new vines are finally producing."

He had seen for himself how critical timing was for grapevines to thrive. Five years ago, he and his crew had struggled to rip out the old, deeply burrowed vines from the land he'd bought in Marlborough. They planted the fields in rye, corn, and clover to restore its nutrients. While the cover crops were nourishing the soil, he found a nurseryman to grow new vines for later transplantation into his own fields. Timing was everything. The fragile young plants had to be handled with the utmost care so they didn't go into transplant shock. There was a short window in which to get them back into the ground.

"What are you going to do about it?"

"As a matter of fact, I have my first date Saturday night."

"That right? Who's the lucky gal?"

"Prudence Mitchell."

"Judge Mitchell's daughter?"

"That's the one."

"You won't have to worry about your girls sneaking out of the house if ol' Pru's around." Alfred grinned.

"That's what I'm counting on," said Jack.

But as he went about hosing down the concrete floors and checking the filled tanks where the wine was already fermenting, Alfred's words began to sink in. Harley had transplanted herself here, on Ribbon Ridge. She was there right now, this very moment, and she would still be there when the crush was over. Even when he couldn't see her, he'd have to drive past the Victorian everywhere he went. He was going to think about her every time he did, imagining what she was doing up there. Wondering if she was thinking about him, too.

Chapter Thirteen

"I don't want to play soccer anymore!"

Jack showed up in the dining room after Mother and the twins had already started eating.

"What's this?" asked Jack, sitting down at his place.

"Mimi says I have to play soccer, and I don't want to."

"Everyone should become proficient in a sport and a musical instrument so they grow up to be well-rounded," said Mother. "That's the way I raised your father, and it's the way you'll be raised."

Emily had gone along with Mother's ideas about child rearing. She had moved straight out of her own family home onto the estate. From the very outset of their marriage, she and Jack had had someone to clean and someone to cook, even a nanny to help with the twins when they were tiny. She had never re-arranged the furniture or added any of her own personal touches to make the home hers.

Jack sat down and reached for the pasta dish in

the center of the table. "I thought you liked soccer, Frankie."

"I never liked it!"

Freddie took a drink from her water glass. "That's why she can't sleep," she said, licking the excess from her lips. "She doesn't want to play anymore."

Lately, Frankie had been waking in the middle of the night, coming to Jack with vague complaints of stomachaches or that she was too hot or too cold.

"Frankie?" asked Jack. "Is that right?"

She shrugged.

"Mm. Try some of that pasta," he said.

Dutifully, Frankie picked up her fork and pushed some food around on her plate. "There's red peppers in it. I don't like them."

"Here," said Jack, spearing a tiny red fleck on her plate. "I'll eat your peppers."

"When I was a girl, I ate whatever was served without complaining," said Mother sternly. "It wouldn't have done any good if I had."

"Sports are good for you. They help you grow up healthy and strong," said Jack, careful to keep his tone light.

"Why does it have to be soccer? I want to take modern dance so I can dance in music videos."

"Even if I did allow you to take dancing lessons, the likelihood of you actually dancing in music videos is slim to none. But playing soccer will look good on your college application. And it builds self-confidence and competitive drive."

Frankie dropped her fork, leaped from her chair, and ran from the room, crying, "Why do you have to keep picking on me?"

Jack's fork stopped midway to his mouth. He looked at Freddie, who kept eating.

"Frances!" shouted Mother. "Come back here and finish your dinner right now."

"I'm not hungry!" came Frankie's voice from the stairs.

"Don't expect to get anything else until breakfast, then," Mother called.

"I'll go check on her," said Freddie, slipping from her chair.

"No—oh, go ahead," said Mother, changing her mind in midsentence.

When Freddie had gone, she said, "Those girls are growing cheekier by the day, seeing what they can get away with. They're testing you, Jack."

"They're just normal kids, Mother."

Still, he thought, that date with Prudence couldn't get here fast enough.

Jack had only known Prudence casually in high school, but he'd been aware she'd had a bit of a crush on him, even if she'd been too backward to do anything about it.

She still lived at her father's home in the better part of Newberry. To Jack's pleasant surprise, when he picked her up, instead of her usual sweats she had on a wrap dress with a deep V-neck.

"So," he said on their way to the country club. "Are you still playing sports?"

"I'm an assistant coach at the college," she said in a deep voice. "Last season we finished 15-3-2 overall."

"Congratulations."

She raised her hand. "Up high."

It took Jack a second to realize she meant to slap palms with him.

"My twins play soccer."

"So I hear. What positions?"

"Both forwards."

"Scorers." She nodded approvingly. "Are they those big, aggressive strikers who hold the ball up? The fast attackers who blow past the opposing team? Or are they a couple of those tricky ones who get creative on the dribble?"

Wishing he'd paid closer attention at games, Jack shrugged. "Just plain forwards."

"If you want, I can evaluate their skills," she said graciously. "Speed, coordination, hustle . . ."

He nodded. "We'll see." Maybe that's what had been missing in the girls' game. Maybe some individualized instruction would make all the difference.

He had to hand it to Mother. Prudence sounded promising.

"I always felt a connexthion with you," Prudence said once they'd been seated at their table.

Was that a lisp? He didn't remember her having that. Now that he was facing her, he looked closer and saw a clear, plastic coating on her teeth.

"I used to think you were everything," she said.

Jack shook the folds out of his napkin and placed it on his lap. "You never said anything."

"I was too shy. I would have been terrified to approach you."

"Nobody's perfect. Especially me."

"I know."

"Huh?"

"Now I realize I was wrong. It's gratifying to see you have flaws."

"I do?"

"For exthample, your hair's too long. It should end right above your collar. I know this great barber. Here. I'll texth you his number." She whipped out her phone, and a few seconds later, his phone dinged.

"Thanks for clueing me in. The guy I used to go to retired when I was overseas. I'll be sure to give this one a call."

"Another thing. One of your teeth is slightly crooked."

"It is?" Jack picked up his spoon and smiled into the underside of the bowl.

"The one on the bottom. You can hardly see it, but being a CPA, I pick up on details like that. They have new ways of fixthing them that they didn't even have when we were in school. Invisible trays. As a matter of fact, I have them on now. I'll bet you didn't even notice."

"No. Not at all."

"Only takthes a year or two and, prestho." She made a motion like shooting an arrow from a bow. "Straight as can be."

"Hm. Maybe I'll give them a try."

"Before we go any further, there are some things you should know about me. My great-grandfather's name is Gusthave, my grandfather's name is Gusthave, and my dad's Gusthave, so we have to name our first son Gusthave."

Perusing his menu, Jack chuckled and lifted a brow. "I guess Gustave's not a bad name."

He raised his finger to a passing server. "Excuse me? I'll have a glass of pinot noir. Pru?"

"Just water for me. Alcoholism runs in the family. My mother?" She shook her head gravely. "Not good. She thinkths Dad and I don't know, but our neighbor spotted her disposing of her empty vodka bottles at Safeway."

Jack nodded. Mother had failed to mention that when she was promoting Pru. But he was definitely going to mention it to her.

"It's always been kept under tight wraps. Information like that tends to work againstht you when you're running for public office. But when it comes to personal relationships, I'm all for transparency. Better you find out now than after we're married."

"Married?"

"Do you like porn? Fun fact: I don't have a gag reflex."

Jack looked wildly around the room. "Where did that waiter get to? Hold on. I'm going to go get him."

When Jack found his server, he slapped a twenty-dollar bill into his palm.

The server frowned, confused. "I haven't taken your order yet."

"This is in addition to your regular tip. The second my date is finished with her entree, you're going to spill a glass of wine down the front of my shirt."

"But—"

"Understood?"

Jack's pocket dinged again. Irritated, he pulled out his phone.

I miss you.

He glanced over at his table to see Prudence winking and waving.

* * *

Even with his wine-stained shirt sticking to his chest, it wasn't in Jack not to walk Prudence to her front door.

"Nice to see you again, Pru. It was good catching up after all this time."

"So, when should I look to see your munchkins to evaluate their skills? I have a battery of tests that can predict their game condition rank in any given league."

"I'll be sure to check my calendar. Well, g'night." He stuck out his hand.

"Hold on." Prudence put both hands into her mouth. With some difficulty, she worked out the plastic retainer. Slurping up the excess saliva, she swallowed, cleared her throat, and closed her eyes.

Peering down at her upturned face, Jack steeled himself, summoned his strength, and gave her the quickest peck in the history of kissing.

He hadn't pulled out of her drive yet when his phone dinged.

When can we go out again?

"How did it go with Prudence?" asked Mother the next morning, when Jack came in from walking the girls to the school bus.

He slid out of his jacket, careful to place it on the coat hook behind the door. "I don't think Pru's going to work out."

"Why not? On paper, she's perfect."

"Let's just say there were some warning signs."

Mother poured him a fresh cup of coffee and blew gently on her own cup. "What do you mean, warni signs?"

Why couldn't Mother ever take him at his word? So be it. "Did you know Mrs. Mitchell has an alcohol problem?"

"There are alcohol problems, and then there are alcohol problems."

"The kind where you hide your empty bottles?"

"There are clinics for that, some very discreet. Besides, you're talking about Pru's mother, not Pru."

"And after I got home last night, Pru texted me pictures of her breasts."

Mother's cup paused halfway to her lips. She sat it down. "What am I supposed to tell Gustave? He sold his practice for a mint. They have a chalet in Vail. Are you sure you want to leave all that on the table?"

"Tell him anything you want. They can have their chalet. I'm looking for the best woman to raise my daughters. Period."

"Don't sell yourself short. My mother always said, 'It's as easy to fall in love with a rich woman as a poor one.' "

"You know as well as I do that I could sell everything and I'd never have to work again."

"But the idea isn't to settle. The idea is to build on what we have."

"I'm open to your suggestions, but I'm the one who has to marry this person, not you."

Mother sighed. "I'll take another look at the club membership roster to see what else I can come up with."

Chapter Fourteen

In keeping with long tradition, when the crush was over, Alfred and Jack walked through the vineyards, examining the lot of grapes intentionally left unpicked.

From the time Jack could walk, he'd tailed his dad everywhere on the estate, from the vineyards to the winery and the tasting rooms. When Dad died, Alfred became his natural, if unofficial, successor.

"This all started the year your father went back during daylight and found an entire row of grapes that had been completely bypassed by the pickers. Anyone else would've wasted no time picking them. Instead, your dad decided to let them continue to ripen, to intensify the sugars and the flavors. That's how Bella was born. And every year after that, Don held back a lot of his total bottling to experiment with. Everyone said he was a fool, wasting good juice. What he was, was an original thinker. A risk-taker, open to new ideas. To this day, Bella's still our most famous bottling."

Alfred never tired of telling Jack that story.

And Jack never got tired of hearing it.

"You didn't have to let me follow you around all those years after Dad died. I must've been a royal pain in the ass at times."

"No doubt about it." Alfred chuckled, turning away, suddenly noticing a rotten grape that needed discarding.

The ground sloped gradually upward until Alfred's breathing became audible. At the top of the vineyard, Jack stopped and propped his hands on his waist, pretending it was he who was out of breath.

"Should be a banner year," Alfred panted. Above them sat the Victorian, dominating the skyline. Alfred squinted toward it. "That looks like our new neighbor."

Shielding his eyes from the sun, Jack followed Alfred's line of vision to where a figure on a stepladder worked a long-handled tool back and forth. His heart beat faster. And it wasn't from the climb.

"Don't know why she didn't hire someone to paint the porch ceiling," said Alfred. "No job for a woman. If she fell, could be days before she was found."

"Better not say that too loud." Jack chuckled. "Haven't you heard? A woman can do anything a man can do, and better."

"No one, man or woman, ought to be up on a ladder by himself." Alfred started toward the house.

"Where are you going?" Jack's heart raced harder. Harley did something to his insides. Something he still didn't know how to deal with.

"Can't just pretend we didn't see her. That wouldn't be very neighborly, now would it?"

Jack hesitated as he watched Alfred stride through

the high grass. But his feet seemed to have a mind of their own. They struck out after him.

Harley's move out of her Seattle apartment was simple and straightforward. After she got rid of her secondhand furniture, most of what was left was clothing and art supplies and her precious fiddle-leaf fig that was the closest thing she had to a pet. She and her mom and dad had made it to Newberry in one trip with a U-Haul.

When they got to the Victorian, all three of them unloaded the boxes into the rooms marked on them. Mom helped her put the sheets on her bed and hang her clothes in the closet, while Dad went through the house, opening and closing windows and jiggling pipes under the sinks.

Over the next few days, Dad dug holes and put fence posts in, and she and Mom strung an electric wire along the top to keep the goats in and the coyotes out.

"They'll need something to climb on," said Mom. "That's what the pallets are for. We'll set them sideways for the walls and lay some across the top and cover it with plywood. Your kids'll be happy as clams in there."

But sometimes, as Harley continued to unpack, she found herself turning objects over in her hands, forgetting what she was going to do with them.

Now, the pickers had moved on to other estates. The vineyards on Ribbon Ridge were quiet again, the leaves beginning to yellow and crisp as summer ebbed.

Harley lowered her paint roller, wiped her brow

on her arm, and squinted at the two figures coming up the hill. So far, the only people who had driven up Ribbon Ridge Road were its handful of residents, wineaux in search of a tasting, or lost tourists. The Victorian was a point of destination. Nobody simply showed up there.

She saw the silhouette of a driver's cap. That would have to be Alfred. And that was Jack's unmistakable long stride.

Hurriedly, she tucked in her shirt and brushed her hair back off her face.

"Howdy," she said when they got within speaking range. "Except for my parents, you're my very first visitors."

Alfred peered up at the porch ceiling. "How's it going up there?"

"Last coat. The Grimskys took good care of the place. Not much needs doing except this ceiling and some minor touch-up work inside."

She looked down from her perch on the ladder, where Jack stood stiffly. She could almost feel the tension in his body, sense his hesitancy.

"Do you guys want to come in?"

"No—" Jack said.

"Always wondered what the grand old lady looked like inside," said Alfred, wasting no time mounting the porch steps.

Jack paused, reluctant to follow him. Only when Harley started down the ladder did he come up and steady it as her feet descended the rungs. "I've been trick-or-treating up here with the girls, but only just inside the front door."

Alfred stomped on the porch a couple of times. "No sign of rot."

"You sound like my dad," said Harley. "He's a mechanic, and amazing at using his hands. There's nothing he can't fix."

"Alfred's the same way," said Jack.

"Given you live so close to one another, it's a wonder you two don't know each other better."

"Does your dad like wine?" asked Alfred.

"Not particularly."

"I never had a thing for motorcycles either."

"And probably while you're up here, Dad's at his shop."

Inside was a mountain of still-unpacked moving boxes and cleaning supplies and packages containing the new guest towels and sheets she'd ordered.

Jack eyeballed the sideboard. "They leave this?"

She nodded. "They left quite a few nice pieces. There are just a few holes that I need to fill in."

Alfred promptly disappeared to investigate, leaving her alone with Jack, standing awkwardly in the center of the foyer with his hands in his pockets.

"So, you say you've never been in here?"

He shook his head. "We ran into the Grimskys at the club and downtown from time to time, but it's like Alfred said. They pretty much kept to themselves."

"Follow me," she said.

She showed him the living room, the parlor, the kitchen and the dining room.

When they circled back to the foyer, he said, "Wonder where Alfred got to."

"He has to show up eventually."

Jack peered up the staircase.

It was natural that he would want to go up there. But what about the nursery? It had never occurred to her that Jack would ever set foot in her house. She didn't relish the thought of standing in that empty nursery with him.

Jack put a foot on the first step. "Okay if I—?"

She could hardly tell him no. She squeezed past him in the stairwell and jogged up the steps. Flying into the master bedroom ahead of him, she yanked up the covers over the pillows. When she turned around, she found him standing in the doorway, staring at the pile of disheveled sheets and blankets that looked like she had just crawled out from under. She felt exposed, as if he could see her plain as day, naked in that bed, arms and legs askew, her hair in a tangle.

"Here're the other rooms," she said, slipping by him again and leading him back into the hallway.

She gave him a quick tour of the other bedrooms, carefully avoiding the nursery. Finally they came to her studio.

"So. This is what you do," said Jack, gaze traveling over her desk littered with notes, sketches, and watercolors in various stages of completion. There were also a half-dozen mismatched mugs containing pens, drawing pencils and paintbrushes.

She spread her hands. "This is where the magic happens."

He picked up one of her most recent drawings. "You've gotten better."

She huffed a little laugh. "I hope so."

"No. I mean, these are really good." Her drawing still in his hand, he turned to her.

She felt her cheeks warm with pride at his compliment. "The best ones are hanging on the corkboard."

On his way to the wall to look at them, he stooped

to pick up one of the many government forms for operating a business that had fallen onto the floor.

"Just lay that on the pile. Turns out, opening a B and B is a tad more complicated than I thought. Seems like every day I get another licensing regulation or insurance form or whatever. You practically have to have a law degree to fill them out."

"Tell me about it."

Of course Jack would know. He had a business, too.

She'd shown him every bedroom except the nursery. She should have thought ahead and shut the door. She could have passed it off as a closet. "Well. Should we find Alfred?" She headed back toward the top of the stairs.

But Jack had stopped outside the nursery and was craning his neck around the doorframe. "What's this?" He questioned her with his eyes. "I thought the Grimskys didn't have any kids."

She drifted over to him, a sinking feeling in the pit of her stomach. "They had always hoped to. It just didn't happen for them."

"Seems like it'd be more practical to turn this into another guest room."

She glanced over her shoulder. "I wonder where Alfred got to?" she repeated. Much to her relief, she heard the sound of boots on the floor below.

"Up here," she called.

Alfred ascended the steps and stood on the landing, squinting up at the ceilings. "You were right about the place being well-maintained. No flaky plaster or water stains." Thankfully, he was more interested in the house's bones than its trimmings. He gave the bedrooms a cursory glance without mentioning a thing about the crib and pale blue walls in the one bedroom.

"How's the basement?" Alfred asked Harley, as the three trooped back downstairs. "Any strange puddles? Clogged drains?"

"I don't think so," said Harley.

"If you don't mind, I'll just run down and have a look."

"Be my guest."

Again, Harley and Jack were left alone, this time in the kitchen. Jack strolled to the window, held back the curtain, and peered out at the view.

"Jeez," chuckled Harley, to fill the awkwardness. "You would think Alfred was buying the house himself."

"That's Alfred for you," said Jack. He dropped the curtain and turned to her. "I can't believe we're both back here on the ridge. Remember when we used to play pirates in the hedgerow?"

She smiled. "How could I forget?"

"Remember ninth grade? My first day at public school. I didn't know where to go for history, so you walked me there. As soon as I walked in, the bell rang. In helping me, you made yourself late."

"No big deal. It was English, and I was pulling an A. How about all those times, after school?" At first, Jack stayed after with student council, while she hung out in the art room. But as they grew closer, Jack often skipped his club and they went riding around on the back roads in his truck, windows down, music cranked up.

He pictured Harley in the passenger seat, his ball cap turned around on her head, pink toes on the dash, bopping to the Backstreet Boys. Sometimes he parked, and Harley surprised him by entwining her arms around his neck and kissing him like it was as natural as the sun coming up in the morning. As that rainy winter revolved into spring, their curiosity turned to desire and then a pulsing need. They grew ever more brazen. Especially Harley. But his father's death and later, the float wreck was proof of his mother's constant warnings that disaster lurked around every corner. At the last second, Jack always slammed on the brakes.

He ventured a step in her direction. "There's something I want you to know."

She watched him suspiciously, standing with her back against the sink as he closed in on her.

"Don't think I don't have regrets. I had to go to work, learn how to be a dad while I was growing up myself. I was a faithful husband to Emily. But that doesn't mean I didn't think about us a million times, and wonder how it could have been."

"We all make choices. Then we have to live with them."

They stared at each other for a long moment, lost hopes and dreams swirling thickly between them.

"What I'm trying to say is, don't think I don't think about where we'd be if I'd never . . . if *you'd* never . . ." Jack continued toward her cautiously, as if she might spook any moment and take off again in a blaze of taillights. His eyes burned into her, his chest rising and falling.

She swallowed.

Jack could see her pulse throbbing in the small hollow at the base of her throat. Inch by inch, the space between them dissolved until he could feel the warm aura surrounding her body.

Their heads moved closer . . . closer, until they were breathing the same air, the space between their lips too small to measure. His hand rose toward the lock of hair curling around her shoulder.

"Ahem. Tight as a drum."

At the sound of Alfred's voice, Harley whirled around as Jack's hand fell to his side.

"Oh," said Harley. "What is?"

"Hot-water heater." He looked at Jack. "You about ready?"

With a nod, Jack followed Alfred to the foyer, Harley bringing up the rear.

Out on the porch, Jack took a last look at the house and said, "It's a lot for one person to take on, but once word gets out, you're going to be beating them off with a stick."

She grinned. "Especially when they find out I'm offering goat yoga."

"Is that what that new pen's for by the little barn?" asked Alfred.

She nodded.

"You going to be okay finishing your painting?" asked Jack.

"Like I said, this is the second coat. It's all but done."

They had seen all there was to see. It made sense for them to leave. But Jack wasn't budging. His feet seemed glued to the floor of the porch.

Alfred descended the steps first. "See you around, neighbor," he with a wave. "Need anything, holler."

Jack seemed to come to his senses. He followed behind Alfred.

She watched them trudge down the steep hill, growing shorter and shorter until they disappeared altogether, then went back to her painting.

So. Jack had regrets, did he?

But if his regrets were that deep, it was interesting that Alfred had been the one to offer help should she need it, and not he.

Chapter Fifteen

Harley donned her waitress uniform and studied her reflection in the mirror with a feeling of déjà vu. The year her dishes took off, she'd thought her waitressing days were over. But with her first mortgage payment soon coming due, she'd wasted no time in applying for her old server's job at the country club. Her previous manager was long gone, but one of the older career waiters had vouched for her. The crush was the start of the busy time of year for eating out, followed closely by the holidays. The club needed experienced help, and they hired her on the spot.

An hour later, she was hefting a tray full of salads out from the kitchen when behind her, the hostess escorted a customer into the dining room.

She set down her tray and glanced discreetly out of the corner of her eye and a feeling of dread washed over her. She'd known when she took the job that there was a chance of running into Jack's mother, but it couldn't be helped. The club was only a couple of miles from the Victorian, the pay was decent compared with other restaurants, and they had taken her back instantly.

Yet of all the tables in all the dining rooms of the club, why did Melinda have to be at one of Harley's? And why today, of all days, her first day back?

Harley served the salads, dressing on the side, to the foursome in lime and pink golf togs who had just come in off the course. Then she took a deep breath, squared her shoulders, and turned to wait on her former nemesis.

The sight of Melinda's stiff blond helmet of hair brought back another time when she had waited on Jack's family, soon after Dad caught her and Jack kissing. In fact, Melinda had gotten her the job here, ostensibly as a favor. But Harley knew the real reason was to keep her busy and away from Jack.

It was Harley's very first job. Melinda knew it, and yet she kept her hopping. Her drink was made wrong. Her order was mixed up. Everything she could find to complain about, she did.

When Jack spoke to her like the old friends they were, his mother told him in Harley's hearing that it was bad form for members to get too familiar with the wait staff.

Seeing Harley stutter and flush, Jack later excused himself to use the men's room and caught her arm in the hallway. He whispered to her that he'd pick her up at midnight, after her shift. Then they'd gone parking up along Ribbon Ridge.

*Meanwhile, Melinda complained to the manager
about Harley's mistakes, resulting in a reprimand
the next time she worked.*

"Good afternoon, Mrs. Friestatt. May I get you something to drink?"

Melinda arched a brow and looked her up and down. "Well. Hello, Harley. I hear we're going to be neighbors again."

No thanks to you, thought Harley.

"I'm curious. How is it that a waitress can afford to purchase a house like the Grimskys'?"

Harley's face heated. She wanted to rip off her apron and storm out of the country club and never set foot in it again. But when she pictured herself rocking her son in her beautiful nursery overlooking the vineyards, she managed to swallow back her outrage. "Waitressing is just one of my jobs. It doesn't define me."

"Sit down for a minute. Let's talk." Melinda motioned to the chair across from her.

Harley looked around, hoping to see someone with his finger in the air signaling her for more water or ketchup, but for once, every diner was contentedly forking food into her mouth or sipping her drink.

"You're not indispensable," said Melinda. "They can do without you for a minute."

Reluctantly, Harley sat.

"Tell me. Why did you come back to Newberry?"

"I wanted to open an inn." Melinda already knew that much. The rest was none of her business.

"Why here? Why now?"

"Why not?" She was Melinda's captive. If they'd

been anywhere but here and she wasn't wearing her drab brown uniform with her manager standing sentinel, observing her on her first day of work—but she had to take whatever Melinda dished out. She had no choice. When it came to her franchise deals, there were so many variables. How effective would the marketing plan be? Would the products strike a chord with buyers? Were they priced right? Even if sales met the manufacturer's projections, it would take a while for her to start making money.

"Somehow, you heard Jack was coming back to the States and you saw an opportunity."

"That's not true. I wouldn't have come back if I'd known Jack was going to be here."

"It's no secret I wanted the Grimsky property for myself. Unfortunately, Jack has always had a weakness where you're concerned, so he didn't do a very good job of making my case. But it's not too late. I haven't seen an 'Open' sign out front yet. Do you know what you're getting yourself into?"

Harley thought about the growing pile of regulatory forms on her desk.

"Most small businesses fail, and fail fast. Tell me, Harley. Are you a numbers person?"

The fact was, she had only passed Algebra II after being tutored.

Reading the answer in Harley's expression, Melinda smiled smugly. "Most entrepreneurs aren't. They only find out the hard way, when it smacks them in the face that they've underestimated how much money they're going to need and overestimated how quickly their business will catch on. It's nothing to beat yourself up over. I had to learn that lesson myself when Don died. So, let's do each other favor, shall we?" She slipped a pen and a brown and gold Louis check-book out of her bag. "I'll save you the tedium of start-ing a business—" she scribbled an amount and signed her name with a flourish "—in exchange for you deed-ing me the property." She ripped out the check and slid it across the table. "This should more than cover any expenses you've incurred so far, plus something extra to get you back on your feet, somewhere far from Ribbon Ridge."

Much as she hated to, Harley couldn't keep from ogling the check. Her eyes grew wide. It was enough money to buy the fanciest place on Bainbridge Is-land. She could do all the things she was doing now, without the risk of running into Jack every time she turned around—to say nothing of his overbearing mother.

Her heart thrummed. She had always believed what she and Jack had had was epic, until he hurt her. Dare she risk getting close enough to let him hurt her again?

All she had to do was slip the check into her apron pocket and there would be no more insurance forms, no more pesky inspectors from the health depart-ment wanting to come to confirm that her kitchen was in compliance. She could quit her waitress job on her first day, walk out of here right now and spend all her time on her art and preparing for her baby.

"Ahem." A few tables away, the brunette in head-to-toe Golftini pointed with a French manicured nail to her empty ice-tea glass.

Stay, and contend with the intrusive regulations and ever-increasing taxes and fees of a small business? Or go, and spend a life of leisure, drawing and playing on the floor with her son—and never see Jack Friestatt again?

Melinda arched a brow. "Well?"

Harley slid the check back toward Melinda and rose. "I'm staying." Pencil poised over her pad, she asked, "Would you like a drink, or not?"

Melinda glared at her with venom in her eyes. She gathered up her sweater and purse. "No, thank you." Tossing her napkin next to her plate, she added, "I've suddenly lost my appetite." She got up and strode out of the dining room, nose in the air.

Chapter Sixteen

When Harley arrived home to find Dad's big pickup in the drive, tailgate down, bed strewn with straw, she forgot all about Melinda.

She hurried past the filbert orchard and around the back.

"I got the gate; go ahead and let her go," said Dad.

Mom's arms opened, and a baby goat bucked and ran to the far side of the pen.

"Goats!" shouted Harley.

Mom grinned from ear to ear. "They were looking for new homes for these at my yoga place. They're fainting goats. They're super playful. Just watch out. When they're startled, they fall over."

"They look like oversized stuffed animals," said Harley. "But do they know how to do yoga?"

Mom laughed. "They know how to climb and be cute. That's all they need to know."

* * *

A few days later, Harley was in the middle of filling orders for her prints, studying her website analytics, and taking conference calls when she found herself staring into space. What was wrong with her? Her plate was full. Her art was getting recognition, she was finally making a decent living, and soon her baby would be in her arms. So why did she sometimes feel like a ghost in her own house?

Maybe she needed to eat. She went downstairs and opened the fridge, only to remember she needed groceries. She really should change out of her ratty old T-shirt before she drove to the market, but whom did she need to impress? She didn't know anyone any more. Her closest friends had moved away, Leslie to Florida and Sarah, Colorado, and the chances of running into Jack were slim. If he needed something in town, no doubt he had people to do it for him. She decided to jump in her car as she was.

The town of Newberry was updating itself. A new coffee shop, a candy store, and a couple of tasting rooms had opened around Newberry Park, the green space in the center of town. When a display of colorful flowers outside Posey's caught her eye, she eased off the gas and swerved into an empty parking space, picturing Mom's face lighting up when Harley arrived at her house holding a cheerful bouquet.

Head bent over the flowers, she noticed movement as a man pushed off the brick building next door, but she paid no attention.

"Harley."

"Jack!"

He had on his tweed jacket and jeans, hair waving over his forehead like a male model's. At the end of a pink leash studded with rhinestones was a Yorkshire terrier.

So much for slipping into town unnoticed.

They stood there awkwardly, neither knowing what to say.

"Flowers, huh?"

No good deed went unpunished. "For my mom." Her hand went to her hair. *Emily probably never had a hair out of place the whole time she was married to him,* she thought. Lovely Emily, of the poreless skin and beige cashmere sweaters. She had never done anything untoward to draw attention to herself.

Unlike Harley, who spent all her tip money on straightening products that didn't work and who'd once caused a minor riot in Biology by excusing herself to go to the lav, then calling the Humane Society over Mr. Graff making them dissect frogs. She was as different from Emily as could be. What man wouldn't have chosen Emily over her?

Suddenly the Yorkie sprang away like a shot, twisting its leash around Harley's legs.

"*Fang!*" yelled Jack.

"Sorry." He scooped up the bundle of apricot-colored fur, disentangled its leash from around Harley's knees and tucked it safely under his arm, its stubby legs scrabbling in midair for purchase. "Don't know how I didn't see that coming."

Only then did she become aware of a passerby and his curious Great Dane.

"Getting settled in?" he asked.

Before she could answer, two freckle-faced girls wearing matching, St. Theresa's School navy plaid skirts ran up to him.

"Finished playing in the park?" he asked, giving them each a squeeze.

Simultaneously, they held up miniature shopping bags, and Harley's heart squeezed. Jack and Emily's twins in the flesh. She hadn't been able to resist checking them out on social media when they were born. The image of them swaddled in pink, one in each crook of Jack's arms, was burned onto her retinas.

Jack's mother had been quick to spread the word that Freddie and Frankie had been born prematurely. But Harley knew exactly when they'd been conceived. And even if the world really was still as archaic as Melinda Friestatt believed, Jemily being the golden couple that they were, everyone in Newberry would have given them the benefit of the doubt.

The twins stared up at Harley with open expressions. One of them scrunched up her face as she scratched her side. Any day now, they would start making the inevitable comparisons with other adolescent girls and realize how beautiful they were. But for today, they were still unself-conscious little girls.

"They just got their ears pierced," said Jack, looking fondly from one daughter to the other, "so of course they had to get earrings."

"Mimi said we could get them done when we were eleven," said one of them with a pronounced New Zealand accent.

Harley smiled benignly. Who knew there was a universal age for getting your ears pierced? It must be true. Melinda Friestatt never put a foot wrong.

Jack rose from his haunches. "Girls, this is an old friend of mine. Frances . . . Frederica . . . I'd like you to meet Harley."

"Nice to meet you," they mumbled politely. Then Freddie—or Frankie—tugged on Jack's sleeve. "C'mon, Daddy. You promised to take us to the ice cream place."

Jack set the animated toy that passed for a canine back on the ground, and, one small hand in each of his, permitted himself to be dragged down the sidewalk. "The park's still a novelty," said Jack. "They were only five when we moved away. It's like they never lived here at all."

"Want to come with us?" Frances called over her shoulder.

Harley hesitated.

"Might as well," said Jack, walking backward. "I have some ideas for how our businesses can help each other."

They had reached the corner. The other twin gestured with her arm. "Come on, then."

Harley shoved the bunch of Shasta daisies she'd been clutching back into the vase and jogged after them.

After she ordered at the counter, Jack ordered for himself and the girls and they found a seat.

"What is it you wanted to talk about?" asked Harley.

"We're both in the tourist trade. And we're right next door to each other. Our businesses feed off each other. We should be thinking about ways to cross-promote."

"I'm listening."

"You're a graphic designer. Maybe you could come up with some brochures, both print and digital."

"That's a great idea. I'll start working on it. While we're on the subject, I'm planning an open house as a way to give people a sneak peek and get them talking. Kind of a housewarming party. I'll have some little appetizers, give tours of the property, and display my artwork. It'll be free and open to the community."

"I'll provide the wine."

"That would be awesome."

Under the table between the twins' chairs, Fang waited for one of the girls to sneak him something.

"This is my lunch," laughed Harley, licking her butter pecan ice cream.

Wide-eyed, the twins looked at each other and then at her. "Reeeally?"

"Sure is. So, girls," said Harley, "tell me about yourselves. What do you like to do?"

"I like dancing," grinned Frankie, fidgeting in her chair.

"I like graphic novels," said Freddie. "And comics."

"I used to love comics when I was your age. I wonder if my mom kept them? I'll have to ask her next time I see her."

"And we're both on the soccer team."

"I wish I wasn't," sighed Frankie. She propped her elbows on the table and sank her chin into her hand.

"We've already talked about that," said Jack firmly. "You're going to keep taking soccer and Freddie's going to stick to piano."

"Piano's dumb," said Freddie.

"Freddie has a hard time sitting still," said Jack to Harley. "She's fallen behind Frankie with her pieces."

"Because I don't like piano. It's boring."

"Is not. *Soccer's* boring," said Frankie.

"Piano's more boring."

"Maybe we'll revisit it after your recital," said Jack.

"When's that?" asked Harley.

"January," Freddie moaned.

"Tell me more about the dancing," said Harley.

"She doesn't really dance," said Freddie. "She just watches videos of people like Selena Gomez and dances around in the bedroom."

"I do, too!" said Frankie. "Just because I'm not allowed to take lessons doesn't mean I'm not a real dancer."

What about you?" Harley asked Freddie. "What kinds of comics do you like?"

"Anything to do with Wonder Woman."

"You should see how many comics she has hidden—"

Freddie glared at her sister, effectively shutting her up. Then she looked at Jack, as if she feared he might scold her.

"One day you'll be glad you know how to play soccer and piano," said Jack.

"The only reason I take them's 'cause of Mimi," Frankie grumbled.

"Maybe it's just me, but it seems like people should be able to choose their own types of lessons," said Harley. She turned to Jack. "What about you? Are you glad you learned how to play saxophone when you were little?"

"You played the sax?" asked both girls at once.

Jack squirmed. "I didn't keep up with it."

"Seriously. If you got to quit the saxophone, how come I can't quit soccer?" Frankie complained, handing Fang a piece of her cone in blatant defiance of the rules.

"Mimi says not to feed Fang at the table," said Jack.

"Why? Why do we always have to do what Mimi says?" she asked, on the verge of tears.

Why were girls so sensitive? "Because Mimi has lived a long time, and she's learned a lot about life."

Though there had been times Jack had asked himself the same thing.

Jack pushed back his chair and opened his arms. "Come here."

Dutifully, Frankie came toward Jack, pain distorting her heart-shaped face, and laid her head on his chest. "Why do I have to do everything everyone tells me to do?" Her voice penetrated his rib cage, into the core of his being. "I hate soccer. I stink at it."

"Is that what this is about?"

She nodded against his chest.

"Even if that's so, you can't quit in the middle of the season."

"Golf," said Harley, out of the blue.

Jack gave her a scathing look.

"I just remembered. You were on the golf team. . . ."

Jack had always wanted to play baseball. But Mother has insisted golf would be more advantageous to him in his career. *"What do people do on the golf course when they're not hitting the ball? They talk. Talking leads to deals. You'll be able to see how people react to pressure and their ability to strategize."*

". . . until you weren't. What happened?"

"Quit when I was a junior," he said sheepishly.

Beneath the table, the Yorkie frowned and nudged Freddie's ankle.

Freddie fed him the last bite of her cone and wiped her hands on her pants. Then she slid out of her chair and reached for Frankie's hand. "Can we go outside and wait on the bench?"

"Okay. But take the dog, and stay where I can see you through the glass."

The bell on the door clanged as they went out.

Jack blew out a breath and scraped a hand across his scalp as he and Harley watched through the glass.

"They're adorable," said Harley wistfully.

"They're getting to be headstrong."

"The soccer?"

"Today it's soccer. Next it'll be something else."

"I never thought about twins being identical right down to their interests."

"No doubt genetics plays a role. But it's not their decision. They're too young to know what's good for them."

"I see." She smiled tightly.

"Clearly, you don't. You will, though, once you have kids of your own."

"You must be right, because you're never wrong, are you?"

Jack ground his jaw. "Is this how it's going to be between us?"

"That's entirely up to you." She stood and slung her bag over her shoulder. "Thanks for the ice cream."

Jack wasn't used to having his judgment questioned. He scrambled out of his chair and followed her out the door.

"Nice meeting you, girls. And you, Fang," Harley said, petting him.

"Nice to meet you," they sang in chorus.

"I just got some adorable baby goats at my house, just up the hill from you. They do yoga with me."

"Yoga?"

"Stand on my back, romp around with me. Come up and try it sometime. It's so much fun. Fang can come, too."

Eagerly, the twins looked at Jack. "Can we, Dad?"

With a wave, Harley turned and walked up the sidewalk in the direction of her car.

Nearby, the door to Zeno's opened. Out wafted the sharp tang of wood smoke from the pizza oven, and it was October of senior year all over again. Sparks from the bonfire outside the stadium flew high into the night sky . . . an amplified voice announced a touchdown and the distant cheer of the crowd filled Jack's ears. Atop the Pendleton blanket spread across his tailgate, he saw Harley's thighs below her cutoffs.

"We'll see," said Jack, unable to tear his eyes away from the sway of her hips and the way her ponytail bounced.

After everyone was safely buckled into the truck, Jack withdrew a ten-year-old mixtape from the glove box and slipped it into the CD player. He'd assembled the playlist himself—a soundtrack from his high school years, the last time he'd felt truly free. He knew every word of every song by heart.

"*Dad*-ah," the twins complained, yelling to hear themselves over their hands clamped to their ears. "Not that again. That music is so old school! Can't we listen to *our* music?"

Jack's first instinct was to say no. But he imagined what Harley might say. Soon the cab was filled with a Selena Gomez reggae-tinged number, the twins bouncing in the backseat.

Chapter Seventeen

The quiet was going to take some getting used to. In Seattle, the nonstop back-and-forth of traffic, the muffled snoring of Harley's downstairs neighbor, and regular footsteps in the hallway and on the stairs of her apartment building were constant reminders that she wasn't alone. Up on Ribbon Ridge, the silence was deafening.

She imagined what Jack's house sounded like, ringing with his girls' voices. She longed for the sound of children here, in her own house.

She was on the phone with Nora, her design team director, when she heard a car pull up. She ran to the window, but she couldn't see the driveway from here, so she waited, eyeing the pen where her goats played.

"Harley?"

"Yes," she said into the phone, peering out. "Sorry."

"The greeting card collection. We need to talk about the direction they're headed in."

"Do we need to do it right now?" From the ground below came the voices of Jack and his twins.

"Now would be good. As you're finding out, these things take time to develop. We're halfway to the deadline."

"It's just that . . . I'm looking out my second-story window, and there are kids in my yard."

"Kids?" echoed Nora from her office in downtown St. Louis.

"Kids. Of both the human and goat varieties."

"Do you need to hang up?"

Harley laughed. "Can I call you back?"

"Call me tomorrow. It's almost five here. We're getting ready to close."

She promised Nora she'd get back to her first thing next morning, then scampered down the stairs. When her eye landed on the box of diapers that had arrived in the mail earlier that day, she stashed them in the closet next to the powder room. Then she dashed out the back door to where the twins were sticking their arms through the holes in the fence toward the goats.

"We came to see the goats!" exclaimed Freddie. Or maybe it was Frankie.

Jack was wearing a white T-shirt and Levi's, a tool belt riding low on his hips. "They wouldn't stop bugging me," he said.

"Aw! Look at her run! She's so cute!" said Frankie.

"They're both girls," said Freddie, bending over at the waist to peer under a goat's belly. "You can tell because they don't have penises."

Jack pinched the bridge of his nose. "The twins have been studying reproduction in health class."

"I see."

"What are their names?" asked Freddie.

"They're brand-new. They don't have names yet."

"I'm going to call this one Daisy," Freddie said.

"And I'm calling this one Tulip," said Frankie.

"Daisy and Tulip it is. Would you like to go in and play with them? They're very friendly. Just don't chase them, or they'll fall over. They're fainting goats."

Harley opened the gate and the girls and Jack filed in behind her.

"Here!" said Frankie to Harley. "Give them one of Fang's dog biscuits. They love them!"

"I keep a supply in the truck. Hope you don't mind," said Jack.

Harley held out a biscuit, and both goats trotted over and pressed their muzzles into her hand, tickling her palm.

Daisy reared up and came down on Tulip's back, resulting in a tirade of squeals and maternal reprimands from the twins.

"How do they do yoga?"

"I'll show you. Who wants to go first?"

"I do!"

"No, me!"

Harley laughed. "Don't worry. You'll both get a turn." Harley positioned Frankie in a downward dog and then went to lift Daisy onto her back, but Jack stepped in. "I'll get her." To a torrent of giggles, he placed Daisy on Frankie's back, steadying her before letting go, while Fang looked on, barking.

"I wanted to follow up with you about the open house," said Jack.

"Right. I'm thinking the second Saturday in October. Does that work for you?"

"Perfect. It'll still be tourist season. The intent is to get people to stop at both our places. I'll send one of our docents over, along with a sampling of wines to pour."

Harley had been secretly hoping Jack would come and pour himself. She tried not to let her disappointment show.

"And I'll have a supply of Honeymoon Haven brochures you can keep at your place," she said.

Frankie turned her head their way, shouting, "Look! Are you watching?"

"We're watching, we're watching," laughed Harley, clapping, just as Frankie tipped over and Daisy leaped out of harm's way, Fang nipping at her heels.

"Now me!" said Freddie. "My turn!"

The girls had taken over. All the adults had to do was stand back and watch.

"No, no, no." Frankie laughed, holding her belly, staggering around the pen till she almost lost her balance. "Not like that!" She shuffled back through the straw toward Daisy, who had skittered to the far side of the pen, and scooped her up.

"Here, I'll help you," huffed Freddie.

With a great deal of effort, the twins managed to carry the goat back to the center of the pen and set her down. "Now. Bend your front legs." They physically folded the poor animal's front hoofs under. It promptly collapsed.

"No! Keep your *butt*—" Frankie moved to the goat's rear and lifted, "—*up*—nnn—"

Watching with her hands on her hips, Freddie got an idea. "Like this," she said, demonstrating where Daisy could see her.

But Daisy simply lay there, Fang sniffing her suspiciously.

"Soccer's not the only way for kids to get exercise," said Harley.

Jack stood with his legs spread, his arms folded, watching. "Come on, girls. Time to get going."

"But we just got here!"

"I just took a break from what I was doing. Now it's time to go back."

"I can watch them and bring them home later if you want," said Harley.

"Pleeeeze?" The twins jumped up and down. "It's not that far. You can practically see our house from here. Bonita Valentine walks to school every day and she's the same age as us, and that's farther than Harley's house."

"Thanks anyway. They need to get back to clean up. We're meeting Mother later for dinner."

Chapter Eighteen

Melinda sipped her wine and perused her menu while the twins chattered between themselves.

Jack opened his menu. "What looks good?"

"I was thinking of the hearts of palm with truffle salad," replied Mother.

"I'm leaning toward the salmon."

"I want a salad, too," said Frankie, a challenging look in her eyes.

"You need meat to build strong bones and muscles," said Mother.

"I hate meat," said Frankie, folding her arms. "It's so gross. And the way they treat the poor farm animals . . ."

"Like the goats at Harley's house," said Freddie. Suddenly she frowned. "Do people eat goats?"

Mother looked at Jack and then Freddie. "You were at Harley's house?"

"After school. She has the cutest little goats!" said Frankie.

"They know how to do yoga!" added Freddie.

The server arrived. "All set?"

"Yes," said Mother firmly. She ordered meat and vegetables for the girls.

The server set down a plate of bread and dipping oil and Frankie tore into it, her attempt at asserting her independence subdued for the time being.

But later on in the meal, Harley's name came up again.

"I like how Harley says people should be able to take any kind of lessons they want," Frankie said. "Like modern dance, for instance."

"You haven't touched your meat," said Mother.

"I told you. I don't like it."

"At least eat your vegetables," said Jack.

"I'm full."

"You ate too much bread," said Mother.

When will this dinner be over? thought Jack.

The girls launched into an in-depth conversation between themselves about their new school and the friends they'd begun to make.

"Yesterday I had a meeting downtown," said Mother. "One of the committee members is Sylvie Collins's mother."

"We just got back to Ribbon Ridge and you're on a committee already?"

"Being involved is the best way to make connections."

Why should he be surprised? Mother had always sought every opportunity to rub elbows with the hoi polloi. Even better if it was disguised as community service.

"You ought to become more active yourself. Have you thought about joining the Newberry Young Professionals?"

"When do I have time for that? Whenever I'm not working, I'm with my girls."

"You would have more time if you had a wife. Back to Sylvie Collins. You remember her."

"How could I forget? Sylvie was the drama queen of Newberry High."

"That was eons ago. Since then, Sylvie's been married and divorced, with kids. She's a mother," said Mother pointedly. "And"—she lifted a brow—"she happens to be a nutritionist."

"Does she wear a retainer?"

"Pardon me?"

"Never mind."

"I could put a bug in her mother's ear."

Jack envisioned his girls eagerly eating meal after meal of tasty yet nutritiously balanced foods. What could it hurt?

"Sure. Set it up."

Sylvie sounded excited to go out with Jack. So that Pru didn't hear about it, Jack thought it best not to take her to the country club. Instead, he chose Tart, known for its extravagant brunches.

The following Sunday, the two of them went up to the buffet and returned with their plates. Jack had loaded his with waffles topped with chicken and gravy and salad.

"I don't consider that brunch food," said Sylvie after they sat down again.

"This is a classy joint. It must be brunch food, or the chef wouldn't be serving it," he replied, tucking in.

"This," she said, indicating her eggs Benedict with her fork, "is brunch food."

"That's more like breakfast food to me," said Jack.

"No. Yours is more like lunch food. Actually, I don't get why anyone would top waffles with a savory sauce. They're supposed to be eaten with maple syrup, period. Not being a purist, I might make an exception for strawberries and whipped cream."

"I disagree. Waffles are bland. They take on whatever flavor you put with them."

"You're wrong. They were first invented to be desserts, and desserts are, by definition, sweet. And another thing—technically, brunch should be served from ten till one, not eleven to two, the way they do it here."

Somehow, Jack no longer had a taste for waffles. He set down his fork and scraped back his chair. "I'm going back up."

He came back with a fresh plate of pasta and oysters Rockefeller. "Starting over," he said, hoping she would get the hint.

"Thank God you seem so normal," sighed Sylvie.

"What do you mean?"

"The men I meet online are crazy. I hate dating. It's soul sucking, having to introduce yourself over and over again to new people. You know what the only good thing about it is?"

"A minute ago, I would have said meeting new people."

"Wrong. Taking different dates to my ex's restaurant, just to annoy him."

Jack took a swig of his mimosa. "If it's not too personal, who broke up with whom?"

"He dumped me. Why?"

"If you broke up with him, I don't see what you would get out of rubbing your new dates in his face."

"Are you implying that I'm not over him?" She huffed. "He wishes."

There was an uncomfortable pause while Jack tried to think of a new subject. "Tell me about your job."

"I work in the health insurance marketplace."

"Mother said you're a nutritionist."

"I have a background in nutrition, but I fainted once when I worked in the hospital, and private practice is too demanding."

"So you're in customer service."

"That's what they call it when you interview. After you're hired, you realize it's selling."

"You don't like selling? People who have the personality to sell enjoy it and can do well."

"Did I mention it's commission only?"

After the Prudence debacle, Jack was determined to make the most of his date with Sylvie. So she wasn't perfect. She might still be a stabilizing influence on his girls. He tore off a piece of his cinnamon roll and stuffed it in his mouth. "Think of it this way. You're educating consumers. You're your own boss. You can make unlimited income if you work hard."

He held out his bread plate with the cinnamon roll on it. "Want the other half of this?"

"No, thanks. The Collinses have a strong family history of diabetes and bipolar disorder." She leaned in. "Two of my cousins are institutionalized."

That raised a red flag. "I'm sorry to hear that."

"Recently, one was allowed to come back for a short visit, and they always come on holidays. You'll meet them at family dinners."

"Family—"

"That's what this is about, isn't it? Your mother told my mother you're looking to settle down."

"Well, I—"

Sylvie sat up, her eyes fixed on a spot over Jack's shoulder.

"What is it? What's wrong?"

"My second ex-husband. And his new girlfriend."

Jack turned around to see the hostess leading a man and woman to a table nearby.

"How many times have you been married?" asked Jack.

But Sylvie wasn't listening. She tossed her napkin on the table. "We're out of here."

Jack had barely made a dent in his oysters. "You can't eat in the same restaurant as him?"

"No. He has a restraining order against me."

She was gathering her belongings as her ex passed by their table.

"Bastard!" Sylvie shrieked, then got up and strode out.

Jack hurriedly took another bite of pasta, slapped some bills on the table, and apologizing to the stunned hostess, followed Sylvie out to the parking lot.

"What was that about?"

"He must have found out I was here and followed me, just to ruin my date."

"How could he have possibly guessed you'd be here?"

"He's the devil! He has dark powers."

"I don't know. Tart's a pretty popular place for Sunday brunch."

"That's why you chose this place. You *knew* he was going to be here."

Realization hit Jack. "I don't think this is going to work."

"You're the devil, too! All men are devils!"

There was a click as Jack pressed the button on his key fob. "You're upset. Let's get in. I'll take you home."

"Forget that," said Sylvie. She whirled around and went back and stood beneath the building's overhang, where she pulled out her phone.

"How are you going to get home?" he called to her from where he stood next to his open car door.

"Don't worry about it." She was already busily tapping away.

Jack's phone pinged.

Why don't you like me?

It was Prudence, texting him again.

Chapter Nineteen

The next day, Jack was taking inventory and the girls were sitting at an outside table visible through the picture windows when Mother came into the tasting room. "How did your date with Sylvie go?"

"Did you know Sylvie's second ex has a restraining order against her?"

"What did she do to him?"

"I didn't ask. I don't want to know."

"Maybe it's something about him."

"She believes he's Satan. Actually, she thinks all men are Satan."

Mother sighed. "Newberry is a small town. There aren't that many suitable women to choose from."

"Maybe it depends on how you define suitable. From now on, I'll do my own date recon. Look. There's Hank." Jack raised a hand in greeting and went outside to meet his cousin.

Mother said hello to Hank and Jamie and then excused herself, saying she had work to do.

"We stopped by to see if you wanted to go to the open house at the Victorian with us," said Hank.

"Got it covered," said Jack. "I sent a docent."

The twins' ears perked up. They'd been hanging out with him at the tasting room for an hour and were bored.

"Come on," said Hank. "Alex is meeting us there with Griffin." Alex was the husband of Jack's cousin, Kerry.

Hank glanced at his watch. "It's going to be over soon. Come on. Can't not stop by and wish your neighbor well."

Frankie's ears perked up. "Are you talking about Harley's house?"

"Forget it. It's almost over," said Jack.

"Not for forty-five minutes," said Hank.

"Is Griffin going to be there?" asked Freddie. The twins adored the baby.

Jamie nodded.

"Oh, please, let's!" cried Freddie. She turned to her aunt for backup. "Harley has goats and everything. Her house is so much fun."

The tasting crowd was dwindling, and even if it weren't, Jack had more than enough staff present. He wouldn't be missed.

"The work'll still be here when I get back, I guess."

"Yay!" shouted the girls, jumping up and down as the three of them followed Hank and Jamie outside to Jack's truck.

"People are going to be here any minute."

Harley's operating permits had finally come through

and her plum-colored Adirondack porch chairs and living room suite been delivered just in time. She'd spent days making sure everything was just so. The house had been cleaned from top to bottom. Her fiddle-leaf fig was content in a window with a southern exposure. Recipes had been researched, beds made, towels folded.

Her talent was for art, not innkeeping. Nothing about running a B and B came naturally. But if that was what she had to do to support her child, she'd do it willingly.

"Don't be nervous," said Mom.

She'd enlisted her parents' help for the open house. Dad was already stationed upstairs, and Mom was headed out to the goat pen as soon as the first guests showed up.

"I'm not."

"Really? You've rearranged those pillows a dozen times."

"People are coming from all over the valley," said Harley. "First impressions are lasting. I need to make a good one. *Kiai!*" she yelled, bringing the side of her hand down along the welted ridge of a velvet cushion, creating a slight indentation.

"What are you doing?"

"What's it look like? Karate-chopping the throw pillows," she panted. "*Kiai!*"

The doorbell chimed, and she jumped and touched her hair. "They're here! How do I look?"

"Fine. I'll head out back to the goat pen."

Mom scurried out the back door as Harley threw open the front. "Welcome to Honeymoon Haven!"

"Hi, Harley. Remember me?" An athletic-looking

woman wearing a tracksuit in the colors of the local college shook her hand vigorously.

"Pru!" Prudence Mitchell, her tenth-grade peer math tutor. "How have you been?"

"Solid. Run my own accounting firm now." She looked around the foyer, nodding approvingly. "Place looks ship-shape."

"Thanks. It's been a lot of work, but I think it's finally ready."

Pru held up a business card between two fingers. "You need help with accounting, here's my card."

"I just might do that. Numbers were never my strong suit."

"I know." Pru grinned, and Harley saw a plastic coating on her teeth.

"Jack been here yet?"

Harley started. Then she remembered: in high school, Pru had had a bit of a thing for Jack, though it went unreciprocated. Poor Pru had always been a little backward when it came to guys. Harley assumed it had something to do with having been raised without a mother. Her parents were divorced and her dad had sole custody.

Then again, lots of the girls had had minor crushes on Jack. No one thought they could compete with Emily.

"Er, I'm not sure if Jack will be here in person. But the docent's pouring his wines, right over there. You're welcome to sample some."

The next group arrived, and then another.

Three hours later, the line had finally begun to taper off when a group of five trooped in, some looking familiar, others Harley had never met.

"Jack." *He came.*

With a jerk of his thumb, he said, "The girls are out with the goats." He gestured toward a tall man in a ball cap with a Textron logo. My cousin, Hank. Hank, you remember Harley."

"'Course." Hank's Grandmother Ellie had raised him at The Sweet Spot. Harley remembered him as a friendly but unsettled kid who bounced from interest to interest, trying to find what he wanted.

"Hello again, Hank."

"Harley. Meet my wife, Jamie. She teaches music at Newberry Elementary."

Jamie's belly was so big, Harley could barely tear her gaze away from it long enough to focus on her face.

"Nice to meet you," said Jamie in a crystalline voice.

"And this is Alex, husband of my cousin Kerry. Alex is one of our local men in blue."

"Griffin," Alex said, nodding to the baby he held.

One look at Griffin's dimples had Harley reaching for him. "Well, hello there, little man!" she cooed, stroking his chubby cheek with a finger. "Aren't you something?" As always, she was thinking of her own, unborn son.

"He's all yours," said Alex, easing the baby toward her. "Kerry's working on a case and the older kids are at a birthday party."

But Harley barely listened to what he said. She was too wrapped up in examining every inch of the baby in her arms.

"How old are you?" Why had her tone suddenly risen two octaves?

"Four months," Alex answered.

"Four months! Such a big boy," she said, bouncing him on her hip, giving him her thumb to wrap his tiny fingers around. "And so strong!"

"He's big for his age." Alex hooked his thumbs through his belt loops and puffed out his chest. "Already has his own football. Just sayin'."

"Listen to this." Jack chuckled. "Papa already has him playing linebacker for the Seahawks."

Alex tipped his head toward Harley, and from behind his hand said, "Could his jealousy be any more obvious? Not my fault all he can make is girls."

"I wouldn't mind balancing out the estrogen pool with a little testosterone," Jack admitted.

He wanted a son. Jack wanted a son. Harley hoped no one noticed the throbbing of her pulse in her neck, the flush in her cheeks. She hid her frenzied excitement behind a smile as Griffin reached for the button on her sweater.

"Watch out. He loves anything shiny," said Alex.

The baby smiled a toothless grin. "Kuh."

"He's talking!" exclaimed Harley.

"Mostly he tries to copy what's said to him."

"Aw. I could eat him up. Would you like to see the goats?" She looked up at Alex. "Do you mind?"

"Let's do it."

"Dad," she called up the stairs. "I'm going outside. Cover for me?"

She turned her back on the others, delighting in Griffin's slobbery smile as she made her way out the back door toward the goat pen.

"Harley!" Jack's twins threw their arms around her, and for one magical moment she was completely surrounded by children. Tears stung her eyes.

She squatted with Griffin to bring him to eye level

with the goats, while Jack and Hank stood back and watched, swirling and sniffing Jack's wine in their glasses, talking about the new vintage, and Alex listened.

"They can talk wine until the cows come home." It was Jamie, standing beside her. "Hank said the three of you went to high school together."

Harley nodded.

"What have you been doing since then?"

"I was in Seattle for a while, but now I'm back, making my living doing graphic design."

"I've heard a lot of good things about Seattle. I'm from back east. I met Hank when I came out here on summer vacation and never left."

"Sounds like there's a story there."

Jamie's laughter was like the tinkling of piano keys, drawing Harley's eyes to her face and, inevitably, back to her stomach.

Mom must have noticed. She reached for Griffin and nodded. "Go 'head. I've got him."

Harley stood. "When are you due?"

"Not until February. I know, I'm already bigger than a house. Do you want to touch it?"

Without waiting for a reply, Jamie took Harley's hand and laid it flat against her belly. "I have this theory that *every*body wants to touch a pregnant woman's stomach, but they're too afraid to ask. I hear some women consider it an invasion of privacy. But I love it when people rub my belly. Why not spread the joy?"

Jamie's middle felt warm and hard against Harley's palm. She gasped.

"Did he kick you?" Jamie moved Harley's hand to

a different spot. "Be real still and he might do it again."

She was, and he did.

"It's a miracle, isn't it? Aww." She laughed. "Don't cry."

Harley blotted an eye with the side of a finger. "Sorry. I get all choked up around babies for some reason."

Jack appeared at her shoulder holding a glass of wine. "Here," he said softly. "For you."

Harley accepted it gratefully. "I guess it's okay. Things seem to be winding down."

"And water for you," he said to Jamie.

Jamie sighed. "I'm counting the days until I can have a glass of wine again, but it'll be a while until I stop nursing."

Nursing . . . yet another thing Harley could never do. She would have to settle for bottle-feeding.

Hank had drifted back to his wife's side.

"You know what you're having?" Jack asked him.

"Boy," replied Hank proudly. "Henry Friestatt the ninth."

"First the vineyards, now a baby. I always thought you'd be piloting an airliner by now. Flying was all you ever talked about."

"That was before I met Jamie." His eyes shone on his wife.

"And now there's going to be another little Friestatt," said Jack. "Just wait. From the moment they put him into your arms, you're going to be able to pick out traits from each of you. The shape of his nose, the length of his fingers . . . you better hope and pray he gets his mother's ears."

Hank lashed out to cuff him and Jack angled, barely missing getting swatted, both men laughing.

"Wonder what it's like?" asked Jack, wistful now. "Dressing up like Batman at Halloween instead of princesses. Peeing in the woods together. Burping contests. Teaching him how to swing a bat . . ."

With every clichéd pastime Jack mentioned, Harley's pulse quickened.

"Sounds like you've given this some thought," chuckled Hank.

"Maybe." Jack got a faraway look in his eyes. "A little."

I'm having a son, she wanted to blurt out to the world. *I'm having a son! He's on his way! He'll be here even before Jamie and Hank's!*

But given Jack's emphasis on eye color and hand shape, he was thinking of a son of his own, not the adopted son of the woman he had already rejected once.

Alex gathered Griffin up from Mom's arms. "Time for us to pick up the kids from the party. Nice meeting you, Harley. Give me your number, and I'll text you mine."

The twins ran over, out of breath from romping with the goats. "We're hungry."

"Mimi had a meeting. She won't be home yet." Jack hadn't thought about dinner. "We could go downtown and get tacos."

"Yeah. Let's!"

"It was nice seeing you again, girls," said Harley.

"Where are you going?" they asked.

"You're my last guests. When you leave, the open house will be over. Time for me to clean up."

"Come with us," they pleaded.

"Thanks for asking. But I have a lot to do."

"Go ahead," said Mom. "I'll get things started."

"No. I can't let you—"

"What's there to do? The house is already spotless. It's just put the leftovers in the fridge and lock up."

"The docent'll take care of the wine," Jack added.

Harley hesitated. "All right." She turned to Mom. "Can I bring you something?"

"Not a thing."

"At least take the leftovers home with you," said Harley.

"You won't get any arguments from your dad about that," said Mom.

Chapter Twenty

At the taqueria on Main, Jack, Harley, and the twins stood at the counter peering up at the menu on the wall.

"What looks good, girls?" asked Harley.

The twins looked at each other, fingers to lips. "Ummm . . ."

Maybe they don't have Mexican food in New Zealand, thought Harley. *Maybe they've never been to a taqueria.* "A burrito is a tortilla wrapped around beans or meat. A taco—"

"We know what they are," said Freddie.

"It's just that we've never ordered ourselves," said Frankie. "Mimi always orders for us."

"Oh." Harley looked at Jack, hoping she hadn't overstepped.

"First time for everything, right?" said Jack. "Go ahead, girls. Choice is yours."

Frankie scratched her head.

"I don't know . . ." said Freddie.

They put their heads together and debated the

relative merits of burritos versus tacos versus flautas as, behind them, the line lengthened.

Ten minutes later, the four of them finally sat down at a red-checkered tablecloth next to a picture window, Jack and Freddie on one side, Harley and Frankie on the other, and unwrapped their meals.

"This is really good," said Frankie, relishing her beef taco.

"So's this," said Freddie.

"Thought you didn't like meat," said Jack.

"I like *this* kind of meat," she replied.

When the girls were finished, Jack offered them some quarters to play foosball and they scurried off.

"They like you," said Jack.

"I like them, too."

"It's none of my business, and you don't have to answer. In fact, part of me doesn't want to know. But I have to ask. When you were in Seattle, did you ever . . . ?"

She looked at him. "Have a boyfriend?"

"I know you had a boyfriend. Boy*friends*. I mean . . . were you ever . . ."

"In love?" She smiled. "Yes, I had boyfriends. And . . ." her smile faded. "As for your second question, the answer is no."

Relief washed over Jack. It made no sense, but even though she didn't fit the bill as a mother for the twins, at the thought of her with anyone else he was overcome with a savage possessiveness. He glanced over his shoulder at the twins, but they were busy playing.

Freddie ran over, panting, and said, "I learned something today."

"What's that?" asked Harley.

"Food tastes better when you're the one who picked it."

"Hey," said Harley with a nod to the foosball table. "Who's winning?"

"It's over. Frankie beat me."

Harley fished some quarters from her bag. "Go play another couple of rounds. I'll play the best out of three."

Freddie's face lit up. "Hey, Frankie!" she called, running toward her sister. "Do-over."

"What we had was special, Jack. But we're different people now."

"Harley?"

"Huh?" Something outside the picture window had caught her eye. "What are all those people doing across the street?"

Jack dragged his attention from her to the window. "Looks like a sit-in."

"The signs say, 'Save Newberry Park.' Wonder what's going on?"

The girls came back. "Frankie won."

But neither Jack nor Harley paid any attention to them.

"What are you guys looking at?" asked Freddie.

Harley rose and gathered her things. "I don't know. But I'm going to find out. Who's coming with me?"

"Harley—" warned Jack.

The twins looked inquiringly at him.

"Sorry," said Harley. "You don't have to leave if you're not ready, but I'm going."

Jack, his forehead furrowed with concern, looked from Harley to his twins and back.

"Can we go, Dad? We're done playing foosball."

Harley headed for the door as Jack protectively cradled a shoulder of each girl. "Harley."

"I'm just going to see what's going on."

"Don't get involved—"

Harley crossed the street and asked a woman what she was doing. "They're going to raze our park," she said. "We're concerned citizens rallying to save it."

"Raze the park?"

"Here," said the woman, handing her a sign. "Join us."

"Harley," called Jack from across the street, flanked by the twins. "What are you doing?"

"They're going to raze the park!" she called. "I'm going to help save it."

Jack took a twin's hand in each of his, looked both ways, and jogged across the street with them. "You better think this through before you get involved," he said. "You don't even know what this is about."

"They're tearing down the park. What else do I need to know?"

"Do you know *why* they're razing it?"

"All I know is, this park is a little jewel. An emerald surrounded by concrete."

Freddie looked up at Jack. "*I* want to save the park."

"There's the wrong way to affect change and the right way," said Jack sternly. "Like starting a petition. Writing letters and going to council meetings."

A few more curious people drifted over from the surrounding shops, then more.

"Do these people even have a permit?" asked Jack, to no one in particular.

A smattering of chants began, "Save the park! Save the park!"

"Permit?" asked Harley, yelling to be heard.

Jack reached out and grabbed Harley's arm. "Let's go home. You can read all about it in the news and decide then if and how you want to help."

Harley yanked her arm away. "Why should I go home when the rally is right here, right now?"

The green had quickly filled with people. So many people, they didn't all fit. They spilled into Main Street, slowing traffic at the filled crosswalks and along the berm. A potted arborvitae wobbled and fell, spilling soil onto the street.

"This could turn ugly," yelled Jack. "Let's go."

"I'm staying."

"How are you going to get home?"

"It's not far. I'll find a way." She waved her sign high at passing cars. "Save the park!" she called, while the girls watched, growing more wild-eyed by the minute.

"Don't let go of my hand, no matter what," yelled Jack to them, searching frantically for an opening between cars to get them back to the other side of the street and safety.

But before he found one, two police officers appeared from out of nowhere, waving their arms at the crowd. "Get off the street," they cried to the crowd. "You don't have the right to block traffic."

Harley tried to comply, but she was bumped and jostled by the crowd.

From the distance came the sound of sirens.

"Get off the street!" yelled the cops.

Where had all these people come from?

Cruisers pulled up, lights flashing, bringing more cops with bullhorns.

"Get off the street! This is the last time we're going to tell you before we start removing you by force."

Harley tried repeatedly to comply, but emotions had caught fire. Each time she made it back onto the green, she was shoved off the curb again. The next thing she knew her hands were behind her back and she heard a ratcheting sound. "You're under arrest for disorderly conduct for blocking a roadway and sidewalk," said a voice.

"She's with me," said Jack frantically. "I'll get her out of here."

"Too late. I told her three times to move and she didn't comply."

Now she was being herded toward a police van.

She caught a glimpse of the twins' eyes, wide as saucers.

"Don't say anything without a lawyer," Jack called to Harley. Over the melee, he yelled to the policeman. "What's going to happen to her?"

"She'll be taken to the station and processed on a second-degree misdemeanor. Then she'll be free to go until her court date."

Jack took his kids back to the estate, where they immediately began chattering to Mother about Harley's arrest.

"What is going on?" asked Mother.

"I have to go," said Jack. "I'll be back as soon as I can."

Then he turned around and drove to the crowded police station. Harley wasn't the only one in trouble. A half-dozen others were there, waiting to be processed.

Four hours later, Jack finally drove her home, his mouth fixed in a grim line.

"I could have gotten one of my parents to come get me," said Harley.

"If I didn't want to get you, I wouldn't have."

She gazed out her window without speaking, watching the scenery slide by. "Go ahead and say it."

"What? That maybe you should look before you leap?"

Harley made a face.

"It would be for your own good, you know. When's your hearing date?"

Harley read from the official papers on her lap. "Next Thursday at nine a.m."

"You're going to need a lawyer. My cousin Kerry's one of the best defense attorneys in the state. If you want, I'll give her a call."

"Why? I did what they said I did. I'm guilty. I already told them that."

"I told you not to say anything!" Jack scolded. "Disorderly conduct is a serious charge. You could go to jail. You messed up. But a savvy lawyer might still be able to help you."

"I can represent myself."

"No, you can't! You know what they say. 'Only a fool represents himself, and he who represents himself has a fool for an attorney.' "

"I like to do things my own way."

Jack ran a hand through his hair while he still had some. If he kept hanging around Harley, it was bound to start falling out.

The next evening, the girls were supposed to be doing their homework when they ran downstairs, their arms full. Frankie put her electronic device under Jack's nose. "Dad, look who it is."

Mother peered over Jack's shoulder at the cover of *Newberry Live* showing a close-up of Harley waving her sign.

"Is Harley famous?" asked Freddie, looking up at Jack, her face the picture of innocence.

"More like infamous," Mother drawled, giving Jack an accusing look.

"Look at the signs we made," said Frankie, holding Popsicle sticks glued onto sheets of hand-lettered construction paper.

"We wrote letters, too," said Freddie, holding up envelopes.

"And a petition," said Frankie.

"Have you girls considered that there might be very good reason for eliminating the park?" asked Mother.

"What reason?" asked Freddie.

"Something that would provide a real service, measurable in dollars, not merely aesthetics."

"What's aesthetics?" asked Frankie.

"You've seen all the cars in the parking lot of the tasting room . . . the people inside who come from all over the country, even the world, to try our wines. We need to spread the word to as many people as possible so we can continue to grow. That's what a tourism office does—helps travelers find what they're looking for. The current office is outdated. It's small and hard to get to because it's on a one-way street, and it doesn't have its own parking lot. The purpose for tearing down the park is to build a much-needed new tourist center."

But the twins' eyes had glazed over. They were too young to make the connection between how more tourists contributed to their livelihood.

"Are your backpacks all ready for school tomorrow?" asked Jack.

They shook their heads.

"How about you go back to your desks and get ready for the new school week?"

"But—"

"No buts," Mother said.

Reluctantly, the girls turned to go.

"Hold it. I'll take that," said Mother, holding out her hand for the device.

Reluctantly, Frankie relinquished it, and they disappeared up the stairs.

Mother studied the news story on the screen. "My committee has spent hundreds of hours on this project," she said tightly in a voice that could barely contain its anger.

"*Your* committee?"

"The Downtown Beautification Committee. I happen to be the chair."

So, that was what all Mother's meetings were about.

"What were you thinking today? You put the twins' lives in jeopardy. Emily has got to be turning over in her grave. What if one of them had been trampled by the crowd or run over by a car?"

"I had control of them at all times," said Jack.

"Look at these pictures! Police cars everywhere. It's bedlam."

"Of course the reporters made it look as bad as possible. Don't read more into it than it is. It was a

small-town protest that got a little out of hand," said
Jack mildly. "If this were Portland, no one would
have batted an eye."

"This isn't Portland. It's Newberry, and you're a
Friestatt. Harley was always trouble, and it's clear she
hasn't changed a bit."

"Harley merely sparked the girls' interest. I explained to them the importance of developing a
plan," replied Jack. "Regardless of how it turns out,
it'll be a real-life civics lesson."

Chapter Twenty-one

Harley hung up her phone after talking to her baby's birth mother. Kelly said the baby was about the size of a head of lettuce. He had had hiccups, which felt like a little flutter. Harley spread her hands on her flat stomach. *If only she could feel that.*

She pulled up the picture of the baby's second sonogram, which Kelly had sent her. After she'd decided to adopt, she had spent uncounted hours scrolling pictures of anonymous babies on the internet, wondering what hers would look like. But *this* was *him*. That was her baby. She traced over his little fingers and toes again and again, her heart throbbing with love. He was a miracle in the making. Every day that passed was a day closer to finally bringing him home.

When the day of her hearing came, Harley's parents offered to accompany her to her court date, but their jobs paid them by the hour. She insisted they not take off work.

She rushed around feeding her goats and getting herself ready. By the time she skipped down her porch steps—running late, as usual, she paused when she saw Jack's truck idling in the drive.

His window slid down.

"What are you—"

"Hop in," he said with a jerk of his head.

"I don't need—"

Jack looked at his watch. "It's already eight forty-five. If it were me getting sentenced, I'd have been there a half hour ago."

She hated being told what to do. But she knew he was right.

Neither spoke until they were off the back roads and onto the main two-lane leading to town.

"Have you had a chance to read up on the park situation?"

She nodded. "I still don't see how razing it is a good idea."

"Newberry's the gateway to wine country. That tourist center is long overdue. It will benefit the wine community, which in turn benefits the whole town. Including your bed-and-breakfast."

"It just seems like there has to be a better way."

The courtroom was far from empty. All the protestors had apparently been scheduled for the same day.

Harley sat next to Jack, fidgeting with the fringe on her bag, waiting for her name to be called.

The stern-faced judge didn't smile or look up from the papers he sorted at his raised desk.

Harley wished she had taken Jack's advice and gotten an attorney, but it was too late now.

When the bailiff called out her name, she rose, both relieved and frightened to be the first one.

The judge finally looked up to see Harley standing alone. "Who's representing Miss Miller-Jones?"

Harley cleared her throat. "I'm representing myself, Your Honor."

The judge lowered his reading glasses and sized her up. "Very well."

He asked the bailiff, "What are the charges?"

"Disorderly Conduct in the Second Degree: causing a public inconvenience by blocking a roadway or sidewalk, Your Honor."

"How do you plead?" the judge asked her.

"Well, first of all—"

"Guilty or not guilty, Miss Miller-Jones?"

She gulped. "Guilty."

He took his glasses off and gravely folded his hands atop his desk. "If there is something you would like to say before I pass judgment, now is the appropriate time."

"Yes, there is. I grew up just outside of town. Back then, there were always people walking and talking and playing in the park. Sometimes there would even be musicians and street performers. Later, when I moved away, when I thought about my hometown, it wasn't the businesses or the stores or the restaurants that came to my mind. It was the park, a green, living space in Newberry's heart."

"Is that all?"

"Yes, your honor."

Beside her, Jack was very still.

"Disorderly Conduct in the Second Degree is a Class B misdemeanor, the maximum penalty for which is six months in jail and/or a fine of up to twenty-five hundred dollars."

Panic threatened to overwhelm her. "You can't put me in jail, Your Honor."

"Defendant will remain silent while judgment is being passed."

Harley clutched the back of the pew in front of her. "You can't send me to jail. I just bought a house—the Victorian, the old Grimsky place on Ribbon Ridge?—everybody knows it—and I've turned it into a bed-and-breakfast. But the real reason I came back home to Newberry is because I'm adopting a baby boy, and I promised his birth parents I would raise him in a house in the country, and the baby's going to be here around Christmas. If I'm in jail, how am I going to finish my designs so I can pay my mortgage?"

"What designs are those?"

She faltered. *How could she put pictures into words?* "Here," she said frantically, pulling out her phone. "I'll show you." Scrolling to some of her older work, she started toward the bench, only to be blocked by the bailiff's arm.

Jack half rose, then remembered himself.

To Harley's surprised relief, the judge reached out his hand. "Bailiff? Bring me her phone."

She waited with bated breath while the judge thumbed through picture after picture.

He frowned, enlarging the screen, turning the phone sideways and then upright again. "I've seen these images somewhere before." Then it came to him. "My wife bought a set of these plates. She has them facing out in her china cupboard. Walk past them every day."

He handed her phone back to the bailiff, who walked it back to her.

The judge looked down at his paperwork. "I see by your record that you haven't been in trouble in the past. Given that you're a first-time offender and a productive member of the community, I hereby sentence you to a term of probation of six months. You will report immediately to the Yamhill County Department of Community Justice."

He brought down his gavel and she jumped.

Jack was on his feet, his hand on her elbow.

Harley's breath rushed out as she turned to him, all smiles.

But Jack wasn't smiling. "Why didn't you tell me?"

She was so relieved not to be locked up that she almost forgot about having kept the baby a secret. "You never know what can happen when you decide to adopt. There are risks all along the way. I've been holding my cards close to the vest."

His eyes were full of questions and concern. "A baby is a big deal. It doesn't get much bigger."

But there was no time to talk about it just then. The Department of Justice was only a couple of blocks away.

"Thanks for all your help," said Harley another hour later, when they were finally on their way back home. "Sorry it took so long. You went above and beyond today."

"I want to know everything," said Jack, and she knew he wasn't talking about being drug tested and assigned her probation officer.

She was relieved that her secret was finally out in the open. But she still couldn't tell Jack that her reason for adopting was because she couldn't conceive a baby of her own. So she told him as much as she wanted him to know.

"Thank God the judge was lenient," he said when she was finished.

He was thoughtful the rest of the drive home, making her wonder if she was being judged yet again.

"Thanks again," said Harley, when they reached her house, unfastening her seat belt. She had one leg out the door when he said, "Wait. There's something I want to say."

She braced herself for a lecture on how crazy she was.

"We used to be close friends. We could be friends again. Would you like to go out some time? Not like a date," he added quickly. "Spend some time together, get reacquainted."

Harley looked at him, sitting there in the driver's seat, as handsome as ever. She'd been afraid that he was judging her again. But she should have known better. His silence was his logical mind assessing and reflecting on her news. She had to admit, it was a lot to take in.

There was a side of her that desperately wanted their old relationship back. Because despite all that had happened, she had never stopped caring for him. But she had lived for years with the hurt and bewilderment of his betrayal. Her pain had built a wall around her heart.

"Are you sure that's a good idea?" There was still so much she didn't understand. How long had he been seeing Emily behind her back? After all this time, she wasn't sure she wanted to reopen that can of worms.

"Seeing you again at Ryan's office in September, the past came rushing back to me like it was yesterday. I've tried to hold it in. But I have to talk about it or I'm going to spin out. It might sound weird, but what I felt that day was an overwhelming sensation of *relief.* Because even though we were just kids, what we had back then—I don't know what it was. I don't have a name for it. But it was real, Harley. The realest thing I've ever known." He paused, his face full of hope. "You feel it, too. I can see it in your eyes. Sense it, every minute we're together."

She knew better than to trust him. But hadn't he practically handed her the Victorian on a silver platter?

Harley stood very still, wanting to respond but afraid that renewing their friendship could only dredge all that pain up all over again.

"Come on, Harley. You're supposed to be the impulsive one. With a baby on the way and Leslie and Sarah gone, don't tell me you couldn't use a friend."

He was right. All her closest friends had moved away and she hadn't made any new ones yet. Except for her parents, she was going to be on her own.

"I guess that would be all right. Just as friends, though."

A grin split his face as he shifted into reverse. "Great. I'll call you."

Chapter Twenty-two

In the following days as Jack went about his work, he could think of nothing but Harley's pending adoption. He didn't know why he was so surprised. She'd been a lonely child. She had talked wistfully about someday having a houseful of children. But what had prompted her to take such a drastic step on her own? He could only come up with two reasons. Either she underestimated the importance of a father in raising a child, or she had given up on finding a man. Either way, he had misgivings.

No one knew better than he how hard it was to raise children alone. He should know—he'd been doing it for the past five years.

As for Harley giving up on love, that brought up a confusing mix of feelings. Because while he wasn't accepting of her, he couldn't bear the thought of her with someone else.

All that aside, how could she have kept such an important decision from him, when they had once been so close? Then again, he'd been the one who threw that away. What right did he have to be part of her world? Still, he couldn't keep from doing a little research of his own, in the evenings. He discovered that what she'd said was true—a lot could go wrong. Aside from the challenge of finding a baby, there could be medical problems. Or the birth parents could renege. Some of his hurt at being left out of Harley's life was replaced with respect for her courage.

A week later they were sitting at a table at one of the nicest eateries in town.

But this wasn't like it used to be. In the old days, they'd be riding around in Jack's pickup, not sitting across from each other, a white tablecloth stretching between them.

Conversation was halting at best.

Their server arrived holding two plates. "Roast chicken?"

"That's me." Jack raised a finger.

"And vegetable strata," she said, placing the second dish in front of Harley.

When they were alone again, Jack said, "Maybe we could start over. Pretend the past never happened."

How was that possible? Jack had altered the course of her life in ways he still didn't know about.

She shrugged. The alternative wasn't working very well. Anything would be better than these long, awkward pauses.

"Good." He settled deeper into his seat. "Let's start from the very beginning. Tell me about yourself. Where are you from?"

"Well," said Harley. She took a sip of wine. "Let's see. I had a great childhood. Grew up outside a small farm town in a valley where there were no boundaries—"

"—that you obeyed," inserted Jack, grinning, thinking of all the times she'd trespassed in his family's vineyards.

"Details. As I was saying before I was so rudely interrupted, I had wonderful parents who let me be me. A great teacher-mentor. I'll stop there and let you have a turn." She stabbed a carrot with her fork.

"That's interesting, because I grew up in the same kind of place. Except that I had a lot of boundaries." He switched to a serious tone. "I'm not like you, Harley. We might have grown up next door to each other, but from the way we were raised, we might as well be from different countries."

"For example?"

"Well," he said, munching a bite of his salad, "I always knew that one day I would take over the family business. Everything I did was geared toward that."

"Whereas . . . ?"

"Whereas you could do whatever you wanted."

"You make it sound like your upbringing was better than mine."

"Not better. Just different. It's like the difference between majoring in, say, business and liberal arts."

"I see. So what you're saying is, we never had a chance."

Jack set down his fork. "I didn't say that."

"That's what it sounded like."

"Will you just shut up and let me explain?"

"You want me to shut up?"

Jack rolled his eyes. "I'm making an effort, here. Why do you have to take offense at every little thing I say?"

"You tell me to shut up and I'm not supposed to take offense? I've got news for you, mister. Just because you happen to have been born a Friestatt doesn't make you better than anyone else."

"You think I don't know that? Why don't you just say what it is you're really thinking—that I think our differences are all about wealth? For your information, I don't believe that having money makes one person better than the next one. Everyone has value as a human being."

"Oh, really? Isn't money the reason you chose Emily over me?"

"What? No! That may have been my mother. But that was never me."

People were staring.

Harley threw her napkin on the table and rose. "Take me home."

"Glad to."

They drove to her house without speaking. He'd tried, but this was never going to work. There was just too much against them.

Jack walked her to her door. "Thanks for going out with me tonight," he said by rote.

"Thanks for dinner," she mouthed without looking at him.

"You're welcome." He waited for her to put her key into the lock, then turned to leave for what would probably be the last time, already reviewing the disastrous date and trying to figure out who was most at fault. He was so preoccupied with his thoughts that he must have missed the first porch step in the dark. The next thing he knew he was tumbling down the steps, cursing as his elbows and knees banged against the wood.

"Jack!" Harley's heels clattered behind him. She

squatted beside him, sprawled on the brick walk, her hand on his shoulder. "Are you all right?"

"I'm fine. Fine." He was such an idiot! Quickly he scrambled to his feet.

"Sit down for a minute." She yanked him down next to her on the step and put her arm around his shoulders. Her body felt good against his. Her scent was clean and green, like sheets dried on the clothesline in the summertime.

He blinked at her, bringing her face into focus in the faint glow of the porch light. Her brow was furrowed with concern.

"What?" she asked. "What's the matter?"

"Nothing," he said, studying the spiky shadow of her lashes on her cheeks. She was still the same Harley he'd been crazy about all through school. Being here next to her again felt good and right. Inevitable. Like they'd been running in opposite directions on a circular track and had finally met up with each other again. "Nothing at all."

"I don't believe you." She wrapped her arm around him in a side hug.

"I appreciate what you've done with your life, Harley . . . all that you've accomplished since high school. I know how important your success is to your self-worth. But I never thought of you as less than equal. I always respected you for who you are." He just hadn't known how much. It had taken time and life to teach him that.

"Are you going to be okay?"

He nodded as he got to his feet.

"You sure?" she asked doubtfully, rising with him, her hand still on his upper arm.

He turned to her and gazed down at her face. "I will be."

They both would be, he vowed to himself, despite the rocky start to their reunion. He didn't know how, but he was going to make certain of it.

Chapter Twenty-three

Friday evening, Harley opened the door with a flourish to her very first guests. "Hello! Welcome to Honeymoon Haven! How was your trip?"

"Ms. Miller-Jones? We're the Pettys."

Harley's research told her that what guests wanted most in a B and B hostess was a people person. But it wasn't hard to be personable when you really were excited.

"Don't stand on ceremony. Call me Harley. What should I call you?"

The Pettys exchanged a priggish look. "Mr. and Mrs. Petty," they said in unison.

"Oh." Harley's head swiveled from one to the other. "Mr. and Mrs. Petty it is. All righty, then." She clasped her hands together. "Let's get you settled. Right this way." She kept up a running commentary on the way to the podium that passed for a front desk. "What are your plans for the weekend? Which wineries do you have reservations at? Are you going to go downtown for dinner tonight? I can recommend some great places to eat. Just let me know what you're in the mood for. Sports bar, craft brewery, seasonal American fare . . ."

As Mrs. Petty examined the foyer ceiling with a critical eye, Mr. Petty set down his duffel bag and pulled out his wallet. "We'll figure it out," he said, handing Harley his credit card.

"Of course."

Upstairs, she lingered in the doorway of the guest room she had so carefully prepared for them, but it seemed they were fresh out of compliments.

Jet lag, she thought. *Poor things.*

No sooner had they set down their bags than they were gone again.

Harley went about her day as usual, working at her desk, taking occasional breaks to walk outside in a fine Pacific Northwest drizzle, satisfied knowing that she was making passive income.

Late in the afternoon, she began looking for the Pettys, thinking they might come back to grab a nap or freshen up before heading back out for dinner. But dinnertime came and went with no car pulling up the drive.

Night fell, and though she longed to get out of her clothes, she felt a maternal need to wait up for them, as if they were teenagers. After all, they didn't know the area. They could get lost, or get in the wrong person's car or be tricked into buying drugs or—

The sooner her baby arrived, the better. Her maternal instincts were in overdrive.

Just after midnight, when she had finally washed off her makeup and donned her pajamas, she heard the key in the front door. She pulled on a robe and scampered down the stairs to meet them.

"How was your day? Did you find everything okay? Did you have a nice dinner?"

"Fine. What time is breakfast? We want to get an early start."

"How's eight?"

"We were thinking seven."

She had picked eight arbitrarily, assuming guests might want to sleep in. "Seven it is. Is your room okay? Do you have everything you need?"

"If we need something, we'll let you know," he said, closing the door softly in her face.

Harley stood there, stung. *Clearly, that advice about being chipper was from an unreliable source.* She decided to focus on the part of her that was relieved they'd returned safely.

She returned to her bed with a contented sigh and squeezed her eyes closed. But when she heard the faint sound of conversation and the shower running, her eyes flew open again.

It had never occurred to her to check the solidity of the walls.

She had finally dozed off when there was a knock at her door. She opened it to find Mrs. Petty, hugging herself, her teeth chattering.

"Do you have any more blankets? Our room is like an igloo."

"It's in the fif—" Harley bit her tongue as she retrieved one of her own blankets from the linen closet. She knew from waitressing that the customer was always right.

It was pitch black outside Saturday morning when Harley's alarm rang. She dragged herself from her bed, slapped some concealer on her under-eye circles, and went down to put the coffee on, preheat the oven, and fry the bacon for the quiche, hoping the Pettys would be more cheerful after a good night's sleep.

By six fifty-five, the silver urn was full of freshly brewed coffee and there were two carafes of cold juice on ice. The table was set with the quirkily mismatched china she'd picked up at salvage stores. She straightened a fork a centimeter. And then she took off her apron and glanced up the stairs in anticipation.

Seven o'clock came and went. Maybe she had taken the Pettys too literally. Surely they'd be down any minute.

Seven fifteen. Seven thirty.

At 8:05 she finally heard footsteps on the stairs.

"Good morning!" she chirped, smoothing down her apron with its grape-cluster print. "How are you?"

"My back is killing me," said Mr. Petty.

"I'm sorry," said Harley. Maybe she should have taken all the mattresses for a test drive. But Mrs. Grimsky had assured her that they were like new.

"Does it rain three hundred sixty days a year in the Willamette Valley?" asked Mrs. Petty.

It seemed the only thing that could erase the scowls on the Pettys' faces was a syringe of Botox the size of a cookie press. Harley was a hair's breadth from snapping, *Don't be silly, only two hundred twenty.*

"Do I smell bacon?"

"You do! Doesn't it smell amazing?"

"Not if you happen to be vegan."

Harley's face fell. "Why didn't you tell me?"

"You never asked," they replied. *Did speaking as a unit come naturally to the Pettys, or was it a practiced skill?*

"Got me there," Harley said. *Dietary preferences and restrictions . . . one more thing to check on, from now on.*

"Do you have any steel-cut oats?"

Last week, when Harley was stocking up on groceries, she had debated the box of cereal in her hand, but she'd put it back on the shelf, fearing serving cereal was the mark of a lazy hostess.

"Or at least some fruit."

Harley peered into the fridge, brightening when she spotted a Fuji apple. "Do you like apples?"

They stared at the apple, prompting Harley to do the same. On closer examination, its skin was as loose as Grandma Miller's when she went into assisted living.

"Or not," she said, tossing it into the trash.

The Pettys exchanged their trademark flat affect. "We'll just stop along the road somewhere and get breakfast."

Harley didn't bother asking if they were interested in goat yoga.

When they exited for the last time, Harley slammed the door and flattened herself against it, sighing, "Joy to the world."

She had to spend the morning laundering the sheets and cleaning the guest room before she could get to her "real" job.

But Kelly had an OB visit today and had promised to call Harley this evening with a baby update.

And after that, Jack was coming over. He had called to ask, and she'd said yes.

Chapter Twenty-four

Saturday. Jack had penciled in a date with his daughters. Mother had gone to the farmers market, and for the first time since he could remember, both girls were in a good mood.

"What do you want to do this afternoon?" Jack asked the girls at breakfast.

"Please take us to the park," the girls begged.

Since the day of the demonstration, they'd developed a fascination with the park.

"It's not very nice out," he said, looking out at the drizzle. "Are you sure you wouldn't rather catch a movie?"

"That's okay. We can wear our hoodies," they cried.

Then again, if you waited for a sunny day to go outdoors, you might end up staying inside forever.

"If that's what you want to do, grab your jackets and a couple of softballs."

* * *

The three of them had been tossing the ball around in a triangle for about an hour.

"I love the park," said Freddie. "I would be so sad if it wasn't here anymore."

Frankie sniffed and wiped her nose on the back of her hand and asked, "Tell me, what's aesthetics again?"

"You're asking the wrong person," said Jack. "I never got art myself." He tossed the ball underhanded to Freddie. It slipped right through her hands.

"The ball's slippery," she complained, chasing it with Fang.

"That's because it's too wet. Our feet are getting soaked. How about we find something to do inside where it's dry?"

"What?" they asked.

"A lot of new stores have come to Newberry since we were overseas. I have an idea."

A few minutes later, they left an exhausted Fang sleeping on the backseat of Jack's truck and walked down the sidewalk until Jack stopped beneath a sign that said NEWBERRY ART COLLECTIVE.

"What's this?" asked Frankie, looking around.

"It's a place where local artists can show their work."

"Can people buy it?"

"Of course they can, silly," said Freddie, on their way inside.

Jack followed the girls as they made their way slowly past displays of ceramics and abstract objects and useful, handcrafted wood items.

The walls were lined with paintings and photography. "Look at this!" exclaimed Frankie, pointing at a picture of a dancer. "Is that a photo, or did somebody draw it?"

Jack looked around, but the only shop worker was busy with another customer. He stepped closer to the picture and stared hard at it. "Sorry, Frankie. I don't know."

"Come look at this!" Freddie called from another aisle.

"It started out as a comic book, but the pages have all been folded in different directions and it's been painted on. I wonder why?" She frowned.

Jack searched again for the shopkeeper, but she was still tied up.

But the girls had already found new things they were curious about. Again and again, they threw him queries the same way he tossed them the softball, and again and again, he dropped the ball.

For once, his daughters' good moods overlapped with the window of time he had set aside to spend with them, and he couldn't answer their most basic questions about art. It was frustrating.

Then it dawned on him. He knew someone who could. And she just happened to love kids.

Chapter Twenty-five

On hearing his knock on the front door, Harley jumped up from where she'd been studying her baby's sonogram and wiped a happy tear from her eye.

Halfway to the door she paused, surprised at how much she was looking forward to seeing Jack's smiling, familiar face given their last attempt at getting together. Then again, anybody would be better than the Pettys.

She opened the door to find him holding out a bottle of wine. "This is for you."

"You have great timing. I could use a glass of wine."

"How'd it go with your guests?" he asked, peering tentatively into the living room.

Behind him, Harley closed the door and leaned against it, trying not to stare at the way his broad shoulders narrowed into his waist.

"The Pettys? Let's just say they lived up to their

name. I'll go find a bottle opener. Have a seat in the living room."

"You're going to meet all types in the hospitality biz. Trust me."

There was that word, trust, again.

"How are the girls? I've been thinking about them. I hope my getting arrested didn't traumatize them too much."

"Funny you should ask. You'll never guess who's the chairwoman of the plan to tear down the park."

Harley looked up from where she struggled with the cork pull. "Don't tell me." She sighed and slumped. "I never intended to cause any trouble—" As if Melinda didn't hate her enough before she got arrested. The memory of her telling Harley she had no idea what she was in for with her B and B came back to her.

Jack came over, took the bottle and cork pull from her hands, and expertly twisted it in. "The demonstration was happening right in front of us. There was no way I could have shielded the girls from it. Anyway, that's life. Have you heard any more about why it's being torn down?"

Harley shook her head.

"To make room for a new tourist center."

Harley thought. "The current one is pretty sad. It's been there as long as I can remember. And it makes sense to relocate it to the town center."

Jack sampled his wine. "Right. It's just a shame they have to use up the only green space."

"Can't you do anything?"

"This is my mother we're talking about."

"If it were my mother, she'd listen to me with an open mind."

"Because your mother wouldn't have an ulterior

motive, which is to gain favor with the other movers and shakers on the committee." Jack sighed. "Anyway, witnessing the demonstration opened a discussion between her and the twins. Somehow the topic of *aesthetics* came up."

Harley made a doubtful face.

She took the glass he handed her and sat down on the couch.

Jack lowered himself next to her. "It was Mother who brought it up, but the girls couldn't let it go. That led to me taking them to the new art gallery on Main Street this morning."

"Oh?"

"They loved it. We ended up spending more time there than we did in the park. But I had no idea what I was looking at. They had all these questions, and all I could do was shrug." Jack pointed to her open laptop on the coffee table. "Did I interrupt something?"

Harley beamed and reached for it. "This is him," she said, turning the screen to face Jack.

"Brings back memories," said Jack. "Except he's got a lot more room in there than the twins did."

Gently, Harley closed the lid. "Do the girls still miss their mother?"

"They were only five when she died. They've spent more of their lives without her than with her. Especially when you consider that they have no memories of their first couple of years at all."

"Do me a favor? Don't tell them about my baby yet."

"After the hearing, the cat's out of the bag, don't you think?"

"Among the adults who happened to be present. But that doesn't change the fact that there could still be complications. The less the girls know, the less you'll have to explain later, should the need arise." Whatever this dance was that she and Jack were trying out, it still felt very trial-and-error. Who knew where it would lead—if anywhere?

"If that's what you want."

Then there was the whole thing with Jack's mother. If she and Jack got closer, Melinda would surely have something to say about it.

Jack set down his glass and turned toward her, lifting her chin with his finger. "Hey. You were in such a good mood a second ago."

The Pettys may not have been very perky, but today marked a milestone. She'd had her first guests and she'd seen another baby picture. Everything in her life—her work, this beautiful home, aglow with candles placed around the room—was coming together. She wasn't going to let Melinda kill her buzz.

"You're right." Harley jumped up. "How about some leftover quiche?"

They talked about the new vintage and some new ideas for collaboration among their properties while they ate. Then Jack scraped his plate clean and set it on the table.

"Well," he said, rising to his feet, "guess I should go."

Harley straightened her top and stood, too. "It is getting late, and I have to get up early. I've signed a contract for a collection of twenty-four greeting cards, and the B and B chores have me way behind."

He grabbed his jacket from the back of the couch—unlike Mother, Harley hadn't said a thing about him leaving it there—and made his way slowly to the door, Harley by his side.

"Why didn't you tell me before? That's great! First sketches, then dishes, and what was it? Towels?"

"Linens," she said with a small, indulgent smile.

"Linens. Right."

They had made it to the foyer. "Before I go, I was wondering . . . the girls and I do something most Saturday mornings. Would you be interested in maybe going with us to the art collective some time?"

She bit the inside of her lip. "I'm not sure."

"It's just an art gallery. No big deal."

"Are you sure you want your daughters spending that much time with me? I mean, I would think that someone in your shoes would want to be very selective about who he lets into his kids' world. You know, so that they don't get . . . confused."

"Is that why you're so tense? Come on, Har. I don't know a Rembrandt from a Picasso. Besides, it'll be more fun with you. Everything always is."

"It is?"

"Of course it is." He'd better keep his enthusiasm in check. He didn't want to scare her off before she even got to know the girls.

"I have more guests coming next week, so I'll be tied up then. But maybe the Saturday after that, assuming I don't get another booking."

His heart leapt. *Yes!* "I can't wait to tell the girls." It was all he could do to keep from hooting with happiness. Somehow, he managed to rein it in. "Well, thanks for the quiche."

"Thanks for the wine," she said, nervously ducking her head.

He put his hand on the doorknob. But he couldn't

bring himself to leave just yet. Cautiously, he bent his head over hers.

When her eyelids fluttered closed, he gently, ever so gently, touched her mouth with his. Her lips were warm and soft, and she smelled like shampoo and second chances.

"Night," he whispered.

"Night."

Chapter Twenty-six

Harley's morning shower wasn't as hot as she liked it, but she excused it away as having just run the dishwasher.

She gazed at the stack of folders and forms she'd deposited on Prudence Mitchell's desk.

"It feels strange leaving all this paperwork here."

"Would you rather take it back home with you?"

"Definitely not. I can't make heads or tails of it."

"Have no fear," said Pru, deftly sorting through the papers, separating them into piles. "By tax time, we'll have you all straightened out."

"That's what I'm counting on. Is there anything else you need from me?"

"Just make sure you utilize the program I gave you to track income and expenses and my staff and I will figure out the rest."

Harley rose from her chair in front of Pru's desk and draped her jacket over her arm. "Thanks for your help."

"You got it." Pru came around her desk to walk

her out. "By the way. Heard you spent the night in the slammer for that park thing."

"It was only four hours."

"Oh," said Pru, sounding disappointed. "See much of Jack these days?"

In her need for help with her accounting, Harley had shuttled aside Pru's schoolgirl crush on Jack. She shrugged. "Jack and I are neighbors. That's all."

"Wonder if he found a mother for those twins of his yet."

"What do you mean?"

"That's the whole reason he came back from New Zealand."

Harley blinked. "I thought it was because his work was done, Down Under."

"That's not what he told me. Obviously, I didn't come right out and ask him. But his mother hinted as much to my father."

The Mitchells ran in the same circles as the Friestatts. Harley had waited on them at the club. It wouldn't be surprising if Melinda had run into Judge Mitchell since they'd come back from overseas. Even less surprising if Pru had misconstrued a conversation.

"My next guests are arriving this afternoon and I still have things to do to get ready. Thanks for your help."

Pru might be a little dense when it came to social cues, but she had saved Harley once before, when she was failing algebra. They'd never been best friends and they never would be. But Pru could provide Harley with a service and Harley could compensate her. As long as they stuck to numbers, they would get along just fine.

* * *

Harley spent the morning vacuuming and dusting. As much as she'd wished for guests to start coming, she had also promised to send new sketches to her design team today. She'd been going to work on them last night, but she'd gone down a rabbit hole researching the best kind of disposable diaper. After a quick lunch, she had just sat down at her drawing table, hoping to grab a couple of hours to work, when the doorbell rang.

"This house is a*dor*able!" exclaimed the woman in a yellow sweater set and lavender-framed glasses.

"Oh! That settee! And look, George. That sideboard has got to be an original Biedermeier!" She scurried over to it, examining every inch. "I'm sure of it. And that chandelier with the colored pendants! Where's my phone? I've got to get a picture."

Following the Pettys, Harley basked in the new guests' compliments, seeing no reason to admit that all those decorator touches were the work of the previous owner.

Lisa's partner was still standing in the foyer. "Are you going to spend all day taking pictures of the furniture when there's all that great wine waiting to be drunk? Let's get registered and get going. We're burning daylight." Setting down his duffel bag, he reached for Harley's hand. "George and Lisa Reynolds, Alexandria, Virginia. Tell me everything you know about the Willamette Valley."

Harley lifted a brow. "Well, I—"

"And don't leave anything out."

Harley led George to the window. "See those vineyards?"

George went over and, with one look, motioned to his wife. "Sweetheart. Come here. Check it out."

Harley looked down at Lisa's heels and George's Italian loafers. "Did you bring any sturdy shoes?"

George looked at his wife. "Did you pack my hiking boots?"

"Those ugly old black things?" A sheepish look came over her face.

"Lisa . . . what did you do with my hiking boots?"

"Did those fat, rubber-soled things ever have a fashion moment? Don't worry, honey, the minute we get back to DC, I'll help you pick out a new pair of nice, stylish boots, one that doesn't make you look like an Amishman."

George sighed and looked at the ceiling.

"You were saying?" he asked Harley.

"We're within walking distance of seven excellent wineries. My best advice is for you to put on the sturdiest shoes you have and start walking."

Their eyes glittered in anticipation.

"You heard the lady," said George. "The sooner we get our stuff up to our room, the sooner we can get going."

The following morning, Harley scooped nondairy yogurt into a serving bowl and sliced bananas while the traditional quiche baked. She was looking forward to the minute her guests left and she cleaned the kitchen and threw their sheets in the wash, when she could finally finish up her sketches.

Lisa appeared in the kitchen doorway, wrapped in a fat terry-cloth robe. "I'm sorry to bother you, but we seemed to have run out of hot water."

Remembering her own tepid shower, Harley paused in midscoop, set down her spoon, and using the back of her hand, brushed a lock of hair out of her eyes. *Uh-oh.*

"I'll see what I can do." Thank goodness it was a weekend. She picked up her phone and punched in a number under Favorites. "Dad? Can you come over, please? I think I have a problem."

"Yup. She's dead." Dad squatted next to the tall, gray metal cylinder.

"You can't fix it?"

"Bottom's rusted out. You need a new one."

"Alfred said it was fine."

"Alfred?"

Dad knew how much Jack had hurt Harley. She tried not to mention Jack or anything to do with the Friestatts around him. Now she had no choice.

"Alfred. He saw me painting the porch ceiling and I gave him a tour."

There was a long pause as, just as she'd feared, the old tension seeped back.

"Was Jack with him?"

"Yes."

"You been seeing a lot of him?"

"Not a lot."

The toothpick in Dad's mouth bobbed up and down like a seismometer in an earthquake. "How's Jack doing since he come back from New Zealand?"

"He's fine."

"His twins? Must be getting big."

"They're adorable. A handful, but adorable. They kind of remind me of myself at that age."

"Uh-oh." Dad grinned. "What's Jack's mother think?"

If Harley told him Melinda had tried to bribe her, there was no telling what he might do.

"We're adults now. Does it matter?"

"I guess not. Just tread careful. Melinda Friestatt's always ruled over her realm with an iron fist. I'd hate to see you get your heart broke all over again."

A flash of anger took Harley off guard. "You certainly wasted no time in going to her that time you caught Jack and me kissing."

"You don't think she had the right to know?"

"We were fifteen! Kissing, standing up, with all our clothes on. I don't see what the big deal was."

Harley still felt betrayed over the way Dad had handled the incident.

"Whoa, whoa. Why are you so mad at me after all this time? You know I always had your best interests at heart. I can count the times I interfered with your life on one hand."

Her temper was already subsiding. "I know." Here he was, helping her with her hot-water heater and trying to make conversation, and she had repaid him by jumping down his throat over something that had happened fifteen years before.

She crouched down next to Dad. "How much is fixing this going to cost?"

"If you hire a plumber, about a grand. If your old man happens to be handy *and* a pushover, then just the cost of materials, about three hundred."

"Maybe it's covered under my homeowner's policy."

"Nope. That only covers damage to your house caused by something gone wrong with it."

She groaned.

"Welcome to owning your own home."

The poor Reynolds' had had to start their day bathing with ice water. At least they'd been understanding. She hated to think of how the Pettys would have reacted if she'd had to tell them there was no hot water for their shower.

"If you want, I'll go with you to Home Depot."

"Suit yourself."

A few minutes later, they were in his truck. Dad draped his arm over the steering wheel, his toothpick still hanging from his mouth. "How's the baby thing coming along?"

"Great! I saw his sonogram. Kelly's due date is December 24. Less than three months to go. I can't wait! That reminds me: While we're at the store, I need to pick up a baby monitor."

"How you feeling these days?"

What he wanted to know but was too embarrassed to ask was if she'd started having periods again. Normally, that was information he got from Mom. That he was asking Harley, even in such a vague way, was a further indication that she was now truly grown-up.

"Still no change. Honestly, Dad, I've kind of given up on all that."

"I'm sorry, honey."

"Don't feel bad. Things always work out for the best. I have a little one on the way, don't I?"

He grunted a response, his eyes fixed on the road, seemingly lost in his own thoughts.

Dad had exited the highway and was driving slowly through the parking lot in search of a space. "Just don't want to see you get hurt again, Harley girl," was the last thing he said as he shifted into Park and they got out.

Chapter Twenty-seven

The next morning, Harley climbed into Jack's front seat as planned and turned around to greet the twins. "Hi, guys. How are you?"

"What's it like in jail?" asked Frankie.

"Harley was never actually *in jail*," Jack interjected.

"I was kept in a holding cell for a very short time, just while I was waiting to get fingerprinted. And the answer is, it's very plain. The walls were gray and the floors were gray, and even the benches were gray."

"Fingerprinted?" asked Freddie.

"They press your fingertip into an ink pad and then onto a piece of paper. Every person in the world has her own unique fingerprints. Maybe later, after we get back, I'll show you how it's done. We'll make your own set of prints."

"Really?" The twins grinned.

"Sure. There are all kinds of ways to make prints."

"Don't forget, girls, I have a meeting," Jack warned.

"Another time, then," said Harley.

"Awww," the girls complained.

"Tell me about your favorite artworks at the gallery," said Harley.

"I can't wait to show you the picture of the dancer," said Frankie. "She's, like, doing a backbend, but she has one leg pointing up in the air."

"And I can't wait to show you the folded-up comic book," said Freddie.

Inside the shop, Frankie took Harley's hand and dragged her to the picture and pointed.

"That's a photograph," said Harley immediately. "Let's see where it was taken." She read the caption beneath it. "Read this. It's a company in Portland. Have you ever been to see a performance of modern dance?"

Frankie shook her head.

"Maybe your dad will take you sometime."

Jack hung in the background, listening. Frankie had been talking about dance even when they were still in New Zealand. Why hadn't he ever thought of taking her to see a performance there? There was probably a big performance hall in Auckland. It was too late for that, now. But there were doubtless lots of places to take her in the Pacific Northwest, too.

Freddie had been waiting patiently. "Are you done?"

"Yes. Let's go see yours," said Harley.

"That's what's called an altered book."

"Do you know how to make those?"

"I've never done it, but it might be fun to try."

"Can I do it with you?"

"I have lots of art supplies back at my house. I'm sure we can find something that would work."

Harley led them through the rest of the gallery, teaching them things Jack never could have.

When they were finished, Jack was waiting, having already paid for Frankie's photograph and Freddie's book.

"How come you know so much about art?" asked Frankie when they were on the way home.

"Art has always been a big part of my life."

"Why?"

Harley thought. "How does your photo make you feel?"

"It makes me want to know how it feels to move and sway the way that dancer is moving," she said, waving her arms and twirling down the sidewalk.

"Mine makes me wonder about the words and the pictures hidden inside the folds," said Freddie.

"I have a feeling art is important to you, too. But you just don't think about it because you're surrounded by it everywhere you look."

"What do you mean?"

"What's your favorite color?"

"Easy. Yellow."

"Red!" shouted Freddie.

"Remember when you were asking me what jail looked like and I told you how gray it was? Imagine no more yellow, no more red ever again. In fact, imagine no colors. Instead, what if everything in your life was gray, from your clothes to your bathtub to the walls of your bedroom?"

"Ew," they said.

"That's a little taste of what it would be like in a world without art."

"It's like without the park, the whole downtown would be gray."

"Exactly."

Jack turned into Harley's drive.

"Do we have to go home now?" the girls pleaded.

"Remember my meeting?" Jack reminded them.

Harley looked at him. "I can take the girls."

Leave the twins with Harley? Mother wouldn't like it. But it would be a great chance for them to get to know each other.

"Pleeeeze?" came from the backseat. "We want to make fingerprints."

"Maybe I should have asked your dad first," said Harley. "I tend to make snap decisions, and he likes to consider all the angles."

"Well, Dad? Can we?"

"I guess that would be all right. I'll come back for you right after the meeting."

"Hooray!" they shouted.

Chapter Twenty-eight

Later that night, Jack stood at Harley's door wearing a suit and holding a loosely constructed bouquet.

"What's this?"

"I walked by Posey's after my meeting downtown. The yellow ones are sunflowers. They stand for warmth and happiness. Easy to see why."

Harley caressed their petals. "They're lovely."

"And these are asters. I just liked the purple color."

She smiled. "What about the white ones?"

"Humility," he said, his caramel eyes brimful of sincerity.

She stood back. "Come on in. I'll put them in some water. There's wine in the decanter."

He untied his tie, yanked it through the crease in his collar and slung it casually across his shoulder.

When she returned to the living room, she found him seated on her new, fluffy ivory-colored rug between the couch and the coffee table, his wineglass dangling from his hand draped across his raised knee, a silver cuff link glinting in the light from the candles she'd placed around the room.

"Thanks for everything you did for the girls today."

Harley smiled sideways as she set down a plate of cheese and crackers and joined him on the floor. "How did their grandmother like their fingerprints?"

"Let's just say her definition of art is a little narrower than yours." Jack grinned, set a slice of cheese on a cracker, and handed it to her before making himself one.

She snuggled the small of her back closer to the couch, her legs stretched out straight in front of her.

"Let's not talk about the kids anymore," he said.

She took a sip of the wine he'd poured her. "Then what do you want to talk about?"

"Us."

In the weeks since the open house, Jack had been walking a tightrope. Every moment with Harley, that rush of excitement, that buzz of electricity came roaring back with a vengeance. They couldn't talk long enough or late enough into the night. Any day he didn't see her face was a day wasted.

She felt it, too . . . he could tell by the way her pupils expanded into huge black pools when she looked at him.

His feelings were so close to the surface, the slightest brush of their arms raised goose bumps. He inched closer, caressing her shoulder with the lightest touch of his fingertip. "It's been a while now since we moved back. . . ."

"I know. I have a calendar, too." Her smile was soft and seductive.

"Don't tease me," he cautioned, a hint of danger in his voice. His self-discipline was only so strong.

"You used to like it when I teased you. Like the time I ran circles around your truck with you chasing me."

When he caught her, they were laughing so hard their lips could hardly fashion a kiss.

"How about the time you waded into the Molalla at Knights Bridge Park, peeling your clothes off as you went, until I had no choice but to splash in after you, slipping all over the rocks, almost killing myself?"

"It was your fault for kicking off your tennis shoes. The trick is to keep them on, even if that's *all* you keep on." She eyed the V between the top buttons of his shirt, then locked eyes with him as she ran a fingertip around the rim of her glass. "We had some good times," she said softly.

But the ultimate expression of affection between a woman and a man was something each had learned with another. Now that they knew what they'd been missing, the possibilities hung heavily between them, like a fat cluster of grapes, ripe for the picking.

He leaned forward, tipping his head until his lips were close to her ear. "We can have even better times," he murmured into her hair, his heart slamming against his ribs with every beat. As desperately as he wanted her, he couldn't afford another misstep. He pulled back and cupped her face, searching it like a road map, hoping it would show him the way.

Harley felt her inhibitions slipping away. Yet warning lights flashed in her brain. Old questions still haunted her. A thousand times, she had wondered why Jack had shattered her heart. Now was her chance to ask him. And yet she was afraid the answer would hurt all over again. So instead, she skated around it.

"After you got married and I moved away, I still

thought about you and Emily for quite a while. I used to torture myself, imagining Jemily having the casually elegant life of a style blogger."

"Ha," said Jack bitterly, his head falling back against the seat cushion. "What people called Jemily were nothing more than longtime family friends." An introspective look came over his face. "There're only two people who know what goes on inside a marriage. It might have looked pretty on the outside, but almost from the beginning, there was no intimacy—physical or emotional."

Almost, thought Harley. *Emily didn't get knocked up all by herself.*

"Truth is, I was never lonelier than when I was married to Emily. If I had to guess, I'd bet she was just as lonely as I was. Looking back, we lacked the most basic connection. Hell, when the kids weren't around, things could get downright awkward. Sometimes I thought we must be the only married couple in America in their twenties who slept in different rooms and—here's the kicker—were just fine with it."

"But all those pictures on social media—" Harley blurted out, and immediately felt herself redden.

"Those so-called 'candid' "—he drew air quotes—"group shots of birthday parties and ski trips with the twins in matching outfits? C'mon, Har. You're an artist. You know. People are pros at retouching reality. They don't post selfies of their silent car rides or what they look like watching TV alone, night after night."

"I guess not."

"I admit it wasn't all bad. We never had knock-down, drag-out fights. Maybe we should have. At least that would have been a sign that there was some shred of emotion between us. Emily and I might have shared a house, but we didn't share what was inside us. We put all our focus on the twins. It was a convenient smoke screen—everybody knows raising twins is supposed to be hard. That way, we didn't have to examine ourselves and see that it just wasn't working."

For a moment, neither of them spoke.

"I don't have the words for what I'm about to say. I'm no good at sharing my emotions. That's the way I was brought up. Don't talk about your feelings. Better yet, don't feel. Feelings are overrated. Once you start pretending feelings don't matter, you become numb to them. Don't touch, because it might get you in trouble. That much, I know for sure is true."

"Jack—"

She licked her lips and lowered her chin a fraction of an inch.

"You're flushed," he said. "Do I make you nervous?"

"No."

"I think I do."

"Not nervous exactly." She twirled a lock of hair, trying to get up the nerve to meet his eyes. "Excited," she whispered.

"Me too," he said softly. "Very, *very* excited." He tickled her lips with the tips of her hair and they parted, her breathing becoming labored.

Dropping the lock of hair, Jack reached for her and brought her toward him and kissed her eagerly, their first kiss in ten, long years.

He slipped his tongue inside her mouth, and she reveled in his desire. As exciting and memorable as their first, fumbling attempts had been, as many times as she'd held them up as a standard for other men's kisses, this was infinitely better. Before they were only experimenting. Now, in addition to the lush physical sensations, each kiss held piercing depth and meaning.

"Harley," he said hoarsely, cupping her breasts inside her shirt, lifting them up, and her head fell back and she sighed.

He kissed her neck as he slung his necktie across the room and began unbuttoning her shirt, kissing a trail from her cheek to her mouth to her other cheek, easing her backward as he did.

Jack felt her fingertips race across his back, leaving a trail of pleasure everywhere they went. He had almost forgotten this kind of need existed. Never had he been so aroused, never wanted a woman as much as he wanted her now.

His kisses delved deeper, more urgent, as his fingers fumbled maddeningly with her buttons. Finally, the last one came undone and he rose from her and thrust the two sides apart like curtains letting in the light to a man who had seen only darkness for so long.

Looking up at him, her eyes shone, her breath was audible as her breasts rapidly rose and fell, pressing against their surrounding fabric.

Jack reached behind her and deftly unsnapped the hooks and eyes. Immediately, the bra went slack and he pushed it up, revealing creamy breasts with pointed pink nipples. He thumbed one of them as he took her mouth again and slid his other hand around her waist, pulling her close.

Jack's knee was sliding between her thighs, impatiently nudging them apart as he neared the breaking point.

What am I doing? thought Harley.

"Jack." She planted her palms against his chest and pushed against him.

"What?" he panted, his face the picture of concern. "What's wrong?"

Things are far from resolved between us, she thought. *I can't let myself fall right back into our same old pattern, only to get hurt yet again.*

He turned aside to let her get to her feet and she walked away, fastening her bra, then her shirt, putting distance between them. Most of her buttons buttoned, she turned around to see him sitting with one leg raised, a look of confused concern on his face.

"Did I do something wrong?" he asked.

"I—I'm just not ready."

He rose, shoved his shirttail into his pants, and sheepishly rebuckled his belt, his arousal still very evident.

"Sorry," she said.

"It's okay," he said without looking at her, ruffling his floppy hair into some semblance of order. He snatched his tie off the floor and looped it over his head, flipping up his collar and starting a knot.

"You don't have to go," she said.

"Yeah," he said. "I do."

Hurting him was the last thing she wanted to do. It was half the very reason she had stopped him. And now she had hurt him anyway. He was trying not to show it, but it was plain to see in the way he refused to meet her eyes and in his posture.

"This isn't what I came back to Ribbon Ridge for," she said.

"And you think I did? But since we both are, I thought we could make the most of it."

"Is that all we're doing, here? Having a good time?"

"What do you mean?" There was an edge to his voice.

"Things are different now. We each have our own, separate, busy lives. You live on the estate with the twins, and I have the Victorian, and pretty soon, a son. And we each have our own businesses to run."

"I thought things were going good between us."

"They are."

"Did things go okay with you and the girls the other day? They didn't get out of line, did they? Because if they did—"

"They were perfect angels."

"Do you enjoy spending time with me?"

"You know I do." She placed her hand on his forearm. "Sit down."

Reluctantly he sat next to her on the couch, his back ramrod-straight.

"I can't believe I'm asking you this. Me—the impulsive one. But pretty soon it's not just going to be just me anymore. I'll have a child to consider."

"You're right," he said, catching his breath. In his eagerness to resurrect the good old days, maybe he'd gotten ahead of himself.

"You're not upset?"

"Of course not."

"Then you're okay with us taking it slow."

"Absolutely. Whatever you want." They had come this far. Jack didn't want to risk blowing it.

From the back of his mind came the niggling reminder that he was supposed to be actively seeking new wife—a woman who was the direct opposite of Harley. Somehow when he was with her, that goal receded into the back of his mind, like taxes or jury duty or some equally tedious chore.

If he forced himself to see past her bed-tousled hair, her hint of cleavage above her half-buttoned blouse, she looked so earnest.

She was right. He had to get out of there.

He kissed her cheek. "I'll be around," he said, and he headed for the door.

Chapter Twenty-nine

The girls barreled down the stairs of the estate, dressed for trick-or-treating in the costumes Mother had bought for them.

"*Walk*," said Mother.

Freddie looked down at her long-sleeved, black knit shirt with a giant appliquéd "P" on the front. "I still wish I could've been Wonder Woman."

Mother tsked as she tugged at Freddie's shirt with a critical eye. "Everyone is going to be Wonder Woman this year. Don't you want to stand out in the crowd?"

"I wanted to be a dancer and wear a yellow outfit," said Frankie wistfully in her white shirt and pants.

"Salt and Pepper is timeless. You two look terrific. Stand up nice and tall, now. Shoulders back."

Frankie and Freddie scrutinized each other's costumes, knowing that arguing was futile.

"Here are your treat bags." Mother handed them each a bag, then ducked behind Jack and mouthed, "Two treats a piece. Otherwise they'll be up all night."

Frankie rolled her eyes as she applied yet another coat of clear lip gloss to her lips. "We can *hear* you, Mimi."

"We're not babies," grumbled Freddie, holding out her hand to her sister to use the gloss next.

"Hold *on*. I'm not done yet," Frankie groused.

Mother clapped her hands together, opened her eyes wide, and in a singsong voice said, "All set?" as if they were, indeed, babies instead of budding adolescents.

They looked up at Jack with shiny pouts, faces sullen, their lashes suddenly terrifyingly long and dark and not like little-girl lashes at all.

Jack had a sudden premonition of them driving off in cars with boys and going to dances.

"Come on, then, me hearties." Tonight, they were still his little girls, and he was bound to make the most of it. He was wearing the same costume he always wore, a billowing white shirt with a wide crimson sash tied around his head and an eye patch.

"Put a leash on that measly mutt of yours and we'll be off."

Halloween in Seattle was celebrated with dances, balls, haunted houses, and live performances. Harley's urban neighborhood came alive with the classic ghouls and witches and popular characters from books and films. Each year she handed out enough candy to last until Easter.

She didn't know what to expect this year. In hopes that at least a few intrepid souls would knock on her door, she'd bought treats and dressed up in the long black gown she'd bought a few years back for a Hollywood theme party.

But now it was getting late and she hadn't had a single comer.

She poured herself yet another glass of wine and reached into the candy dish for her fourth candy bar. Then she lay back on the couch and began scrolling through photos of babies in costumes on her laptop, projecting to next Halloween, when she would be deciding whether to dress her little one as an elf or a monkey, or maybe in a simple pumpkin costume.

Ding-dong!

Clicking her laptop closed, she jumped up and hurried to the door.

"Trick-or-treat!"

Harley slung her feather boa around her neck and struck a pose against the doorframe, in part for something to lean on, but also because she was a little tipsy. "Hello, ladies." She eyed Jack up and down, from his eye patch to his tall black boots. "Cap'n. I remember you." In her minds eye she saw again Jack as a kid, posed atop a fallen log 'raft' brandishing his iris-leaf 'sword.' But with those long limbs and broad shoulders, he wasn't a kid anymore. He was all man.

Jack seemed equally pleased to see her in costume. "Ahoy, lass!"

She stood aside. "Do come in," she drawled, fanning herself. "Like I always say, a man in the house is worth two in the street."

Jack let his girls enter before him and with a flourish of his scabbard toward the bowl of candy Harley had set out. "Surrender the booty!"

Harley rolled her eyes and the twins giggled.

"Take what—" But Jack was laughing too hard to

continue. "Let's try that again," he said in an aside. Then, "Take what you can, lassies," he rumbled in a perfect Jack Sparrow voice, "and give nothing back."

"Who are you?" Salt asked Harley, eyeing her gown.

"Why, I'm Mae West, darlin'." She twirled her boa and gave Jack a look. "I used to be Snow White, but I drifted."

"Arrrrr!" He laughed. "'Tis awful harrrrd to be funny when ye have to be clean."

Salt and Pepper looked at each other and shrugged.

Harley went to the kitchen and came back with a tray of drinks. "Now. Here you are, ladies. There are soft drinks and apple cider. Pick your poison." Then, with a bow of her head, she handed Jack a glass of wine. "And for you, Cap'n. Sorry, I'm fresh out of rum."

"What about ye, missus? Aren't ye going to indulge in some grog?"

"I'm way ahead of you. I generally avoid temptation—" She looked him up and down. This was no longer the boy who had cheated on her and broken her heart. This was an unexpected, sexy marauder. "—unless I can't resist it."

"Arrrrr! When yer good, yer verra, verra good, but when yer bad, yer far better!"

"Till now, you've spent all your time here outside, with the goats. Would you like to look around?" asked Harley.

The twins looked at each other, and then, having apparently deduced each other's opinions telepathically, turned to Harley and nodded in unison.

"Right this way." She swept her arm toward the living room, taffeta skirt rustling.

The girls examined the living room approvingly.

"And over here's the parlor," said Harley.

Sipping their drinks, the girls tried out the room's centerpiece, the gold velvet ottoman, before following Harley to the other rooms.

"And what exactly are you dressed as?" she asked when they got back to the living room.

"I'm supposed to be a salt shaker, but I really wanted to be a dancer, and Freddie's Pepper, but she wanted to be Wonder Woman."

"Is that so?" Harley studied Frankie for a moment. "What do you have on under that?"

"Tights and a cami," they said together.

Harley pressed a finger to her lips. "I have an idea." She opened a cupboard in the sideboard the Grimskys had left behind and pulled out a couple of old tablecloths. From the kitchen, she grabbed a pair of scissors and some twine. Then she cut a strip off one of the edges of the cloth, then straight into its center.

"Come here," she told Frankie. "Slip off your costume."

"What are you doing?" asked Frankie.

Harley tied the tablecloth around Frankie's waist, securing it with the strip so the ends fell in an uneven, handkerchief hem.

"Wow!" Holding her skirt out, Frankie twirled around. "I'm a dancer!"

"Do me!" begged Freddie impatiently, already slipping out of her pepper outfit.

"Hold on, here. That's what the twine's for." Cutting two even lengths, she attached them to adjacent corners of the other tablecloth and then secured them around Freddie's neck, creating a cape.

"Cool!"

"And there's something else I've been meaning to give you," she said. She handed Freddie a shoebox.

"What's this?"

"I was a big fan of comics, too, when I was you're age. I've been looking for a good home for these." She cupped her mouth as if telling a secret. "I hear they're great for making altered books."

Freddie's lips formed an O. "Really?" Catching herself, she looked to her father for approval.

"What do you say?" said Jack.

That was all she needed to hear. "Thank you!" she exclaimed.

Jack glowed. "Ye see that, me hearties? What did I tell ye? Not all treasure is silver and gold."

"We forgot one thing," said Harley, looking at Fang, wagging his tail. "I'll be right back."

She dashed up to her studio and returned with some art supplies. A few snips and folds of black and white paper and in no time, she was perching a paper hat on Fang's head and stretching some elastic under his chin. "Voilà!"

"He's a pirate dog!" squealed the girls.

"Yer hands work magic," said Jack. He set down his glass and glanced at his wrist. "Avast, bilge rats! Drink up! She's a school night, she is, and it's high time ye be in yer berths."

"Oh, Dad," said Freddie, cider mustache spoiling the effect of her lip gloss. "Do we have to?"

"Do we have to?" Frankie chimed in. "We want to stay here with Harley for a while."

Harley's heart swelled.

"Maybe ye'll get invited back sometime," Jack said.

"It's scarcely a cable length from the missus's port to ours."

"I think that can be arranged," said Harley, accompanying them to the door, the girls carrying their original costumes and the shoebox. With one last swish of her boa, she said, "Nice meeting you, ladies." She looked pointedly at Jack. "Anytime you've got nothing to do and lots of time to do it, come on back."

"If ye don't watch out, wench, I'll be climbin' yer riggin' and wettin' me pipe."

"Captain!" Her hand flew to her cleavage in pretend outrage. "How you do run on."

He winked broadly as he descended the porch steps. "Keep a weather eye open, ye savvy? Ye never know when ye might see me sails again on yer horizon."

When Jack and the girls got back to the estate, Mother was waiting for them. "What happened to your costumes?" she asked, hands on hips.

"Harley made them for us. Now I'm a dancer," said Frankie, pirouetting across the foyer.

"And guess who I am?" asked Freddie, swirling her red cape.

"What's in the box?" asked Mother, lifting off the lid.

"Comic books! They used to be Harley's. She gave them to me."

Jack ignored Mother's disapproving glare and hurried his daughters upstairs and through their bedtime routines so quickly, he almost felt guilty . . . almost.

He was in such a hurry to get back to Harley's house, he forgot the condoms he had bought weeks earlier and had to run back up the stairs for them.

"You're going out again?" asked Mother as he blew past her in the hall.

All he said was, "Later."

He sped to the Victorian and half ran to her door to find her waiting in the threshold, one hand on her hip, the other holding her fan.

"Why, if it isn't the swashbuckling Captain Jack."

"Aye," he panted, unable to control his grin. "I see ye couldn't wait."

"I heard your truck. You know what they say. Love thy neighbor. And if he happens to be tall, debonair, and devastating, it's all the easi—"

He silenced her by snatching her into his arms, bending her backward, and kissing her senseless, just like in the movies.

She deepened their kiss, arching into him, grabbing a handful of his shirt to pull him closer.

He thrust his tongue into her mouth, sending a current of lust through her, tugging at her core.

The kiss grew, delving, exploring. Their bodies pressed together at every possible point, searching for closure.

"Jack," she murmured, sliding her hand up the back of his shirt.

How many nights had she longed to be back in his arms, the way they'd been before everything went sideways? Tonight, their costumes were a trigger that took them back to their innocent past. The wine had loosened any lingering inhibitions.

In one smooth movement, he swooped her into his

arms, kicked the door shut behind him, and headed up the stairs.

As he climbed, their lips never parted. He cupped the overflowing swell of her breast, his whole body throbbing with lust. *Yes.* He was finally on his way to finishing something that had started a decade ago. This was going to be good . . . *so* good.

He lowered her to the bed, not taking his eyes off her as he stripped off his belt, whipping his shirt over his head, and retrieving the condom from his pocket and tossing it onto the nightstand before swiftly dispensing with his trousers, all the while watching Harley's body reveal its secrets as she shimmied out of her gown.

"Let me," he said, working the material down over her hips and casting it aside, then crawling onto the bed. It had been so long since he'd been with a woman—any woman. His need for her was beyond endurance.

"Strike your colors, woman," he snarled, still wearing his eyepatch. "Prepare to be boarded."

"Captain!" she huffed. "Don't you know? Anything worth doing is worth doing slowly."

"Don't fash yerself," he said with a wicked grin, stroking his hand up her inner thigh. "Captain Jack knows how to make ye smile."

But as it turned out, she was even more impatient than he. He hadn't yet finished his intention when she positioned his hands over her shoulders, took him in hand, and arched against him.

"One sec," he said, reaching for the condom, ripping it open with his teeth.

"You don't need that," she gasped.

With his good eye, he frowned down at her hot

cheeks, the rapid rise and fall of her chest tempting him beyond all reason. He had fantasized about this moment a thousand times. Finally, it was here.

And yet, if anyone knew the consequences of unprotected sex, it was he. "You positive?"

"You don't need it," she insisted, thighs spread, her hand guiding him firmly toward her center. "Now," she panted, "take me as you wish, sir. I ask no quarter."

He flung the condom over his shoulder. Her feather boa draped across the pillow caught his eye, and on an impulse, he deftly hog-tied her wrists and secured them to the headboard, enjoying the look of surprise on her face. Then he lowered himself into position. "Aye, and it's a jolly good thing," he growled into her ear, "because no quarter will be given."

Chapter Thirty

Mother turned on Jack the minute he came in from seeing the girls onto the school bus at the end of the lane. "What were you thinking, staying out all night?"

"I had my cell. All you had to do was call and I'd have been home as fast as if I'd been out in the vineyards. Faster."

"It's not the same thing, and you know it. What if one of them went to your room in the middle of the night and saw your bed was empty? Haven't they been traumatized enough in their young lives?"

"Admit it, Mother. You don't like that I'm seeing Harley. If I'd been with any other woman, you wouldn't have cared."

"The nerve of her—changing the girls' costumes that I spent time and money on. What right did she have to alter them?"

"She didn't destroy anything. All she did was create something new. You're just going to have to make

peace with the idea, because I want to be with her.
I'm *going* to be with her, whether you like it or not."

"That woman is the polar opposite of Emily."

"Harley. Her name is Harley."

As soon as Jack's truck turned out of the lane,
Melinda grabbed a jacket and hurried to the first
place she thought Alfred might be, the cellar room.

One of the seasonal workers looked up from
where he was extracting wine for sampling.

"Have you seen Alfred?"

"Not today. Anything I can do?"

She fled without answering, scanning first the tasting room and then the lab. Where could he be?

She finally found him behind the winery, in deep
conversation with a field hand hired as a temp for
the crush who was still trying to figure out how to
leave. People did that with surprising frequency. No
sense memorizing their names.

She waited some distance away, huddling in her
jacket in the early November chill, doing her best to
look unobtrusive.

Alfred spotted her, in that psychic connection
lovers share. Melinda tried to be patient, but his lack
of urgency, one of the very traits that attracted her to
him, also drove her crazy. As he stood conversing
with his hands jammed into his jacket pockets, rocking to and fro on his heels, it was all she could do not
to storm over there. But she couldn't risk arousing
suspicion.

If not for Alfred, she would have been lost after
Don's death. He had patiently explained things to her

in that calm way of his, until her heart had stopped racing and her breathing returned to normal.

As they spent more and more time together, she began to notice things about Alfred other than the fact that he had an excellent grasp of profit and loss statements and statistics. People said the secret of winemaking was planting great grapes and then getting out of the way. But Alfred did far more than that. Electrical repair, plumbing, carpentry—there was nothing he couldn't fix. In addition to having a fine nose, he was a chemist and a botanist. He could easily have been a winemaker himself, but he was happy to leave the notoriety to others. He preferred working in the fields and behind the scenes.

Perhaps most importantly, he knew how to get along with people. Melinda's occasional temper tantrums didn't cow him in the least. That only made her respect him more.

But when it came right down to it, indispensable as he was, Alfred was still just an employee. If there was a heaven and Melinda's mother was looking down on her, seeing how close she was becoming to Alfred, she would be scowling.

"Dammit, Alfred!" Still waiting, Melinda stamped her fine leather boot. She hated that she had come to rely on him so much.

A minute later, Alfred was finally backing up, raising his hand to the worker in a respectful farewell.

About time. She counted his steps, willing him to hurry up.

"What is it?" he asked when he saw her face. "What's wrong?"

"Jack didn't come home last night."

With a backward glance, he took her elbow and led her into the lab and shut the door. "Where is he now? Is he all right?"

Melinda shook her head impatiently. "He's fine. He went to town, but he'll be back soon. He spent the night with Harley."

"I don't know why you let yourself get so worked up over those two."

"I'm from the old school. I know how hard it is to run a business and raise a child by myself. Why should I want my son to endure that?"

"Let Jack and Harley do as they please. Start thinking about yourself for a change."

"Me?"

"You. When was the last time you did something without your son or granddaughters in mind?"

Melinda drew a blank.

"That's what I thought," said Alfred. "How about this. What say we go down to the Turning Point Friday night and I'll buy you dinner."

At first thought, she welcomed the idea. The last man she'd been out with was Thurston, the owner of a collection agency in Marlborough.

And then she caught a glimpse of Alfred's baggy corduroys, and she imagined the whispers of her committee members and country club friends when word got out that she was dating her vineyard manager.

"How can I relax when my son's getting in deeper and deeper with the wrong person? No. I'm determined to find Jack someone better. And I won't rest until I do."

She strolled briskly out of the lab before Alfred could stop her.

Chapter Thirty-one

"Can we go play with the goats now?" asked Freddie.

Jack and the twins had finished the vegetable soup and salad Harley had made them.

"It's November, you sillies. The goats are snuggled up in the barn," Harley replied. "But you don't have to stay at the table."

"Can we go exploring?" asked Frankie.

"Yeah," said Freddie. "Your house is so cool!"

"Sure."

The girls bolted from the table and disappeared.

"Don't get into anything," called Jack after them. He set down the empty garlic bread basket he'd brought from the table and nuzzled her neck as she was putting the lid on the leftover soup. "You're good for them, you know that?"

Once the floodgates had opened, there was no closing them. Since Halloween, Jack had appeared at Harley's door most evenings, after he tucked in his kids. Just thinking of their nights together as she worked on her designs brought a smile to her lips.

Making love in character had had a freeing effect. In sharp contrast to Halloween night, the second time they made love was sweet and tender . . . a poignant homecoming. And the passion the third time . . . her face heated, thinking about it.

At the sound of giggling from the vicinity of the powder room, Harley smiled. "Hear that?"

"Should I tell them to keep it down?"

"No." She smacked his chest playfully. "I like the sound of happy children."

"When it comes to compromising with Frankie, my mother has dug in her heels. We've always eaten together as a family, and she insists everyone eat a balanced diet. But lately, mealtime has become a contest of wills." He laid his hand on his abdomen. "It's enough to give me indigestion."

She turned the water on in the sink. "I went through my own finicky-eating phase when I was the twins' age. I remember going for months eating nothing but my dad's macaroni and cheese."

Jack's hands inside her waistband distracted her. She shut off the water, turned around, and draped her arms over his shoulders.

"You know who else you're good for?" he murmured.

"Who?" she teased.

He craned his neck, looking around to make sure they weren't being spied on. "Me," he said, and kissed her.

There was more giggling, this time very nearby.

Harley and Jack looked over to see the girls in the doorway, demure and pink-cheeked.

"What are you little imps up to?" asked Jack.

"Nothing," they giggled.

"Don't give me 'nothing.' By the looks on your faces, I can tell it was something. Get your coats. It's time to go. I have some work to do tonight. Did you thank Harley for the meal?"

"Thank you, Harley," they sang in chorus, approaching her with outstretched arms.

Harley bent to their level and gathered them to her breast. "I love you guys," she said.

"We love you, too," they said shyly, while behind them, Jack beamed.

Chapter Thirty-two

"Hello, this is Melinda Friestatt calling. I'd like to make reservations for Thanksgiving dinner. Twenty-eight. That's right. Would it be possible to push some tables together? I'd appreciate it. And one more thing—would you happen to know if Harley Miller-Jones is working that day? She is?" Melinda had been counting on it. Harley had only been back at the club a couple of months. The newest hires always got the shaft during the holidays. Now, she relished the thought of her plan coming to-gether more than she relished the feast itself. "I'd like to put in a special request that she be our server."

"What are you doing for Thanksgiving?" Jack asked Harley, curled up next to him. The movie they'd been watching on TV had ended and the credits were rolling.

"Same thing I do every Thanksgiving," she said, without a trace of self-pity—"working."

Jack pictured Harley in the brown uniform with the club's embroidered logo, setting two plates loaded with turkey and mashed potatoes and baked corn in front of members in sport coats and Fair Isle sweaters.

"Not that postponing my own dinner is easy." She chuckled. "The smell of thyme and sage and onions in the restaurant kitchen drives me crazy. But I'll get my turn Friday."

"I was going to ask you to have Thanksgiving at my house."

Harley paused. "With your mother?" She huffed. "Did you happen to run this idea by her? We both know I'm number one on her hit list."

Jack stroked a lock of her hair over her shoulder. "It's my house, too. And it won't be just her. There's usually a full table. Hank and Jamie will probably be there. And Kerry and Alex and their brood, and who knows who else. It'll be an opportunity to announce to the world that we're together. You know . . . safety in numbers."

"We might be ready, but your mother might resent us using an important family holiday to do it with. Besides," she said, laying her head on his shoulder, "I have to work. I have mountains of bills to pay."

He stroked her forehead. "I don't like it . . . you working on Thanksgiving."

"It's no big deal. That's how we've always done it, even when I was in Seattle. I'd waitress on the holiday, then get up early Friday morning to drive down here and walk in my parents' house as Dad was lifting the turkey from the oven."

He turned to face her. "It doesn't have to be like that anymore. Can't you take a year off? Just one?"

"I just started at the club. I'm the low man on the totem pole. Not only that, I'm single. If I call off, that means some mother or father'll have to come in."

A couple of days later, Jack had just put the girls on the bus and was pouring a second cup of coffee to take out to the winery when his mother said, "I've decided to have Thanksgiving at the club this year."

The coffee pot in Jack's hand halted in midpour. "We never have Thanksgiving at the club." Of all years, why this one, when Harley was working there?

Mother sighed as she set down her newspaper and slid off her reading glasses. "I'm just not up to orchestrating a big meal."

"I don't think restaurants should be open at all on Thanksgiving," said Jack. "It's a national holiday. Everyone should be able to be home, with their friends and families."

"That's rather extreme. It's not like we've never eaten out on Thanksgiving. You never complained before."

That was before he'd found out that the woman he loved had to defer her own holiday to wait on others.

"How about this. I'll chip in. The girls can help cook, too. They're plenty old enough."

"It's nice of you to offer, but even with help, it's getting to be too much. Hank and Jamie are coming."

"You've already started inviting people?" he asked, indignant.

"And Rose and Seamus and their brood."

"The entire Friestatt-O'Hearn clan?" This was going from bad to worse.

"You make it sound as though they're strangers. Besides, it's hardly the whole clan. I'd have to rent a hall for that."

"You've never invited the entire Ribbon Ridge contingent to Thanksgiving."

"We could hardly fit everyone around our dining room table, now, could we? Not only that, half my silver spoons are missing. I wish I knew what happened to them. I tried to find replacements, but the only pieces to be found are monogrammed with someone else's initials."

At the mention of the missing spoons, guilt stabbed at Jack. Aside from that, giving Harley the Victorian had been a step toward taking his life into his own hands. But planning an elaborate feast was way out of his wheelhouse. He didn't know the first thing about how to make turkey and mashed potatoes and stuffing.

"I've already spoken to the club. They're going to push several tables together for us. It'll work out fine, you'll see."

No, it wouldn't be fine. Jack wanted Harley by his side for the annual celebration. Instead, she would be forced to wait not just on him but his entire family.

At the club on Thanksgiving Day, an enormous red and gold floral arrangement sat on a round table in the center of the dining room. Freshly polished

hurricane lamps sparkled atop the linen-covered tables.

Harley checked her watch yet again. The Friestatt
party was due any minute. All twenty-eight of them,
according to the reservation.

She inhaled deeply and smoothed down her uniform. *You'll be fine,* she told herself.

Down the hall, a commotion interrupted the
music coming from the grand piano. Harley peeked
around the corner toward the lobby to see Jack helping his mother out of her coat.

Harley took a deep breath, breezed through the
swinging kitchen door, and stood off to the side, half
hidden behind a large fern on a pedestal.

Melinda led the way, carrying herself like the
queen of Willamette Valley society she was.

Jack walked at her elbow, matching her pace, listening to what were undoubtedly some last-minute
instructions. Though what instructions were needed
for Thanksgiving dinner, Harley could only imagine.
Probably guidelines on who should sit where. Or
maybe she was reprimanding him for something
he'd done in the car on the way over. Failing to signal
or forgetting to open her door.

Behind them came the twins in stiff taffeta dresses.
Harley wondered when they would stop letting Melinda
dictate their style and start dressing like other girls
their age.

Next in line were Rose and Seamus O'Hearn,
Jack's great-aunt and -uncle. Rose walked haltingly
with a cane, but she still looked elegant in low heels
and a satin bow blouse.

Then Ryan O'Hearn, the Grimskys' attorney, and
his wife, Indra, wearing a printed silk. Kerry and her

daughters, Alex, and his foster children. And little Griffin.

Hank and Jamie. At the sight of the basketball under her fitted knit sheath, Harley's breath caught.

Bringing up the rear were Keith, the youngest O'Hearn boy, who'd shared Harley's locker in tenth grade, Marcus, the middle son, and their wives and a tangle of kids of whom she wasn't sure who belonged to whom, but clearly, they were all either Friestatts or O'Hearns. You could tell by their caramel-colored eyes and auburn hair.

Harley couldn't help but wonder what it was like to be part of such a big, tight-knit clan.

And yet there seemed to be someone missing.

Following several false starts, minor arguments, and redirections, the hostess finally got them all seated to Melinda's satisfaction.

It was time. Harley took a deep breath, breezed through the swinging kitchen door, and approached Melinda's chair at the head of the table. "Happy Thanksgiving. May I take your drink orders?"

The second he saw her, Jack was on his feet. "Harley. Good to see you. Happy Thanksgiving." He kissed her cheek in front of her ear, where it tickled.

Her face warmed and she grinned. "Happy Thanksgiving."

"Mae West!" said Freddie. "How come you're here?"

Melinda frowned. "Frederica, remember our little talk?"

"You mean about not talking to the waiters? But she's not a waiter." Freddie pointed, her brow furrowed in confusion. "That's Harley."

Harley smiled at Freddie. "I work here."

"You do?"

"I do."

"Even on Thanksgiving?"

Next to Freddie, Frankie scratched unself-consciously at the seam cutting into her waist where her bodice was sewn to the gathers in her skirt.

"If not for me, now, who would bring you your food?"

Jack looked miserable. But as there was nothing else he could do, he returned to his chair.

"How are you, Harley?" asked Ryan from a few seats down.

"Fine, thank you."

"Happy Thanksgiving," called out Jamie.

"Same to you," Harley replied.

"Nice to see you again, Harley," said Kerry. "Happy—"

"I'll have a Bloody Mary," said Melinda. "And I want it with real tomato juice, not the bottled mix, and plenty of ice."

It took Hank and Jack but a moment to agree on the brand of celebratory champagne for the toast.

When the bartender had filled their order, Harley returned promptly and passed around their beverages.

"How's your drink, Mrs. Friestatt?"

Melinda took a sip and smacked her lips. "A little too much horseradish, but it'll do."

"Wonderful. We have turkey and all the trimmings on the buffet. Is everyone ready to order?"

"What else is on the menu?" asked Melinda.

Harley leaned on her long experience with difficult customers. "Most people will want the buffet, but the chef can make anything you want." One of the benefits of a private club.

Melinda put her finger to her lips and thought. "What about the onion soup?"

"Of course, Mrs. Friestatt," said Harley, jotting it down on her pad. "Anything else I can get for you?"

"I'm not in the mood for turkey. Give me a crab cake, extra crispy, tartar sauce on the side."

Up and down the table, amid giggling children with their napkins draped over their heads, wary eyes turned.

Harley scribbled on her pad. "One crab cake, extra crispy."

"And the Country Club Salad, no anchovies."

Jack clenched his jaw. This was exactly what he had been fearing . . . Mother throwing her weight around. But it was understood that she was the matriarch, and this was her gig.

He could take Mother's antagonism toward himself. But he couldn't abide her dumping on Harley. If Mother only knew—the way Harley took her provocation in stride only made him think the more of her.

Harley moved around the table, smiling and chatting easily. She chucked Griffin under the chin. Asked Jamie how she was feeling these days.

Jack couldn't have been prouder. He also couldn't have imagined Harley looking better than when she'd first come back to Newberry. But a summer on Ribbon Ridge had put some color in her cheeks. She was almost glowing. If not for her hourglass figure, he would almost think *she* was expecting, too.

Kerry's baby let out a wail and Harley jumped. Seemed she could take whatever Mother dished out, but when it came to babies, she was supersensitive.

On Jack's right, the twins had been waiting patiently for Harley to make her way to them.

"And for you?" she asked, finally.

Like everyone except Mother, Freddie ordered the buffet.

Then it was Frankie's turn. "I'm a vegetarian," she announced to the table at large. "I don't eat anything with a face."

Today, of all days, Frankie had chosen today to go cold turkey? thought Jack.

Harley raised a brow and looked inquiringly at Jack. But before he could respond, Mother did it for him.

"Frances. Girls your age need iron in their diets." Without bothering to look at Harley, she instructed, "She'll have the buffet."

"How come you get to have whatever you want and I don't?" asked Frankie.

"You're my grandchild and you'll do as I say. Adults shouldn't have to explain themselves to children."

"But—" Frankie burst into angry tears. Looking around for moral support, she cried, "It's not that I don't like meat. It's just that I feel sorry for the poor turkey." Her fists screwed into her eyes pathetically.

Jack put his arm around her. "Shh. There are plenty of other things on the buffet that don't have, er, faces."

"Come with me when we go up," said Indra. "You can get the same things I'm getting."

Harley had come full circle around the table. She turned to leave, then halted and read over her list, her forehead furrowed. "I feel like I'm missing someone." She gazed around the table until her eye stopped on the empty seat at the far end, opposite Mother's.

"Alfred."

Mother's neck turned the color of pinot noir.

Harley repeated, "Where's Alfred?"

On a piece of grassy bottomland, in a modest ranch house that sat just far enough back from 240 to muffle the road noise, Alfred reclined his La-Z-Boy with only his plate for company.

Out in the galley kitchen, the nicely browned, twelve-pound turkey rested on the stove, the carving knife sticking out of it. Alfred always bought a decent-sized bird at Thanksgiving, to last him through the week. No sense going to all that trouble for one meal. A pot of gravy congealed on a cool burner, and there was plenty more mashed potatoes on the counter.

He sipped his wine and forked a bite of stuffing into his mouth at a leisurely pace while he thumbed through the channels on his remote. There was a feast of football on TV. Three NFL, and one big college game. Which one to watch? Minnesota vs. Detroit? Chargers at Dallas? Washington and the Giants? Or maybe he should go with Ole Miss vs. Mississippi State. But that wasn't on until later that evening. By then, he would be back at the winery, checking to see that everything was stable. He spent most of his waking hours there. So much so that no one had batted an eye when he'd hauled in a secondhand easy chair and floor lamp and installed it in the supply closet. Everyone assumed it was for him to catch the occasional catnap. But it was really for Melinda and him.

If the only place she would be with him was the winery, then he would make it as comfortable as possible for her.

Alfred had only a passing interest in football, and the Vikings were ahead by two touchdowns. And then a golf club commercial came on, and he thought of Melinda, eating dinner with her family at the country club.

Though his stomach was full, he felt somehow hollow. He got up and went to the fridge, grabbed a handful of carrots, and headed out to the stable.

Nowadays, Alfred let the cellar rats do the heavy lifting at the winery. The work following the crush was strenuous. There was a lot of dragging hoses around and moving barrels, not to mention cleaning. Sometimes the young ones complained they spent more time cleaning than they did making wine.

"Here you go, Dave," he said, holding a carrot under the gelding's nose, watching as he nibbled it with velvet-soft lips.

But as long as he'd been at Arabella Cellars, his appreciation of being part of the process never faded. He lived to watch the tasting-room employees pull the cork on a new vintage. He would stand back anonymously and watch the ruby liquid trickle into the glass. The pourer would hand it to one of thousands of annual visitors and say, "Here, try this." Then Alfred would wait for their faces light up.

From beneath Dave's neck appeared another greedy muzzle.

"Wondered where you were, Petey. Hang on a minute. I didn't forget you," he said, feeding a carrot into the donkey's mouth.

"That's it," said Alfred with a pat to Dave's neck.

With no more carrots in sight, Petey had already wandered back to his favorite corner of the stall.

"Happy Thanksgiving."

Back at the club, the adults stopped chatting and sipping their water and they, too, searched for the venerable vineyard manager. Not finding him, they exchanged puzzled looks. It only made sense that Alfred should have a place at the table. He had been around as long as any of them could remember.

"Harley has a point," said Jack. "We should have invited Alfred."

"Thanksgiving is for family," said Melinda firmly. "This is a family dinner."

"Alfred's practically family."

As Alex quietly reprimanded his boys for sword fighting with their butter knives, the other adults decided now was a good time to retrieve their napkins from the floor and remind their kids to hold their hands when they went up to the buffet line and not cut in front of anyone.

Harley smiled. "I'll have the chef put your order in right away, Mrs. Friestatt. The rest of you, feel free to go up to the buffet."

"Crab cakes?" Jack whispered to Mother under his breath, as Harley left to put in her special order. "Today, even Indra's making do with the side dishes."

"I'm paying for this meal. Shouldn't I be able to get what I want?"

Jack just shook his head, then clapped his hands and rose. "Who's hungry?" he asked his girls. "Let's go up and fix your plates."

For her next drink, Mother requested a Rum Martinez, again made to order. More tartar sauce. Another bread basket. *Was there any of that sweet raisin bread? This Portuguese loaf tasted old.*

Thirty minutes later, half the wine had been drunk and the kids had finished pushing their food around their plates and were getting antsy.

"There's no one out on the greens. Why don't I take them outside?" offered Indra. "Let them run off some steam."

"I'll come with you," said Jack.

The twins had to stop off at the bathroom. Indra went ahead, leaving Jack to pace the hallway outside the ladies' room as Harley exited the kitchen carrying a tray full of drinks.

"I won't keep you. I just want to say sorry about my mother."

"Nothing Melinda does could surprise me."

The twins emerged from the bathroom. "Harley!" Freddie and Frankie threw their arms around her waist, causing her tray to tip precariously.

"Girls!" said Jack. "Harley's working."

Harley smiled indulgently. "It's okay."

"When can we come over again and play with Daisy and Tulip?" they asked.

Harley eyed Jack. "You'll have to ask your daddy."

The girls whirled around as one and flung themselves onto Jack. "When can we go? When? Soon? Soon, okay?"

"Shh!" said Jack, a hand on each twin's upper back. "Inside voices." Eyeing Harley, he asked, "Maybe later today?"

"I have guests coming tomorrow. I'm afraid I have to go home and get ready for them."

"Awwww." The girls' faces fell.

"You've been wrestling alligators ever since you got back to town," said Jack.

"What about next weekend?" asked Harley. "Frankie, how about I make you something one hundred percent cruelty-free."

That brought the smile back to her face. "Can we?" she asked Jack.

"All right by me."

"Everything okay?" Gordon, the club manager, appeared from out of nowhere. He lifted a meaningful brow at Harley.

"Got to go, girls," sang Harley, detouring around them. "Happy Thanksgiving."

Under the manager's scrutiny, Jack watched her go, admiring the S-curve from waist to hip as she balanced her tray on her shoulder.

His phone dinged. Prudence, again.

Why did you lead me on?

Chapter Thirty-three

Harley hurried home after her shift at the club to finish preparing rooms for a wedding party. The bride and her attendants were driving up from their homes in California for the destination wedding. Two of them arrived after midnight. Just when Harley got them settled, the third woman rang the bell and she went through her routine once more.

At least they left shortly after breakfast for the wedding venue.

Later that night, when the reception was over, they returned barefoot, dangling their high heels by their straps, their dresses creased and makeup smeared.

"Looks like you had a good time," yawned Harley, tightening the sash on her robe.

Then came the men in their shirtsleeves, loosened bow ties draped around their necks.

"Where's the room?" one man, apparently the groom, asked his bride.

"Follow me," she replied, gathering her skirt and ascending the stairs.

Not only the groom but his male friends trooped after her.

"Excuse me," said Harley. "I believe some of you don't have reservations."

The women exchanged perturbed looks. "We paid cash for the rooms."

"I charge by the person, not the room. Are you forgetting about breakfast? I have to buy enough food to serve everyone."

"No problem. We just won't eat," said one of the men. At that, they laughed and continued up the stairs.

Harley didn't know what to do. She knew better than to argue with drunks. She hadn't asked for a credit card, so she couldn't add the charges. She decided to bill the bride, hoping she would pay it when she came to her senses, and chalked it up to another lesson learned. From now on, she would make her guest policy crystal clear.

She was exhausted from the cumulative effect of working Thanksgiving, staying up late last night, and again tonight. Hopeful the wedding party would pass out, she fell back into bed.

But it wasn't long before she heard the front door opening and closing, followed by music, laughter and the loud voices of yet more people. It seemed the party was only just getting started.

That's it. She threw off her covers and marched downstairs in her T-shirt and flannel pants to find four more people lounging in the living room with their feet on the coffee table. One of them popped a cork to a rousing volley of cheers as champagne sprayed in an arc, landing on her yellow velvet ottoman.

"What do you think you're doing?"

"Hey! Who are you?" asked a man jovially. "Who cares who you are—we're having a celebration! Come join the party." The man thrust one of her own glasses, obtained from her china closet, into her hand.

"This is my house, and that's my furniture you're ruining," she said, pointing to the ottoman.

"Sorry. My bad," he said, chugging from the bottle until his laughter forced him to stop and wipe his mouth on the back of his hand.

She hurried to the kitchen for a tea towel. The guest was always right. That's what the guides to running a B and B said. When she got there, she found a couple making out against her counter.

"Do you mind?"

"Oops," hiccupped the woman. She had the decency to lead her beau out of the room.

Harley wondered where she was taking him. But she had to blot the wine off the ottoman before it stained. She grabbed a couple of towels and headed back to the living room, and when she got there, her jaw dropped when she saw a man standing on her beautiful ottoman with his shoes on, peeing into her fiddle-leaf fig.

"Get out! Everyone, out! Now!"

But her words were drowned out in the commotion.

Then someone mentioned going out to see the goats. Her property was one thing, but her animals were another. She had visions of the poor creatures fainting in terror. She had to defend them. But how?

If you ever need anything, holler. At the time, she had chalked up Alex's offer to polite neighborliness. Only now did it occur to her that, as both a cop and a friend of Jack's, Alex was serious about looking out for her.

With shaking fingers she punched Alex's number into her phone.

"Harley," he answered in his officious voice after the first ring. "'Course I remember you. What's up?"

Minutes later, Alex pulled up in his unmarked car, lights flashing, a backup officer close behind him. And following *them* came Jack.

It had taken some good-natured cajoling by the men, but soon the house was emptied of everyone but the bride and groom, who the whole time had been closeted in their room, presumably doing what all brides and grooms do on their wedding nights, and the original two women members of the party.

Still in her bathrobe, Harley breathed a sigh of relief as she thanked the men. "I hated to call for help, but when they started talking about the goats . . . I was picturing it turning into a free-for-all, with you throwing them bodily off the porch. I can't believe it ended peaceably."

"You were right to call. As for defusing the situation, when you're outnumbered, you have to use brains instead of brawn," said Alex.

Alex and the other cop left, but Jack stayed behind.

Harley pinched her temples. "If I'd known this was what running a B and B was like . . ."

Jack escorted her to a kitchen chair. "You've been drinking from the fire hose ever since you got back to town. What are you going to do when the baby comes?"

"I don't know," she confessed. In Seattle, all she had was a one-bedroom apartment and her design business. Now she had added another full-time business and—Jack.

"I know," said Jack.

She searched his face.

"Quit the B and B."

She shook her head. "I can't. At least not until my royalties start coming."

Jack looked down at her, so strong yet so vulnerable. When Alex had called him and told him there was trouble at the Victorian, he didn't think twice before jumping into his truck.

"Besides, what about goat yoga?"

"Those goats won't miss doing yoga with strangers. They'll be just as happy to do yoga with you and the girls." He took her in his arms. "What can I do to help you? Whatever you need. I'm here for you."

Without thinking, she replied, "I can do this on my own, the same way I've made my career on my own. I don't need you or any other man to help me." She had started with nothing. She hadn't just beaten the odds against a starving artist making a living. She'd smashed them out of the park.

"You don't have to be so defensive. I'm asking you to lean on me, and let me lean on you. What more do I have to do to convince you that you can trust me?"

It was because of Jack that she was standing in her dream house. He'd seen to it that everyone in his family welcomed her.

Everyone except Melinda, of course.

"There're some things you need to know about. Things I probably should have told you before, but everything was going so well for us, I didn't want to ruin it."

"What could possibly ruin what we have?"

"The first day I went back to work at the club, your mom was there."

He exhaled loudly and pinched the bridge of his nose between his eyes. "Great."

"She tried to bribe me to leave town again."

Jack set down his glass and went over to gaze out the window. "Why didn't you tell me?"

"You knew I was in her crosshairs. Like I said, I didn't want to spoil things. Anyway, it didn't work. I didn't take the bait. It's over now."

He came back to the couch, sat down beside her, and took her hands in his. "I've given this a lot of thought. You're great with the girls. They're much happier than when we first came back. Their grades are improving and they're easier to get along with." He hesitated. "What would you say to us moving in together?"

Harley slipped out of his grasp, tightened the sash on her robe and angled away from him. There was a time when she would have jumped at the chance. The irony was, now that Jack was finally ready, she wasn't. Why couldn't the two of them ever be on the same page?

"I know you're determined to be a one-woman band, doing your artwork, running a B and B. But why run yourself ragged if you don't have to? I thought you were the open minded one. What's the down side? The house is plenty big enough."

"I don't need anyone to take care of me."

"What if I were to tell you I need you to take care

of me? And the girls, and your son. *Our kids.* We can be a family."

Waking up next to Jack every morning . . . the patter of three pairs of little feet down the hall? Ending each day together? It was everything she had ever wanted.

"You won't have to open your house up to strangers any more. The only people you'll have to take care of are the people you care about and who feel the same way about you."

They had found their way back to each other against all odds. She should be ecstatic. But there was still something else that nagged at her, kept her from going along with Jack's plan. She bit her lip. "You make it sound so perfect . . ."

"It is perfect. Why are you so against it? Who knows? Maybe one day we'll even have another baby."

She hadn't told Jack that she was infertile. Because letting him in on her secret would lead to him insisting on taking the blame for having made her that way. And even though his marrying Emily had cut her like a knife, she couldn't bear the thought of hurting *him.*

There was something Jack still hadn't told her either: what he was doing with Emily while he was seeing *her.*

He put his arm around her and pulled her close. "Harley. You make me very," he kissed her lips lightly and unbuttoned the top button of her shirt, "very," kissed her again, and undid the next button, "happy."

He cupped her head, his mouth hungrily seeking hers. A minute later, he pulled back and asked, "Tell me I make you feel the same."

"You know you do. You always have." He untied her sash, slipped his hands into her robe and pulled her body flush with his. He was larger than she remembered. Any hint of boyish wiriness was gone, replaced by slabs of solid muscle from years spent hefting bins full of grapes and barrels full of wine. She felt ultrafeminine in comparison. "You're very persuasive. You know that?"

Gently he peeled her robe off her shoulders, held her at arm's length and examined her, surrounding her breasts with his warm hands, making her nipples tighten. "Then it's a done deal." He kissed her again and slowly lowered her backward onto the couch cushions.

She pressed her hands against his chest and wrested her mouth from his. "Wait. There's something you should know—" She'd rehearsed the words over and over in her head.

"Whatever it is, it can wait." He nuzzled her neck, slipping his hand between her legs.

She inhaled sharply. A moment later, her head fell back and her eyes closed, reveling in the sensations swirling through her.

"Nnnnnn." Harley groaned into her pillow.

"What's that?" panted Jack. He lay next to her in her bed with his hands behind his head, feeling exceedingly smug. "Did you say you wanted to do it again?"

"Nooooo." He might have had his way the first go-round, but she had made him pay, and pay dearly. "I cry uncle."

He grinned into the darkness, absentmindedly trailing his fingertips lightly across the small of her back. He hadn't felt so satisfied, so hopeful, in years.

And then he felt something . . . something that wasn't supposed to be there. His hand stopped on an elevated ridge along Harley's spine.

Her muscles tensed. "Whad?" Though muffled in her pillow, her voice held a distinct edge. He sat up and fumbled with the lamp on the nightstand until he found the switch.

Then he leaned over her lower back and ran his finger over the four-inch scar.

There were a couple of closed head injuries when the Homecoming Court was thrown from the float. Jimmy Polanski fractured his right thumb when he broke his fall, costing them the game against Barlow that night. Jane Zhou, whom the mean kids called "Plain" Jane, sustained a broken collarbone. At halftime, when Jane walked out to the fifty-yard line with her arm in a sling and was crowned queen, word circulated through the bleachers that she'd got the mercy vote.

Slowly, Harley rolled over onto her back and stared up at the ceiling. The moment she'd been dreading was here.

She began speaking in a monotone. "After the accident, my periods stopped. The doctors assured me they would come back in a year or so." She swallowed the lump in her throat, unable to continue. Every month she waited, watching for the slightest cramp, the merest trace of pink. "I'm still waiting. I've done some reading. The medical term for it is post-spinal cord injury amenorrhea. In a small percentage of cases, periods never resume. It's being studied extensively overseas. They think it has something to do with the effect of trauma on prolactin levels. Too much prolactin inhibits menstruation."

As the upshot of her words hit Jack, his self-satisfaction vanished, replaced with self-loathing. "If you don't have periods . . ." His conclusion was too devastating to give voice to. "But . . . I thought your back injury wasn't that serious. I thought the surgery fixed things."

"All the surgery did was take out the tiny fragments of fractured vertebrae. The body is a complicated machine, Jack. Even the slightest trauma to the spinal cord can throw things off. And when you toss hormones into the mix . . ." She winced. "Bottom line is, I can't get pregnant. I'll never carry my own child."

"Aw, Harley. Jesus." He cradled her cheek, searching her face with silent tears streaming down it. "This is my fault. I did this to you."

She removed his hands and squeezed them between hers. "Jack, no. It's nobody's fault. It was a freak accident."

All these years, she'd been suffering in silence. He sat up on the side of the bed, put his feet on the floor, and hung his head. "Don't tell me that! If it weren't for my carelessness, this never would have happened."

She rolled onto her side and propped herself up on her elbow. "Stop kicking yourself. I was the navigator—"

"I was the one behind the wheel. The driver is always the one responsible."

"If you want to go assigning blame, I'm every bit as culpable as you are."

But he'd been raised to take responsibility for his actions above all. Nothing she could say would ever convince him of that.

Chapter Thirty-four

Jack had taken the girls to Harley's house for dinner. Now they were back at the estate.

The girls were in the living room, whispering when Frankie jumped up.

"Freddie! That's my favorite pencil! Give it back!" Freddie ran around the coffee table, her twin hot on her heels, both giggling.

"What did you have to eat?" Melinda asked, imagining Harley stuffing them with sugary desserts.

"Soup," said Freddie.

"And salad," finished Frankie.

"Hmph," said Melinda.

The timer on Jack's phone buzzed. "Listen up, girls. I have a call scheduled with my man Down Under. Get ready for bed and I'll come up and kiss you good night when I'm finished."

Jack grabbed his jacket and headed out for his office.

"Girls," Melinda repeated. "It's time for you to go upstairs and get your baths."

But instead of complying, they continued chasing each other around the furniture.

"Frankie! Did you hear what I said?"

The more time they spent at Harley's place, the more headstrong they were becoming.

Out of breath, Freddie said, "You tell her."

"No, you," panted Frankie.

"Tell me what?" asked Melinda.

"Let's do rock-paper-scissors," said Freddie.

The first two attempts were ties. Not surprising, given their telepathic bond.

"Rock crushes scissors," said Freddie. "You lost."

"What is it you're dying to tell me?" Despite their silliness, Melinda filled with foreboding.

They drew out their competition for another half minute, clearly enjoying the drama.

"Just tell her!" said Freddie finally.

Frankie turned to Melinda. "Guess what? Harley's having a baby!"

Later, when Jack came back downstairs after kissing the twins good night, Mother was waiting for him.

"We have to talk."

Jack plowed a hand through his hair. "Can it wait till tomorrow? I'm bushed."

"No. It can't."

With a sigh, he followed her into the living room.

She turned to him with a scowl on her face.

"Is it true? Is Harley having a baby?"

So, that was the secret the girls had been buzzing about that night at Harley's, when she let them loose to explore.

"It is."

"She can't do that."

He could tell Mother that Harley wasn't giving birth. But why should he? It was none of her business. Besides, after all her meddling, she deserved to stew a little.

"When are you going to stop trying to control everyone in your orbit?"

"You can't have a child with her."

Annoyance changed to suspicion. "I don't like what you're implying."

"She's wrong for you. And bringing another child into the world will only make it worse. Jack, you have to put a stop to it."

"Stop it?" he snapped. "When are you going to start trusting me to run my own life?"

"When you start showing me you can." She picked up his jacket and dangled it in the air between her thumb and forefinger.

"Because I threw my coat on a chair? Did it ever occur to you that I might pick it up myself if you'd give me half a minute?"

"What if someone comes in and sees it before—"

"Who cares? Who the hell cares? You're so worried about appearances. I wish you cared more about my feelings . . . the girls' feelings. But it's never been like that, has it? All you ever cared about was that we live up to some impossible standard that only exists in your mind."

Mother glanced over her shoulder toward the kitchen. "Lower your voice this instant. The help—"

"I don't care about the help or anyone else. The help is human, just like us. Human, Mother. We fall down and we bleed . . . and we cry and we throw coats on chairs. We *fall in love*." He recalled his parents' chilly relationship and added, "If we're lucky."

"Are you quite through?"

"No." Jack squared his shoulders and looked her in the eye. "I'm not. You're such a hypocrite. All my life you acted like we're better than Harley, and yet you're running around with the vineyard manager."

The color drained from her face.

"You think I didn't know about Alfred? How could I not? Whenever you're not in the house you're in one of the outbuildings with him. It's been that way ever since I can remember."

"Alfred and I have to work closely together. How can I not be expected to spend time with him?"

"It's more than that, and we both know it. Tell me. How long has it been going on? Since before we even went to New Zealand?"

Mother's mouth was a tight white line. "Leave Alfred out of this."

"Why? Isn't that what we're talking about here? The fact that in your warped mind, class trumps genuine feelings?"

"That's *not* what we're talking about."

"Then what?"

"If I had married a man like Alfred instead of your father, we wouldn't have any of this—" she spread her arms wide in reference to the heart of the house, with its antiques and its crystal chandelier.

"I've had *this* all my life," he spat, gesturing angrily to the room. "But *this* never made me happy. I was an empty shell before Harley came into my life. She makes me whole. We were meant to be together. If only you would have let me live my own life without your incessant interference."

He headed out of the room.

"Jack!" she called, running after him.

At the door, he turned back around and pointed at her. "Harley's adopting," he spat. "But I'll tell you something. I wish that child *was* mine. No matter how much you have against her, you're going to have to get over it. Because I love her. I've always loved her. And whether you like it or not, we're going to be together. In the beginning of the year, I'm taking the girls and we're moving in with her."

Chapter Thirty-five

In his closet office, Alfred shushed Melinda with long, slow strokes of his hand over her hair, down the nape of her neck, until her heart stopped racing and her breathing returned to normal.

When she had finally quieted, he pulled back and looked at her face. "There, now. You okay?"

"Alfred. What would I do without you?"

She took off her ever-present strand of pearls and poured it from hand to hand. "You see these? Growing up, my Grandmother Esther never lacked for anything. Her father was one of the wealthiest men in McMinnville. He started out raising beef cattle. Then, realizing that timber was Oregon's main natural resource, he started a trucking company to haul logs to the mills. He was able to send Esther to private school. As she got older, he screened all her acquaintances. That was much easier to do, back in the forties. He chose a man, a decent man he knew would be able to provide the kinds of things his daughter was used to having.

"But youth is foolish. Esther rejected the man her father chose for her and married a boy she knew nothing about. A lay about and a gambler who swore he loved her but, she soon found out, loved a lot of women. They lived in one rented house after another, skipping town in the dead of night when they couldn't fend off the landlord any longer. Esther took in laundry and ironed tablecloths for a local hotel until she died a painful death from diverticulitis, thanks to her abysmal diet. These were the only thing of value she had left."

Alfred stared at the pearls. "What happened to her father's money?"

"The business went to her brother. You know how it was in those days. It wasn't considered proper for a lady to work. Women were at the mercy of men. First their fathers, and then their husbands. It wasn't like today, with the internet making it possible to market ideas without ever leaving the house, and women becoming educated and receiving fair pay."

She sighed. "In every day and age, once you're down, it's hard to get back up. Instead of learning from her mother's mistakes, my mother followed in her footsteps . . . fell in lust with a man whose paycheck barely made ends meet."

"Were your parents in love?"

"Love?" she huffed a bitter laugh. "Love doesn't keep the wolf from the door." She thought for a minute. "Were yours?"

He shrugged. "I like to think so. Doesn't every kid? What good's money if there's no love? I didn't grow up rich and I turned out just fine."

"Unless you've been truly poor, you don't know what it's like. You live in a constant state of insecurity.

It's a sick feeling in the pit of your stomach when you go to the fridge yet again and there's nothing to eat. Not seeing a dentist for years at a time . . . opening your dresser drawer to see the bottom of it showing beneath the same old rags, season after season . . . never having anything new. It's like a heavy secret you carry around, embarrassed people will see. It makes you feel less than. Beneath.

"And even when you've finally made it and you live in a beautiful home and your pantry is stocked full of nutritious food and you can give your child golf lessons and music lessons and take exotic vacations, even then, that knot of fear never goes away.

"I was determined to be stronger than my mother. To get back what my grandmother had thrown away. I was hell-bent on rising above my circumstances."

There was a heavy pause.

"If that's what will make you happy," Alfred said, rising from his chair with a small groan at the ache in his knees.

"Where are you going?"

"If I don't get back to work, what'll happen to all that success of yours?"

He walked out of the tasting room, leaving her there to think.

Chapter Thirty-six

On a frosty December morning, Jack called Harley to say he was taking the twins Christmas shopping at the mall in Tigard and to ask if she wanted to come along.

"Thanks, but you guys go ahead without me. I'm putting the finishing touches on my greeting card collection, and I just looked at my planner and remembered I promised to stop by one of those home parties where women sell things like makeup and Tupperware."

"You're making some friends."

"Dad!" shouted Frankie before Harley could reply. "We're ready. Are you coming?"

"I'll be right there."

"Go ahead. Have fun," said Harley.

She was drawing when the phone rang.

"Harley? Stacy Rubenstein."

"Yes!" Harley leapt from her desk chair. It had been a while since she and her adoption attorney had spoken. Now that the due date was only three or four weeks away, she shouldn't be terribly surprised to hear from her. But she began pacing her office. "Hi, Stacy."

"How are you?"

"I'm fine." *Whatever you're calling for, please . . . get to the point!*

"We're at T minus two weeks and counting. Just checking in to see how things are going on your end. You ready for the holidays?"

Stacy's voice was maddeningly calm.

"I think so." Harley looked out the window at the inflatable snowman in the yard. Downstairs in the living room, the tree glistened with lights and shatter-proof ornaments.

"Have you talked to the people up there lately?"

"My latest contact with the birth father before he went back overseas confirmed their intentions."

"What about Kelly?"

There was a pause.

"I called Kelly a week ago and left a message. I'm still waiting for her to call me back."

Mind racing, Harley clenched the phone so hard it might break. As the due date had drawn closer, her fears of the adoption falling through had receded further into the distance. She dreaded asking, but the only thing worse than knowing was *not* knowing. "Why would Kelly keep us on hold like that?"

"I wouldn't read too much into it. She has two little kids, her husband's deployed again, and it's almost Christmas. Plus, she's gained twenty-five pounds and she's ready to pop."

"Okay. If you say so."

"Meantime, is there anything I can do for you? Anything you need?"

"N-no, nothing."

"I don't have to tell you that due dates are only estimates. If you're not already, be sure to keep your phone turned on and with you at all times."

She laughed. "I've been doing that for months."

"Perfect. The next time we talk, then, will be when Kelly goes into labor."

"Wait! W-will you let me know the minute Kelly gets back to you?"

"Oh. Yes. Sure thing."

She exhaled. "Thanks."

She hung up and gazed down at her work, but despite her looming deadline, she couldn't focus. She went to the nursery and opened the drawers where the tiny undershirts and sleepers lay neatly folded. Screwed open the top of the baby lotion, closed her eyes, and gently sniffed. That was what her baby was going to smell like. Soon, he would be here. How could he not be, when she had gone to such effort to make a cozy, safe home for him? There was absolutely no need to worry.

At the mall, Jack stood behind the girls as they pressed their hands against a glass case and peered down into it.

"See something in there that catches your eye?"

Immediately, they dropped their hands, expecting to be told it was time to move on. But Jack had another idea.

"What were you looking at?"

Freddie pointed shyly into the case. "Those fur earrings."

The silver dollar–sized disks might just be the tackiest thing Jack had ever seen. "You think Mimi'd like those, huh?"

Freddie nodded. "They're beauuuutiful."

"What about you, Frank? Something in there you like?"

"That pin," said Frankie, pointing to a red enamel chrysanthemum brooch.

He was wrong earlier. *That* took the prize for most tacky.

"You want to look around a little more before you make a final decision?"

They had never selected gifts without his or Mother's direction. They looked at Jack and then at each other, trying to comprehend.

"Tell you what. Why don't we meet back here in, say, forty-five minutes?"

"You mean . . . walk around by ourselves, without you?"

"Why not? That way I can do a little shopping, too. You never know what I might come up with." He winked as he slipped two crisp fifty-dollar bills from his wallet and handed one to each of them. "Here you go. Don't spend it all in—" He caught himself just in time. "Have a ball."

"Ta!" they thanked him, in their excitement reverting to the Kiwi expression. He watched them saunter away with their heads together, giddily gazing down at the most money they had ever handled and debating over what each planned to buy with it.

Jack headed back to the teen department, snapped up the sweaters he'd seen the girls admiring earlier and had them gift wrapped, then bought his mother yet another bottle of the scent she'd been wearing forever.

At the appointed time, he returned to the jewelry counter, half expecting the girls to be late. His eyes lit up when he saw they had beaten him there. But instead of multiple shopping bags, they held only one small bag between them.

"What'd you get?"

"It's for Christmas," said Frankie.

"We can't tell," said Freddie.

He suppressed his curiosity. "Are you finished shopping, or do you need more time?"

They looked at each other. "We spent everything we had," they said.

Jack sighed. "All right, then. Let's go home."

Harley arrived at Pru's father's stately home to find it packed with women in festive attire, tippling wineglasses, voices raised to be heard above the din.

Pru reached for her coat. "How's it going at the Victorian?" As usual, she looked like she had just come from the track. "Rakin' it in?"

"Not exactly," said Harley, slipping off her coat and handing it to Pru as ordered. "Turns out running a bed-and-breakfast isn't as easy as I thought."

Pru slapped her on the back. "We'll talk."

Recovering her bearings, Harley glanced at the booklet Pru handed her. "Pure Delights," she read aloud. *Sounded like some kind of food product.*

"Grab yourself a drink and some food. The presentation's about to start."

Harley speared a couple of sausages and cheese cubes from the spread on the dining room table, then carried her paper plate to the living room and looked around. Apparently, the wine boom had brought even more newcomers to town than Harley had thought. She didn't recognize a single face.

Weaving through the crowd, she found a seat on a low footstool between two women gossiping about the extramarital affair in the neighborhood.

As Harley opened her booklet, Pru asked everyone to pick teams for an icebreaker game.

Not surprisingly, Harley was the last to be picked.

"Now, ladies," said Pru. "I'm going to describe a product. If you know what it is I'm describing, call it out. The team that finds the most products first wins."

Harley sat up. This might be her chance to ingratiate herself to her team and, in the process, make some new friends.

"The first item might come in a tube or a bottle. It's used to alleviate friction."

Harley shouted out the first thing that came to mind. "Lubricant!"

The next thing she knew, a tube was flying through the air, straight into her lap. Her teammates cheered.

"Taste it!" shouted Pru. "It tastes like strawberry."

She examined the label. *So that's what this party was about.* "I'll take your word for it," said Harley, feigning a smile.

"Taste it! Taste it!" The chant spread throughout the room.

Far be it for Harley Miller-Jones to be thought of as a poor sport. She opened the cap, squirted a pea-sized dab on her finger, and touched it to her tongue. Harley smacked her lips and nodded feebly. "Strawberry."

The room erupted in cheers of approval.

"What did I tell you?" demanded Pru. "Next up. This handheld item requires a battery—"

An hour later, when Pru's sales team captain disappeared into an adjoining room to take orders, Harley said farewell to her teammates with the excuse that it was feeding time for her goats. But she couldn't leave without saying good-bye to the hostess.

"Did you have a good time?" asked Pru, handing her her coat.

"Lovely. Such a surprise."

"You said the B and B business isn't all it's cracked up to be. Well, I have an offer just for you. If you join my team of sellers, you can earn commissions on our sales."

"Er—what are we talking about?"

"It all depends. Say you throw a party. If you sell five hundred dollars, you'll earn fifty dollars toward your own merchandise, plus a half-price item plus twenty percent off additional purchases plus—"

Harley held up a halting hand. "What with my design work and waitressing and the inn, I've already got a lot on my plate."

"Don't think of it as selling. Think of it as performing a genuine service to the community."

"No, thanks."

"Suit yourself. See you at the office." Pru disappeared into the melee.

"Harley?"

She turned around from where she was buttoning her coat. "Sylvie Collins," said the woman.

How could Harley forget? Back in high school, stirring up trouble and causing arguments was Sylvie's favorite pastime. That ensured she'd be the center of attention. It was a wonder her performance after being thrown from the parade float hadn't won her an Academy Award.

"Just when I thought I didn't know anybody here," said Sylvie. "It's been a long time."

"Ten years." By the looks of Sylvie, the wreck had left no lasting scars.

"Nice catch with the lube."

Harley shrugged. "Pru's got one hell of an arm."

"I hear you bought the old Grimsky place."

"That's right."

"What a coincidence. You coming back to Newberry at the same time as Jack."

So, Newberry still hadn't tired of talking about them. "Coincidence, that's all."

Sylvie arched a brow. "If I remember right, you two were always hanging around together after school."

"It was nice seeing you. I have to get—"

"Has Jack interviewed you yet?"

Harley halted in her tracks and turned back around. "Excuse me?"

"He interviewed *me*."

"What do you mean—interviewed?"

"Word at the club is, he's on the prowl for a new partner." She rolled her eyes. "Let's face it. He needs a stepmother for his daughters, to share the load. Think of the timing. He comes back to town just as they're about to become teenagers."

Was that why Jack had set her up with his girls at the art gallery—to see how they'd get along? If Harley might be the missing puzzle piece?

Her blood rushed in her ears. "I don't know what you're talking about. Now, I have to get going."

She squeezed the polished brass door handle.

Behind her came Sylvie's voice. "He interviewed Pru, too. She didn't tell you?"

Adrenaline coursed through Harley, making her pulse race. Rather than fight, she flew to the refuge of her car. Jack didn't want her for her. Now that he had kids and no mother, he needed a helpmeet. A nanny. And it just so happened that she and the girls had clicked.

That evening, when Jack came over to Harley's, before he even took off his coat he said, "I was thinking. When the call comes about the baby, I don't think you should drive up to Seattle and back by yourself. I remember driving the twins home from the hospital. I was so nervous, I only drove like five miles an hour. And that was just from downtown. You're going to have a good two-and-a-half-hour drive, and that's doing the speed limit. I want to drive up with you."

"I appreciate you thinking of me. But it's all worked out. My dad offered to drive my mom and me up. Besides, it'll be Christmastime. You should be with your girls."

"Hey." Jack took her in his arms and, with a fingertip, turned her chin. "Look at me. I can't wait until we're all together."

Harley broke free of him and stepped out of his reach.

"What's the matter?"

"We need to talk."

He frowned. "Okay." In the corner of his eye, he spotted the decanter filled with wine he'd gifted her on the breakfront and headed toward it. "Can I pour you a glass?"

"Yes. No. On second thought, I'm having vodka."

Jack's hand paused in midpour. "When did you start drinking vodka?"

"Today. After Pru's get together."

She found a rocks glass left behind by the Grimskys and cracked open a bottle of Grey Goose she'd received as a housewarming gift.

"Vodka neat," he chuckled nervously. "This sounds serious."

They settled on the couch, facing each other.

"I ran into Sylvie Collins today."

Jack averted his eyes and tipped his glass. "Yeah?"

"She told me you 'interviewed' her," she said, drawing air quotes. "And she wasn't the only one. I heard it from Prudence Mitchell, too."

Jack snorted. "Is that what this is about? Here's what it is. Since we got back from New Zealand, Mother's been trying to fix me up."

"Let me guess. With a woman like Pru or Sylvie?"

He shook his head. "It doesn't matter. I'm not the least bit interested in either of them."

Harley slammed the rest of her drink, went to the mantel, and refilled her glass with wine. "It's obvious why your mother chose Pru and Sylvie. They come from established Newberry families. What about you? Didn't you have any say in the matter?"

"Well, I—"

"It's not like she put a gun to your head and made you go out with those women."

"No, but—" How could he explain? "It's all about the twins. They're entering a crucial stage in their development. I know, they've got me. But they need a mom, now more than ever. Someone who can talk to them about things they wouldn't be comfortable talking to me about . . . who can advise them . . ."

"Melinda always thought she knew better than you what was good for you. Now she's projecting it onto her granddaughters."

"No. Yes. But—"

Harley stopped him with her hand, ignoring the wine sloshing around in her glass, threatening to stain the new white rug. "Let me get this straight. All autumn, while we've been seeing each other, you've been going out with other women? Interviewing them for the position of your girls' new mother, so to speak?"

At a loss for what to say, he stood and started toward her, halting when she turned aside.

"A couple of times I said we might be rushing things."

"That was before," Jack pleaded, panic rising in him. "Before the girls got to know you and like you, and we started talking about moving in together."

Harley backed up until she hit the fireplace, protecting her space, eyeing him skeptically.

It was all Jack could do not to go to her. This was the third time he'd hurt her. Wrecking the float, rendering her incapable of having babies, marrying Emily, and now, yet again.

He swallowed, his throat dry as dust. "Come on, Harley. I'll do anything, pay any price. Trust me—"

"*Trust* you? Trust *you*?" She came toward him with fire in her eyes. "How could I ever trust you? You remember that condom you kept in your back pocket at all times? Typical Jack, like a Boy Scout, always prepared. You always reined yourself in short of needing to use it with me. But with Emily, you apparently got so carried away you couldn't even stop and fumble with a square of foil."

"Harley—"

"Let me ask you something . . . something I've been dying to ask you for ten years. How many times were you with Emily before she—before you—"

Jack screwed up his brow. "What? You think—she and I—" He shook his head. How could he have been so blind? All these months, no wonder she'd been so reticent. "*One time*, on that trip to Mexico she and my mother cooked up. The real kicker is, I don't even remember it."

He reached for her, but she flinched in disgust. "I swear to you, Harley. Somehow that night, Emily and I ended up the only ones left at the pool bar. The bartender never let our mai tais get empty. When I finally staggered back to my casita, my key was missing. Emily invited me to crash in her place, next door. The lobby seemed like it was a mile away. I was too drunk to make it all the way there, so I thought, what the hell. Next thing I know, I'm waking up with the mother of all hangovers, and worst of all, Emily's lying next to me."

"You must have been pretty drunk not to remember having sex."

"Wine's like food in my family. They teach you to drink for exactly that reason—so you won't abuse it, starting with a spoonful in your water glass as soon as you can sit up at the dinner table. They add a spoonful a year until you're a teenager and you finally get your own small glass. You know me, Har. That night was the first of only two nights in my entire life I've gone overboard. The second was the night of my bachelor party. That time, I *wanted* to get drunk. I knew in my gut that marrying Emily was wrong."

"Do you remember what you said to me that night?" she steamed.

"I remember being surprised to see you, given that you weren't on the guest list."

"Believe me, it wasn't my idea. I happened to be in the car with some kids who crashed it. You told me if Emily weren't pregnant, you'd be with me. Well, you could have had me as soon as we got back home, but you still couldn't leave any stone unturned, could you? You had to make sure you'd picked the best of what Newberry had to offer. What is *wrong* with you, Jack Friestatt? What's wrong with *me* that you couldn't commit to me without shopping around?"

He ducked as her glass went flying past his head, shattering against Mrs. Grimsky's classy black and white wallpaper.

"And to top it all off," she screamed, "I can't even get pregnant, and you produce multiples without even trying!"

Jack drifted through his days, lost at sea. Surrounded by people, yet alone in his own home, his own town.

Why had he kowtowed to Mother's dating advice?

Why? Because their lives were so interdependent he felt caught up like a fish in a net. They lived in the same house, ran the family business together, and she was the twins' grandmother. He was stuck.

At least he could draw the line when it came to

Mother's match making advice. He had no desire to be with Pru or Sylvie, or any other woman except Harley. But after what he'd done, could he blame Harley for doubting him?

And if he was through dating the women Mother chose for him, and Harley no longer wanted him, then he might as well face it—he was bound to end up alone.

Mom plopped down next to Harley on the couch and gave her a side hug. "Aw, honey. I know you're hurting."

Harley's head fell sideways onto Mom's shoulder. She pounded her thigh with her fist. "I just need to keep telling myself I didn't come back to Ribbon Ridge to be with Jack. I don't know why I'm so surprised. I need to carry on as if this never happened. Like everything that happened with us this fall was just a detour, a blip on the radar." She squeezed her hands between her knees. "You still have so much going for you," Mom said. "This beautiful house, your business . . . that little baby. Have you heard from your lawyer lately?"

Harley sat up straight and wiped away a frustrated tear. "That's the other thing. I haven't. It makes me worry that the birth mother hasn't been in touch with *her*."

"I wouldn't worry about it. What with the holidays and all, it probably slipped Kelly's mind. Why don't you call her?"

"I don't want to seem overly anxious." But eight months of waiting had stretched Harley's nerves to the breaking point.

"Anyone in your shoes would be anxious. You and Kelly are friends, right? Call her direct. That way you'll get it straight from her, without it being filtered by your lawyer. Go ahead, while I'm here."

"Maybe you're right." She sighed. "Give me a minute to collect myself."

"That's it. While you're doing that, I'll go make us a nice cup of tea."

Mom disappeared into the kitchen. Her herb tea might taste like compost, but Harley needed to talk in private. She blew her nose. Then she took a deep breath, punched in Kelly's number, and pasted on a smile, hoping it would come across in her voice.

"Kelly! How are you?"

"Harley! I'm so sorry."

Harley's heart leaped into her throat.

"I was supposed to call your attorney back a week ago, and what with Mattie being sick and trying to find a sitter so I can finish my shopping and—Aiden! Get off the table!—Sorry. I'm a little overwhelmed at the moment."

Relief battled with empathy in Harley. "That's okay. Don't worry about it. I didn't mean to bother you. I just—well, it's just that naturally, I've been thinking of you and the baby and I wanted to make sure . . ."

"Aiden! I said, get down. The elf is watching, and if you don't listen, there'll be no Star Wars Mega Playset for you. No, the pregnancy is fine. My heartburn is easing up. This kid is so jumpy, I feel like I'm carrying around a joey in my pouch."

A pang of jealousy swept over Harley. If only she were lucky enough to be so miserable. "Okay. Well, I know you're busy. I don't want to keep you."

"That's all right . . ." There was an odd lack of finality in Kelly's tone, as if she were considering adding something. But as hard as Harley pressed her phone against her ear, all she could hear was Kelly's toddlers playing in the background.

". . . nothing. Never mind. If you talk to your lawyer, tell her we spoke, would you? Save me a call."

Harley's body slumped as she let out her held breath. "Will do."

"All right. Talk soon. *Aiden! For the love of God—Put. Down. Your. Sister!*"

Chapter Thirty-seven

Harley used to count the weeks, and then the days. Now, she counted the hours.

The Victorian was baby ready. The downstairs cupboards had child locks installed on them. Upstairs, in the nursery, the changing table drawers were stocked with diapers and wipes and powder.

After studying dozens of online reviews, she'd chosen a pediatrician; Dr. Brown, a grandfatherly man with twinkly eyes and years of experience under his monogrammed lab coat.

Christmas Eve day, Harley checked her phone every thirty minutes to make sure she hadn't missed Stacy's call. Between checks, she roamed the cavernous Victorian like a caged animal, mentally checking off the items on her to-do list. *Car seat installed, check. Bag packed with formula and diapers, check. Extra blankets, check.*

When the phone rang at around eleven in the morning, she jumped.

"Dad! You almost gave me a heart attack."

"Mom and I were wondering if you'd heard anything yet."

"You know I'll call you the second I do."

"All set?"

"There's never been a more prepared adoptive mother."

Her phone buzzed, jangling nerves that were already on the brink. "Dad! Hold on."

"Harley?" Stacy's voice was brimming with positivity. "I bring you tidings of great joy. Yesterday afternoon Kelly gave birth to a baby girl."

"A girl?" Harley's whole body tingled.

"Those sonograms don't claim to be a hundred percent accurate."

"But—"

"I know, she said she'd call us when she went into labor, but it's her third, and there was no advance warning. She barely made it to the hospital."

"A girl!" she exclaimed, still absorbing the news.

"That's right. A girl. Blond. Seven pounds, seven ounces, nineteen and a half inches long. Everyone's doing fine. The hospital is releasing her later this afternoon. They'll be waiting for you as soon as you can get there."

It was a wonder Harley didn't drop her phone as she somehow reconnected with Dad. "It's a girl!" she cried, hands shaking, tears running down her cheeks. "I have a baby girl!"

"A girl? But you said—"

"I know, I know," she choked. "They said it looked like a boy. But it doesn't matter. All that matters is that I'm a mom! The waiting's over. I'm a mother!"

"Aw, Harley girl," he said gruffly, his voice cracking. "You're gonna be the best mama any little girl ever had."

"Never mind that!" She was jumping up and down in her excitement. "Just hurry! How soon can you get here?"

Bursting with gratitude and goodwill, Harley embraced a groggy Kelly in her hospital bed. "You've given me the best present anyone could ever give another person."

Kelly smiled weakly and patted her hand. "Take care of her for me, won't you?"

Thank goodness for Dad driving and Mom in the front seat, talking Harley down when she cringed at every bump in the road, afraid it would somehow jar the precious bundle next to her in the car seat.

Halfway back to Ribbon Ridge, it began to snow.

It was well after midnight by the time they got home. Harley carried the baby upstairs to the waiting nursery.

"Careful," said Mom, watching as Harley nestled her in her all-blue crib when they finally got home. "Lay her on her back."

"Don't worry," said Harley. "I think I've read every book ever written about how to take care of a newborn."

"Do you want us to stay?" asked Dad, looking around bleary-eyed. "You got enough bedrooms around here, that's for sure."

"No, you don't have to. You've already done so much. We're snuggled in safe now. You go home to your own bed and get some rest."

They kissed her good night. "Merry Christmas, Harley."

"Merry Christmas, Mom. Dad."

Harley listened to their feet on the stairs, cross the foyer and out the door, and then it was just she and her daughter. She gazed down at her baby in her crib in the soft light as the snow fell gently outside her window. Her cheeks were downy soft, like peaches, each tiny finger a miracle.

The only way the moment could possibly be better was if Jack were there to share it with her.

Jack sat on the couch savoring his coffee, watching his girls rip open their gifts and exclaim at the trinkets that tumbled from the stockings they'd dumped onto the Oriental rug whose pattern was quickly being obscured by wrapping paper. In spite of the twelve-foot Douglas fir glittering with ornaments and the blazing fire in the fireplace, inside he felt cold and empty.

Luckily, what with the excitement of the holiday and shopping and practicing for their school pageant, the twins didn't seem to notice they hadn't seen Harley lately. As long as there was a chance they might get back together, he didn't want to say anything that might ruin the bond they had formed.

As for Mother, they weren't on the best of speaking terms these days.

So, he had ended up not saying anything.

Yet he shouldn't have been surprised when Freddie turned to him from where she sat cross-legged on the living room floor, immersed in a new electronic device, and said, "Oh my gosh. I just remembered.

Did Harley get her baby? He was supposed to be here on Christmas."

"That's right!" shouted Frankie. "Can we go see Harley and him?"

Mother looked up from her chair, curiosity on her face.

He was dying to see Harley, too. But not for the same reasons as the twins. He longed to cup her face in his hands and take her features apart, one by one. Kiss her soft lips . . . hold her tenderly in his arms and wish her a Merry Christmas in a very special way.

"Why did Harley have to adopt a baby?" asked Freddie, her brow wrinkled.

"Because she doesn't have a husband," said Frankie matter-of-factly. "Sister Mary Margaret told us how it works. The husband puts his penis in the wife's vag—"

"Harley's probably really busy," Jack interjected. "Maybe we'll go see her another day. Babies are a lot of work. Especially when they're brand-new."

Harley's parents returned late Christmas morning, weighed down with gift bags, large and small, and Dad's macaroni and cheese. While Mom fed the goats and Dad busied himself in the kitchen, Harley concentrated all her attention on the baby.

After a late lunch with her parents, Harley reluctantly left her daughter's side to allow Mom to take over while she did the dishes.

She was getting a taste of how completely children took over your life. But now, staring out the window at the sleeping vineyards covered with snow, she wondered what Jack and the twins were doing this Christmas Day. And then she remembered Jack's many cousins and nieces and nephews. She imagined the grand estate, alive with the voices of adults and the excited chatter of children. She doubted that Jack had time to be thinking of her.

Dad came up behind her and slung his arm around her. "If you're okay, we're going to head home. We're beat."

"Of course. Just let me finish washing this casserole dish and you can take it with you."

Alone again, she changed the baby's diaper and laid her in her bassinet. She told herself she was grateful for the quiet, when there was a knock at the door.

She scurried toward it, heart pounding.

"Merry Christmas."

"Frankie! Freddie!" Harley peered over their heads expectantly.

"It's just us," they said in answer to her unasked question.

Her heart sank.

"Can we see the baby?"

"Of course," she said, opening the door wide.

Their noses were red with cold.

"Did you walk?"

They nodded.

Jack and his mother must have loosened the reins a bit. *About time.*

"Come on in and get warm."

They stomped the snow from their boots onto her hardwood floors.

"Why don't you take off your boots, and I'll make us some cocoa?"

* * *

"Have you seen the girls?" asked Mother, peering out the window at the back of the house in the early twilight.

"Last I looked, they were making snow angels," said Jack.

"I can't see them anywhere."

There was a sharp rap at the front door.

"I'll get it," said Mother.

"Alfred," he heard her say.

"It's getting dark. I wasn't sure if you knew. Just saw the girls walking up the meadow."

"What?"

"Cutting across the vineyard toward the Victorian."

Mother looked worriedly at Jack, who was already out of his chair. "I'm on my way," he said, yanking open the coat closet, pulling his coat off the hanger.

His headlights shone hazy cones through the fog. As he drove through the dreary evening, his gaze swept the fields, concern for his girls uppermost in his mind. But he had little doubt where he'd find them. The second he knew they were safe, he would be able to appreciate seeing Harley again. It was Christmas, after all. How could she turn him away?

Minutes later, he was striding up her porch steps and stabbing the bell, trying to ignore the pounding of his heart.

"Jack."

Harley looked cozy and natural, wearing a pink sweater with her hair piled up on top of her head. She didn't seem surprised to see him.

"Are the twins here?"

She turned so he could see into the living room. "They're here."

The house smelled like peppermint candles and hot chocolate. Jack crossed the foyer, stopping at the entrance to the living room, and a scene of light and warmth and his daughters bent over a cradle by the decorated tree, giggling.

"Your father's here," called Harley, passing him in a cloud of fragrance that tempted him to grab her and pull her into his empty arms.

"Dad!" They grinned and waved him over excitedly. "Come see."

He used to be welcome here. Now he felt like a formal guest. He meandered to the cradle and peered down into it, his hands in his jeans pockets.

"Look how tiny she is!" exclaimed Frankie.

"Her name's Angelica," said Freddie. "Isn't she cute?"

Jack glanced at Harley. "She?"

Harley nodded. She hesitated briefly before asking, "Do you want to hold her?"

No. He knew what babies did to you. Sucked you in . . . grabbed hold of your heartstrings and didn't let go. He couldn't afford to get attached to this one.

"Go ahead. We already had our turn," Freddie assured him.

He glanced at Harley to make sure.

In response, Harley reached into the cradle, gingerly picked up the bundle and deposited it into his waiting arms.

The baby's eyes were shut tight. From within her cocoon of blue, she worked her tiny rosebud lips. She smelled milky sweet . . . a Christmas miracle, altogether innocent of the mixed-up, muddled-up world into which she'd been born.

"Hey there, little one." Tears sprang to Jack's eyes. He bounced her expertly, like the experienced father he was.

Frankie gasped. "The present! We almost forgot."

Freddie dashed to her jacket, lying across a chair, and dug through the pockets, returning with a battered, misshapen gift box.

"What's this?" asked Harley. She looked at Jack questioningly.

"Don't ask me," he said. "The girls picked it out."

"It's for Angelica," the girls replied. "Sorry, the bow fell off. Open it."

She sat down on the couch and patted the cushions on either side of her. "Here," she said. "Come sit by me."

Happily, the girls flanked her, bouncing in anticipation.

She tore back the paper and lifted the lid on a velvet box to reveal a silver rattle.

"Oh, girls." She hugged them one in each arm in exactly the same way Jack did. "I will treasure it always."

The girls hugged her back.

Jack cleared his throat.

Harley looked up at him as if only now remembering he was there.

"She's asleep," he said.

"I'll take her." She took her from him and returned her to her bassinet.

"We should get going," Jack said to the twins. "Mimi'll be wondering where we are."

"Can't you call her and tell her?" they begged. "Pleeeeze?"

"No. Let's let Harley and the baby get some rest."

"You girls are always welcome to come visit," said Harley.

You girls. *Not him.*

When they were all bundled up again, Jack tried one last time to catch Harley's eye. But while she squeezed the girls yet again at the threshold, she sidestepped his awkward attempt at an embrace.

It was Christmas, and Harley wouldn't even hug him. Pain stabbed at his heart.

"Come on, girls." Jack herded his magpies out into the bleak night and down the steps, shivering as the cold seeped through his jacket and settled deep in the marrow of his bones.

"Whose car is that?" asked Frankie as they pulled into their driveway after being at Harley's house.

Jack's headlights shone on an unfamiliar sedan parked in the drive.

"I don't know," said Freddie.

"It's still early. Probably someone stopping by to wish us Merry Christmas." Most likely a relative. But the person Jack most wanted to spend time with didn't want anything to do with him. "Guess we're about to find out," he said, putting the truck into Park and getting out.

The girls followed the sound of women's voices to the living room. Jack trailed not far behind, despite wishing he could disappear to his office. He'd had enough of this Christmas. He just wanted it to be over.

"Frankie! Freddie!"

The blonde who rose from her chair and opened

her arms to the twins looked so much like Emily it stopped Jack in his tracks.

"Remember me?" she asked, giving the girls a squeeze.

But the girls only stared, confused.

"Aunt Cait!" she said, as if it were obvious.

"Girls. You remember Mommy's sister," scolded Mother, embarrassed.

"I don't blame them if they forgot. It's been a while. A couple of years, the summer you came back to Oregon to visit."

Before that, it was Emily's funeral in Marlborough. The girls had only been five. Still, Cait's resemblance to Emily was almost spooky.

Jack and Cait exchanged holiday greetings and the briefest of hugs. "What brings you to Ribbon Ridge?" he asked her.

"There's a new rollout in Newberry. I'll be working here for the next couple of months."

"What's a rollout?" asked Frankie.

"It's when a company adopts a new computer software system. My job is to train the employees."

"Cait travels all over the country—" said Mother.

"—which is why I'm only now getting to see you since you moved back to the States. I spent the fall in the New Orleans area."

"Where were you before that?" asked Freddie.

"Chicago. Before that, New York, and before that . . . well, you get the picture. But now that I'm going to be back home in Oregon for a while, I'm hoping to spend some time getting reacquainted."

Chapter Thirty-eight

The day after Christmas, Harley hummed along with a chorale singing "Joy to the World" in the background, while the glass balls on the tree danced in the reflection of the lights.

She had just fed Angelica her bottle. She was gliding across the parquet floor in her furry slippers, her baby on her shoulder, listening for that satisfying *burp!* when her phone rang.

"Oh! Who's that calling us, angel? Must be Grandpa or Grandma. Hold on here."

She was still new at this mothering stuff. Between juggling the baby, the burp towel, and the phone, she had all she could handle.

Angelica mewled.

"Don't fuss, now. Mommy has to get the phone. Hello?"

"Harley."

At Stacy's tone, Harley's slippers halted in midstep.

"This is the hardest call I've ever had to make."

Angelica started wailing as panic struck Harley. "Shh. It's okay, baby," she said, jouncing her up and down. "Don't cry."

"I just got off the phone with Kelly's attorney."

There was a distant roaring in Harley's ears, like an approaching storm.

"Dragging this out would only be more cruel. I'll get straight to the point. Kelly and her husband have decided they want to raise the baby after all."

The room began to sway.

"Harley? Harley, are you there?" Stacy sighed. "You have my most profound sympathy. The husband and their attorney have already left for Newberry. You should expect them within the hour."

Three hours later, in the glow of a Peter Pan night-light, Harley rocked in a melancholy rhythm, staring at the empty crib.

She was vaguely aware of her father hunched next to her on the knitted pouf, head hanging, arms draped across his knees, and her mother standing helplessly in the nursery doorway, hugging herself, watching her rocking . . . rocking.

She held a blue blanket to her nose. The sweet smell of baby lotion was the only thing she had left of the daughter she had had for one idyllic day. All the gifts . . . the stuffed lion in the crib, the giant giraffe propped in the corner from her parents . . . she'd sent them all with Angelica—if that was still her name.

All that she had left of her was the silver rattle. She rolled it back and forth between her fingers like a lifeline, the metal warm from her touch. It was the only thing keeping her sane.

Harley's parents had no reason to hide what had happened with the baby. Once the news leaked out, it spread quickly through Newberry's taverns and tasting rooms and shops.

Jack was at the gas station pumping air into his truck tires when the owner of Ruddock's restaurant came up and asked how Harley was doing.

When he told him Harley lost the baby, Jack immediately called her. He stood outside his truck in a fine drizzle, listening to her phone ring. When it went to voice mail, he punched End and tried again. And again. He was wracked with guilt. If he had never wrecked the parade float, she wouldn't be infertile. She wouldn't have had to adopt in the first place.

A voicemail couldn't begin to express the depth of his concern. But at the same time, she'd told him in no uncertain terms that she wanted nothing more to do with him.

He climbed back into his truck, racking his brain. Her parents' house was on his way home. He'd stop and ask them how she was doing.

But when he slowed down to turn in at their unpaved driveway, neither of their vehicles was there. He continued onto Ribbon Ridge Road, swerving a hard right at the last minute, downshifting to climb the steep hill that led to the Victorian.

Cindy Miller opened the door, looking years older than the last time he'd seen her.

He wondered what, if anything, Harley had told her about their breakup.

"I just heard."

Cindy stepped aside for him to enter.

"How's she doing?"

"She's in bed."

"It's been, what? Three days?"

Cindy nodded.

He knew what a death in the family felt like. He'd gone through it twice before. Though Angelica hadn't died, Harley was mourning, just the same. But he'd never lost a child. He couldn't imagine that kind of agony. Three days was hardly enough time for the reality to set in.

"I tried calling her, but she won't pick up. Do you think there's a chance she'll see me?"

Cindy sighed. "I'll ask. But don't get your hopes up."

She disappeared, leaving Jack to stare blindly out the window onto the sleeping vineyards, wishing he could ease her grief, if only a little.

He heard returning footsteps and turned and gazed anxiously up the staircase.

But when Cindy was only halfway down and her head was shaking, her lips in a straight line, his hopes plummeted.

"Tell Harley that I care, would you?" he asked, fists balled inside his coat pockets. "And that I'm thinking of her, and if there's anything she needs, anything at all, I'm there for her."

"I will, Jack. And thank you."

Chapter Thirty-nine

Around Jack, life went on.

Cait started her new job. Mother had all but insisted she stay with them at the estate. But Cait's company paid for her apartment and she said she didn't want to be any trouble.

The twins went back to school and their evening and weekend classes.

Mother had extended Cait a standing invitation for dinner, however, and she showed up like clockwork, every Tuesday, Thursday, and Friday at seven-thirty on the dot.

"Frankie. Elbows," said Mother.

Cait gave Frankie a look. From her blond good looks to her slightly monotonous voice and quiet mannerisms, she bore an uncanny resemblance to Emily.

Frankie removed her elbows from where she'd propped them on the dinner table.

"Tomorrow night, I think we should go out for dinner instead of dining at home," said Mother.

"The taqueria!" shouted the girls simultaneously.

Mother raised an eyebrow. "I was thinking more along the lines of Ruddock's. What do you think, Jack?"

"How about Tart? It's not as casual as the taco place but less formal than Ruddock's."

"Cait?" Mother asked. "You grew up here. Is there a place in Newberry you haven't been back to in a while, or a new place you've been wanting to try?"

Cait kept her eyes on her plate. "I'll go along with whatever you decide," she said.

Just like Emily.

Mother glanced at Jack, a satisfied smile on her lips. "How is your piece coming along, Freddie?"

"Fine."

"I want you to play it for me after dinner."

"You don't have to check on me."

"Yes, I do. Your recital's coming up soon. Next Wednesday, and I want to make sure you've got that F-sharp down."

Jack looked up from his dinner. "Wednesday?"

"It's been on the calendar for months," said Mother.

He knew that. He set down his knife and fork and pulled out his phone to check his calendar. "I don't know how I did this, but I committed to that wine dinner at Visaggio's. They booked a hundred people. It's sold out."

"Wine dinners give vintners a chance to talk about their wines directly to consumers and win converts," Mother explained to Cait. "They're a key part of the slow winter months."

"We've been jockeying to get in Visaggio's for years," added Jack. "Last year, we lucked out when another winery canceled at the last minute and we got their slot. But being that we were out of the country, we had to send a representative."

"So, this year, you should definitely make an appearance," said Cait.

"I should, too," said Mother.

"You two go. I'll take the girls to their recital," said Cait.

Jack turned to the twins. "Would you mind terribly if we missed this one?"

"I don't care," said Frankie, picking up the green bean she'd dropped and popping it into her mouth.

"How about I go to Visaggio's, too?" asked Freddie, brightening.

"You're going to the recital," Mother stated unequivocally. "Aunt Cait will take you. She can record your performances, and your father and I will watch them later, when we get home."

There were days when Harley never got out of bed.

Her parents took shifts being with her, doing whatever they could to make her comfortable.

Mom held spoonfuls of chicken soup under her nose. "There's babies born all the time," she said. "You can always try again. Don't give up."

Yet, even if she were to start the whole adoption process all over again, and if this time it went through, there would never be another Jack. And if she couldn't trust him, whom could she trust?

Dad called the club. "They said given January's a slow month, they can furlough you till the weather warms up," he said.

She resigned herself to a solitary existence.

She had no guests scheduled and no prospects for them, given the Willamette Valley's cool, misty winters and wet springs. There was no sense rambling around in this expensive old house alone. Maybe she could swallow what shred of pride she had left and crawl to Melinda on her knees and beg her to take it off her hands. If she knew Melinda, she would offer her a pittance of her original check.

She went to church.

Quit church.

Went back. That time, she returned home feeling a little better. But after a month of doing nothing, she was weak. She propped herself up against her pillows and opened her laptop, only to be faced with the smiling Jamie and Hank flanking their newly born son. She eased the lid down and crawled back under the covers.

Harley rolled away from the wall long enough to see Dad standing at the foot of the bed, his capable hands hanging helplessly at his sides. He talked about how soon the Chinooks would be running again, and if she wanted, they could plan a trip over to Tillamook.

She rolled back over, nodding her head on her pillow to be polite. With no routine, she had lost track of what day it was . . . what week.

But neither Mom nor Dad had ever lost a baby and the love of their life in the same week. How could they understand how she felt?

How could anyone?

Chapter Forty

The day after the recital, the girls were waiting for Jack at dinnertime.

"Well?" asked Freddie. "Did you watch us?"

Cait had sent it to him, but he hadn't yet opened it. "I was waiting to watch it with you. Did you hit your F-sharp?"

Instead of answering, they exchanged anticipatory smiles as Jack watched his screen.

"Here it comes. Andddd . . . yes!" He high-fived Freddie. "You did it."

"Brunch is served," said Mother, arriving from the kitchen holding a casserole dish in gloved hands.

Frankie climbed into her chair across from her sister. "Do you still want to quit, now?"

Freddie looked at Jack, and then at Cait next to her, her hands folded in her lap, then back at Jack.

Until that moment, Jack hadn't even noticed Cait, sitting across from him. In a matter of mere weeks, she had blended into the household so seamlessly, it seemed as though she had always been there.

Freddie sighed. "I don't have much choice, do I? It's three against one. Pass the butter, please."

He'd been bracing himself for an epic battle over getting Freddie to keep playing, once the recital was over. He hadn't counted on Cait's influence. It almost seemed unfair.

Mother made the sign of the cross, and they dutifully bowed their heads and chanted, "BlessusOLordandtheseThygiftswhichweareabouttoreceivefromThy bountythroughChristourLordAmen."

Without thinking, Frankie reached for the serving spoon lying next to the casserole dish.

Mother tsked. "Uh uh uh."

Frankie's hand sprang back as if scalded.

"Your father goes first."

"Hungry?" With a sympathetic smile, Jack scooped a serving of baked French toast onto Frankie's plate, then Freddie's, and then his own. If some of the twins' ideas might be uninformed and contradictory to his, he still liked them to express their opinions. He was proud they had minds of their own. Yet since Cait arrived, they were becoming less combative and more pliable in general. They didn't argue any more when nagged to clean their rooms or do their laundry. In fact, sometimes they seemed like little robots, meekly following the rules.

Probably they were just growing up, he thought as he ate. That was why they were less silly, more serious. That's what it was. It had to be.

After dinner, Jack sat in a comfortable chair skimming through a stack of trade journals. Cait had pulled her knitting project out of her bag to work on while listening to Mother talk about the wine dinner.

"Cait," she said, "why don't you go up with Jack when he wishes the girls good night?"

Jack froze. Between work and school and lessons, he barely saw his girls all day. When he did see them, Mother was almost always around. Bedtime was a ritual that was universal and yet so personal and unique to every family. To him, it was sacred.

Cait waited for him to approve. What could he say? After all, she was their aunt.

He watched Cait smooth out the girls' blankets, brush their hair from their brows, and kiss their foreheads, the same way Emily used to.

And then, just as they were about to turn off the light, Frankie looked up at Jack from her bed and asked, "How come we never visit Harley anymore?"

He had told Mother and the twins—separately, of course—about the birth parents taking the baby back. The girls had expressed sympathy for Harley, but a month had passed, and they hadn't brought it up again.

Cait cocked her head at Jack. "Harley? The same Harley I remember?"

"The Harley that lives up the hill," said Freddie.

"Even though she's an ex-con, she's still our friend," said Frankie conspiratorially.

"We'll talk about it later," said Jack. "Right now, it's time for you two to get to sleep."

When Cait and Jack got back to the living room, Mother was gone.

"Do you mind seeing yourself out?" he asked, stretching and feigning a yawn, "I have a little more work to do in my office, and then I'm going to hit the sack. See you tomorrow."

"Wait," said Cait, sitting down on the couch, patting the cushion next to her. "Can we talk for a minute?"

With mounting suspicion, Jack perched on the edge of a leather armchair.

"The girls are so polite and well-mannered. Emily would be proud."

"Thanks," he replied, feeling more awkward by the second.

"I know you have things to do, so I'll get right to the point. I like what I do, and I'm well-compensated. But I've been on the road for a long time. Traveling isn't conducive to meeting someone. Especially not the kind of person I'm looking for." She paused meaningfully.

"What kind is that?" asked Jack, because he had to say something.

"Someone who's bright, and independent, yet at the same time solid and steady. Those kinds of men are few and far between. If I don't do something about it, I'm going to wake up one day to find I'm a middle-aged woman, still alone."

Jack squirmed. "Why're you telling me this?"

"As you know, when Emily died before coming into her trust, her share of my parents' assets went to me. Marry me, and you'll double all that Emily would have given you."

For a long moment, Jack was speechless.

"But . . . I don't *love* you, Cait. For that matter, you don't love *me* either."

"Jack. Don't be naïve. Marrying for love is a recent phenomenon. You know that. Even today, arranged marriages are still the norm in many cultures. Smart people have always married strategically. If that means you're not madly in love, well, it is what it is. The goal is to lift the family to a higher level, generation after generation. Marriage is a sacrifice you make for your family."

Jack shook his head, trying to absorb what she'd said. "What is it that *you'd* be sacrificing?"

She smiled wistfully. "Like you said . . . there may not be sparks between us—at least, not yet. But I wouldn't mind having a child one day. Giving my parents a grandson, because they never had a son. How about you? Haven't you ever thought about giving the girls a brother . . . a boy to carry on the Friestatt name?"

Rubbing a hand down his jaw, Jack rose and went to the window, then turned to face the couch where Cait lounged easily. "I can't say the thought of having a son hasn't crossed my mind." He would never love anyone the way he loved Harley. But Harley had rejected him in no uncertain terms. And unlike his other random stabs at dating, with Cait there would be no unpleasant surprises. He'd know exactly what he was getting.

Cait smiled, cat-like. "I don't expect you to give me an answer tonight. I only wanted to plant a seed. Give it some thought. I'll be around another couple of months. Meanwhile, we'll go on as we have been. Get to know each other a little better in the process."

Chapter Forty-one

"Mom, I don't know what I would have done without you this past month. My design team director has been more than generous with her extension, but now it's coming up and I can't push her any further. It's time to get back to work."

Harley's mom objected with every step, but Harley kept her hand planted firmly on her back as she accompanied her to the door.

"Are you sure?" Mom asked, turning her head around even as Harley kept up her forward momentum. "Why don't you just go up to your office and I'll bring you some tea and come back down and leave you alone. I promise, I'll be quiet as a mouse."

Harley had managed to get Mom to the door. "You're going to Spain in a week. You have things to do to get ready." Besides, one more cup of Mom's compost tea and Harley would sprout leaves.

"Go." Gently, she pushed Mom across the threshold.

Mom turned around one last time. "Are you sure?"

"I'll call you later," she said through a crack in the door just big enough for her lips.

Finally, she closed it, turned the bolt, and slumped against it for a moment.

Then she showered, dressed, dragged herself to her office, and pushed some papers around, trying to get back into the swing of things.

But the half-finished sketches she'd been so excited about mocked her with their insignificance. What good were greeting cards in the greater scheme of things? Come to think of it, what good was art itself?

There was a knock on the door.

"Coming," she called out, sighing, wondering what Mom had forgotten.

Jack had lost count of the number of messages he'd left for Harley over the past month. Finally, he'd stopped calling her. Thinking about her grief couldn't help but dredge up what it'd been like for him, losing his dad and then his wife. He remembered that sometimes, no matter how well meaning others were, the best medicine was time alone to think, to process, and eventually, to learn to accept.

But Harley was never far from his thoughts. He was growing desperate to see her face again, hear her voice.

Even though she'd made it clear she'd given up on him, he was determined to try to get through to her one last time.

Now he stood on her doorstep, praying she would open up.

Footsteps from within sent his pulse thrumming.

"Mom. What'd you for—" Her eyes flew open. "Jack."

"I take it you were expecting your mom?"

"She just left."

"Can I come in?"

"I have work to do."

"I promise, I won't keep you long."

She hesitated, then stepped aside. But she made no move to go beyond the foyer.

"Is it okay if we go in and sit down?"

"Jack. We've said all there is to say. It's not going to do any—"

"Please?"

She sighed. "For a minute. But then I have to get back to work."

In the living room, he sat down next to her. "There was a reason I came back from New Zealand, aside from the new vineyards being established."

"We've hashed this out. To find a replacement for Emily."

"That's right. But I had no way of knowing I'd find you here. You were never factored into it."

"But when I did end up being here, that didn't stop you from interviewing other women, did it?"

"The date with Pru was set up before I ever set foot on American soil."

"What about Sylvie?"

"Guilty as charged. But that was way back before your open house. You and I were just getting reacquainted."

"Why didn't you tell me?"

"What was the sense in telling you, when we weren't a couple?"

"You could have told me after the fact. Besides, how do I know you weren't intending to use me the same way you planned to use them? As some glorified nanny . . . a dutiful sidekick?"

Jack couldn't help but laugh. "You? Dutiful? Let's be real."

"The bottom line is, I couldn't trust you before, and I still can't."

"I didn't know you'd be here!"

"But I was. I am. If I caved now, I'd always be thinking about what you did with Emily, and waiting for the other shoe to drop."

They sat there for a full minute, neither willing to give ground.

Finally, Jack smacked his hands to his thighs and rose. "Well . . ."

She rose too and faced him squarely.

"I guess this is it, then."

"I guess so."

Jack wanted to cry. But instead, he moved toward her door with long, slow strides, Harley following behind.

When they reached it, he turned to study her face one last time. And then he forced himself to walk out of her life, once and for all.

Chapter Forty-two

The winemaking season was at a lull. Last season's cellar rats had finally moved on. The full-timers were out in the vineyards, pruning dead wood, and the previous vintage was maturing in the barrels.

"What's eating you?" asked Alfred, straddling the stool next to Jack's.

"What are you talking about?" Carefully, Jack withdrew the long glass pipette from the bunghole in the barrel and released the ruby liquid into the glass Alfred held out with a knobby-knuckled hand.

"Don't give me that," said Alfred. "Only one thing makes a man mope around like that, and that's woman problems." He held up his glass to the light and swirled. "Color's bright."

Jack reinserted the wine thief into the bunghole, obtaining his own sample, squirting it into his glass. "It's Emily's sister, Cait."

"Your mother said something about Cait working in town for a while. I've seen her coming and going.

Getting out of her car. Looks like a dead ringer for Emily, at least from a distance."

"She *is* a dead ringer."

"It that a good or a bad thing?"

"That's what I'm trying to figure out."

Alfred lowered his nose into his glass, an act that always made Jack think it was a good thing they made wineglasses bigger than they used to, else it would never have fit. "Smell that bouquet?"

Jack sniffed, nodded, and together, they tasted it, smacking their lips.

"Starting to develop," said Alfred. "Your mother says Cait's in computers or something."

"She's an IT expert. Portland's her home base, but she's hardly ever there. She spends all her time traveling, teaching people how to use software. Right now, she has a client here in Newberry."

"Teacher, huh? Must be smart . . . good at getting along with people."

"She's that. And more. She asked me to marry her."

If Alfred was surprised, he didn't let on. He only massaged his jaw and considered. "How's Harley doing?"

Jack started. Was it that obvious that Harley was always on his mind? "You heard about them taking her baby back?"

Alfred nodded. "Sad. It was all over town. Every time I look at the Victorian, I think I ought to go up there to see how she's doing, but what can I say to make it better? Figured I'll give it a little more time and maybe something'll come to me. Then again, if anyone knows what it's like to lose someone, it's you. How's she doing?"

Jack stared into his wine. "Don't know."

That wasn't what Alfred had been expecting. "Thought things were going great guns for you two."

"She dumped me."

"What'd you go and do to her?"

"Nothing!" He blurted. Then, he hung his head. "She heard I went out on a couple of dates. She blew it all out of proportion."

"I always thought you and Harley made a good pair."

"One of the main reasons I came back to the States was to meet a woman. The right kind of woman."

"What kind's that?" asked Alfred in an admonishing voice.

Never had Alfred used that tone with him before. Jack glanced up in surprise and saw Alfred's faded corduroys, his worn boots, his hardened hands that had toiled for years in the service of his family. There weren't many men in a position to reproach Jack, but if there was one, it was Alfred. He had loved him like his own son.

Yet unlike Mother, Alfred didn't pick and choose people for what he could get out of them. Jack's face heated.

Alfred didn't have to ask Jack who was behind the marriage scheme. He pictured a young Melinda as she had described herself to him: a strong-willed girl born into tough circumstances, struggling to get by, and a ferocious protectiveness came over him. He was far too loyal to Melinda to malign her, especially to her own son.

"And then along comes Harley and throws a monkey wrench into it," Alfred continued, his momentary disapproval already gone.

Jack set down his drink. "Best-laid plans."

"Plan too much, there's no room to experiment." Alfred slapped Jack on the back. "I ever told you about how Bella came to be?"

"Only about a hundred times."

"Never would have happened if your dad hadn't found that row the pickers missed."

"Make that a hundred and one." Jack grinned and rolled his eyes.

"If your daddy had kept to the plan, he'd have picked those stragglers right then and there. But he had the courage to change course, even though he didn't know how it was going to turn out. Took a risk. That was Don Friestatt's genius—knowing when to play it safe and when not to. I don't need to tell you what happened next. Pure magic."

Jack appeared to consider that.

"There's a place for planning. Without planning, your dad wouldn't have had any grapes to begin with. But you can't anticipate every curve life throws at you. Sometimes going off-road helps you see through the bullshit to what really matters."

"And just how am I supposed to do that? It goes against everything I've been taught. Everything I am."

"You gotta stop listening to other people and learn to trust your own gut. Take Harley, for instance. If you'da stuck fast to your plan, you'd have walked right by her. But something made you stop and look. Trust that."

"It doesn't matter now," Jack said miserably. "Whatever chance I had with her, it's gone."

"Nah, don't say that. Something'll come up. You'll see."

Chapter Forty-three

Early one evening a week later, Mother came downstairs more dressed up than usual.

"Where are you off to?" asked Jack.

"Debora has dinner already in the oven. I have a committee meeting in town, and afterward, a few of us are going out to eat."

"It's Friday. What about Cait?"

"You and the girls will be here, won't you?" she asked, checking the mirror in the hall as she tied a scarf around her neck. "Besides, it's not like Cait needs to be entertained. She's not a guest. She's family." She opened the door to leave. "Don't expect me till late."

Jack opened his mail and tried to concentrate on an important business letter. Without Mother as a buffer, dinner was going to be awkward. Despite what she'd said, he wasn't sure exactly where Cait belonged in the scheme of things.

He was on his way upstairs to change his shirt when he passed a window and saw Cait's car drive up.

She might be his sister-in-law and the twins' aunt, but she still didn't come into the house without knocking. He took a detour, opening the door as Cait came down the walk carrying a large tote bag.

When Cait saw Jack standing in the doorway, her smile reached her eyes. "You were waiting for me."

"No, I was just on my way to—" That sounded rude. "I mean, yeah."

She deposited her tote onto a chair and began pulling things out of it Mary Poppins–style.

"What all have you got in there?"

"Just a few things. Some oranges, a new piano book for Freddie, and this board game." She held up a cardboard box and read from the back. "It says it's easy enough for kids and tricky enough to keep adults entertained."

He had to hand it to her. She was really trying.

"The girls are upstairs."

She glanced at the letter in his hand. "Don't let me interrupt what you were doing. I'll call you when dinner's ready."

To Jack's surprise, dinner wasn't bad. The twins were in a rare, upbeat mood. And afterward, Cait brought out her new game.

They played for over an hour. After the third round, Jack said, "Okay, girls, that's it. Time to go up."

"Do we have to?" whined Freddie, looking sideways at her aunt.

"I want to stay up till Mimi gets home," Frankie pouted.

It was almost as if they were testing Cait.

Without saying a word, Cait raised an eyebrow as she began putting the game pieces back in the box.

On cue, the girls rose and pushed in their chairs.

"Carry your plates out on your way," said Cait. "Don't forget to brush your teeth. We'll be up in a minute to kiss you good night."

After that first time tucking them in with Jack, Cait had made it a habit.

Jack rose and started clearing the table. Cait came into the kitchen behind him, carrying the rest of the dishes. As they rinsed and scraped, she bumped arms with him. "Oops."

And then, again.

"Well, that's it," said Jack when they were done, hanging up the dishtowel.

"All set," said Cait.

He realized being alone together made her a bit nervous, too.

Cait followed him up the stairs.

Jack still said good night first. But afterward, he watched from the doorway as the twins hugged Cait around the neck.

Often, Jack left to do work after the girls went to bed and Mother sat with Cait. But without Mother, he could hardly leave her by herself, even if she was family.

"That wine at dinner was really good. Is there any more of it?"

There was a twinkle in her eye. She knew very well that when it came to wine, he had an unlimited supply.

"I think I can find some," Jack replied.

He poured them each a glass and they carried

them to the couch, where Cait slipped off her shoes and curled her feet beneath her legs.

"Have you thought any more about what I asked you?"

Jack sipped from his glass, not sure how to answer. He felt nothing for Cait. But earlier that night, as he looked around the table at his girls laughing and talking, he couldn't help but wonder if maybe this was as good as it got.

"I know what you said about not being in love. But maybe, in time, we could grow fond of each other."

"Cait—"

"Is it that you're not over Emily? You still miss her? I understand. I miss her, too. I'll never stop missing her."

The fact was, Jack had stopped missing Emily a long time ago. "Emily was a devoted mom and a welcome firebreak between my mother and me."

Cait gave him a sideways look. "Melinda can be a touch overbearing. I mean, it's no wonder you feel the way you do, after what happened."

Jack blinked, confused.

A sound halfway between a cough and a laugh of disbelief came out of Cait's throat. "Don't tell me Emily never told you."

"Told me what?"

Cait leaned back into the couch cushions, still not believing what she was hearing. "I'm sorry. I never should have assumed—never mind," she said with a wave of her hand. "It's nothing."

"It's something or you wouldn't have mentioned it. Tell me what you were going to say."

Still, Cait hesitated. Finally, she sighed. "I guess it

doesn't matter now. Emily was everything Melinda
ever wanted in a daughter-in-law. She told her as much,
very early on. Inheritance aside, she was just easy.
Melinda wasn't the only one. My parents saw it, too.
They knew exactly what kind of life Emily could have
with you; the security a life with you could offer. Why
do you think we went on all those joint family vacations?"

"Our parents liked each other?"

Cait smiled patiently. "Of course they did. But lots
of people who like each other don't vacation together."

*Emily's parents were in cahoots with Mother? Jack had
never had a chance.*

"There was just one problem."

Jack met Cait's eyes, reading what was in them.

Harley.

His mind raced.

"Melinda and Emily had to come up with a work-
around."

As Cait's story unfolded, her voice took Jack back
in time until he was hearing her words through a
long tunnel. Finally, all the puzzle pieces fit together.

His heart slammed against his ribs. With long
strides, he headed out of the living room.

He needed to see Harley.

Now.

He was already in the doorway when he remembered the twins. Torn between the things he loved
best, he braced his arm against the doorframe and
gritted his teeth.

"Jack . . ."

Cait's voice was close behind him.

"Go to her."

He turned his head and looked at her, to be sure he'd heard her correctly.

"I'll stay here with the twins. Go to Harley . . . the one you love."

Chapter Forty-four

Harley snapped off her desk lamp and padded downstairs. She had worked until well after dark. Finally, her greeting cards were finished, her contract fulfilled.

She scooped herself a bowl of ice cream for her supper, carried it into the living room, and cocooned herself beneath a throw. Lately, she found perverse satisfaction in watching shows about women who gave birth without ever realizing they were pregnant and expectant teenagers.

When the doorbell rang repeatedly during the third episode of *17 and Pregnant*, Harley didn't even consider answering it.

She heard the door click open and footsteps. *Dad*, she thought. Mom had left for Spain and her hiking trip. She waited for him to appear.

But instead of Dad, it was Jack, wild-eyed and out of breath.

Harley licked the ice cream from her lips. "This

better be important, because Bambi's about to tell Summer she's secretly in love with her and not her baby daddy."

"It's important. It's real important."

Something about his manner made her sit up. She picked up the remote and froze the action.

He sat down next to her. "First, how are you?"

"My parents aren't baby-sitting me anymore. And I'm back to work."

"That's a good sign. Take it from someone who knows—these things take time."

"What's going on?"

Jack held out his hands and let them fall again. "I don't know where to start. I thought my future was carved in stone. I know now that I wasn't living. I was just existing. Going through the motions, ripping off the pages month after month, year after year, until my calendar was used up."

"Jack. You're not making any sense."

"I just got through talking to Cait—Emily's sister. After the parade, Mother panicked. She realized she couldn't keep me away from you, that my feelings for you were too strong.

"She took Emily into her confidence. They set up the plan for our families to go to Mexico together over Easter. Bribed the bartender to overserve me. Emily stole my room key off the bar so I'd have to spend the night in her room. You know why I don't remember having sex that night? *Because I didn't.*"

Harley couldn't think clearly. Her brain had OD'd on junk TV and it was wobbly, like Jell-O. "But the twins . . . "

"Emily didn't get pregnant until *after* we were married. The twins weren't premature after all."

Harley shook her head. "How can that be? How could they . . ."

"Cait told me. If they hadn't tricked me, I never would have married Emily. We'd probably still be together. All this time . . . wasted."

All the things Harley had blamed him for—none of them were his fault. She ignored the throw slipping off her shoulder.

"I know there were times when I took us for granted, back when we were teens. I didn't know any better then. But now I do. Now that I'm free, I want that back. I want *us* back, Harley. We have so much to catch up on. We have our whole lives ahead of us. Nothing but time."

She was still trying to absorb everything.

He brushed a strand of hair back from her face. "I love you, Harley. Don't you see? I never stopped loving you."

"I'm no traditional, soulless, hostess wife. I've always had my own identity."

"That's what I love about you. You might not be what I was looking for. But your return to Newberry was like a gift that I didn't even know I wanted but was exactly what I needed. When it comes to a place in my heart, no one else could ever compete." He took her hands in his. "It's going to take a while. I don't expect you to trust me right away. But in time, I'll make you see that you're all I ever wanted."

He studied her anxiously. "What are you thinking?"

She slipped a hand from his grasp to swipe at a

rogue tear. "Do you know how long I've waited to hear you say those words?"

"Get used to it, because you're going to be hearing a lot more of them."

He took her into his arms, squeezing her with a ferocity that took her breath away. Then he gazed into her eyes. "Marry me."

Her head spun. "What?"

"Marry me. Right now. Let's not wait another minute."

"But—"

"Let's hop a flight to Vegas."

"Jack!" She chuckled doubtfully, but it was just the kind of thing that revved her motor. He could already see her turning it over in her mind.

"What about the kids?"

"We'll take them with us! Why not?"

A laugh burst from her. "Because you never do anything spontaneously, that's why not."

"It's high time I started."

Harley rose and walked toward the fireplace, hands praying against her lips, thinking.

Jack stood, watching her every move, hoping against hope.

She turned to face him from across the room. "I always pictured myself walking down the aisle in a long white gown in front of a church filled with people, my groom's hand over mine as we cut the cake, dancing to a live orchestra . . ."

"Uh . . ." That was the last thing he'd expected her to say. "Is that really what you want?"

A grin spread across her face. She ran to him, laughing, and leaped into his arms, knocking him backward onto the couch in a cloud of feminine scent. "No, you idiot."

"Then—"

"Yes."

"Yes?"

"Yes! Let's do it. Vegas," she thrust her pointer finger to the ceiling, "here we come!"

Jack flipped her over onto her back, their eyes smiling into each other's. The whole world was wrapped up in the kiss he gave her. He reached beneath her bottom and brought her hips flush against his.

"I've missed you," Harley said.

"I've missed you more. Can you tell?"

The unmistakable evidence of his arousal prodded her lower belly. "I didn't know it was a contest," she chuckled.

But he was no longer in a laughing mood. His breathing had grown heavy. He drew his palm along the curve of her hip to her waist and slipped it between their abs into her waistband and then, lower, lazily parting her.

At the intimacy of his touch, she sucked in a breath.

"Well, I'll be," he murmured. "Seems like you might be the winner after all." He buried his nose in her hair. "What should we do about that?"

She pressed against him, forcing him up, and she stood over him. "It's too late to get a flight tonight, especially one with four seats together. Come. Let's go to bed." She took him by the hand and led him upstairs.

* * *

Twenty minutes later, Jack was lying naked between Harley's clean sheets, his shape fitted against
her hourglass curves, and she was drawing little circles between his pecs with her fingertips.

"We're going to be so happy."

His words flowed through her like a fortifying
broth, nourishing her, body and soul.

"What are we going to do about the twins, later?"
asked Harley.

Jack propped himself up on his elbow. "You're an
enigma, you know that?"

"I am?"

"I'd have laid odds you weren't thinking past deciding whether you wanted to say our vows at the
Graceland Chapel, in a gondola at the Venetian, or
in the Grand Canyon."

"As ready for this as we are, that doesn't mean the
twins are. We can't just drag them away from the estate. Their grandmother is a big part of their lives. It
wouldn't be right for them—or for her."

Jack gazed down on her. "After the way my mother's
treated you, I don't know of anyone else in the world
who would take her feelings into consideration."

"Don't get carried away. I don't exactly see Melinda
and myself relaxing at a spa day or baking cookies together."

"You're suggesting you and I live at the Victorian
without the girls?"

"You and I will have each other. As for the girls, I
would never want my stepdaughters to feel manipu-
lated into doing this or that. That would only lead to
them resenting us.

"The Victorian and the estate are within walking
distance, and even if your mother can be difficult,

she loves them. The girls have choices. Why not take advantage of that? We'll make our home a warm and welcoming refuge where they can feel free to come and go as they please, and then trust them to do what's right for them from day to day. They'll know better than anyone else."

Chapter Forty-five

The twins dragged their rolly bags out the door of the estate and down the walk, chattering excitedly about taking a helicopter ride to Tower Butte, innocently oblivious to Melinda behind them, taking in every word.

At least Jack and Harley had been compassionate enough to tell her where they were taking them.

Powerless to stop them, she followed them all the way out to Jack's truck. After Harley and the twins were seated and their doors *thunked* shut, she tried one last time to talk some sense into her son. "Jack. Are you positive this is what you want? Harley's never been anything but trouble. Starting way back with you sneaking out at night with her, and the float wreck."

Jack turned to face her. He squared his shoulders, surprising her with how much he'd matured in the past six months since they'd come home. "I don't want a type. I want Harley, with all her impulsive, reckless ways. There is no better wife, mother, or lover for me. As for what you think of her, I really don't care.

"But just so you know, Harley doesn't deserve all the blame. She didn't sneak out that night we wrecked my minibike. She had no curfew; she had no need to sneak around. And she didn't coerce *me* into sneaking out. I did it of my own volition. What's more, *I* was the one who wrecked the float, not Harley. She took the blame for me without being asked."

He reached for the truck's door handle, but Melinda stopped him with a hand on his arm.

"Wh-what's going to happen with the girls when you get back?"

"If you're worried that we'll keep them from you, that was my initial thought, too. Don't worry. Harley thought a gradual change would be better for them. Let them come and go as much as they want, at least until school gets out. After that, we'll see. Right now, I have a plane to catch."

Melinda's hand fell away from Jack's arm.

The second his truck was out of sight, she went looking for the one person she could always count on.

She found him in the vineyard, pruning and tying up trellises.

"I don't know why you're so surprised," drawled Alfred when she told him about the elopement. "Most men Jack's age don't live with their mothers. About time for him to remarry."

But despite Jack's admissions, her opinions were stubbornly fixed. She couldn't just turn on a dime. "Our family isn't like most families," Melinda snapped, blotting her eyes with a tissue.

Alfred dropped his shears. Singling out a vine, he slowly, gently bent it toward the trellis wire and, holding it in place, wrapped a length of twine around it, securing it with a knot.

"What's it going to take, Melinda?"

She stared down at his serviceable boots. "What do you mean?"

"When are you going to learn to accept people at face value?"

She didn't respond.

"I might not fit in with your country club crowd. But I care for you, even if I don't meet your standards. Standards you can't seem to let go of, even when they thwart your own happiness and that of your son."

"I—I care for you."

"You're only saying that because I put you on the spot. I've given you the last seventeen years of my life. Everyone thinks my loyalty is to the winery, but they're wrong. It's you that's kept me here, year after year. But all I am to you is someone to run to when things need fixed."

"That's not true!"

"The only things you want from me are help with business and the occasional roll in the hay. Whenever I ask you to go out in public or to my place, you close up like a liquor store in Salt Lake City on a Sunday."

A sob escaped from her. "I've thought about going out in the open with what we have. But every time I think I'm ready, I panic."

Mascara ran down her red cheeks.

Alfred pulled off his gloves and put his arms around her. "Stop crying," he said, slowly stroking her hair. "It pains me to see you like this."

When she had calmed a little, she pressed her

palm to his chest, flirtatiously fingering his shirt collar.

But Alfred was determined not to fall back into their stale pattern. Jack had taken a risk. It was time for him to take one, too.

"If you care for me like you say you do, come with me now."

"Where? I only came out here for a minute. I have things to do . . ."

"Suit yourself." Alfred picked up his gloves again.

Melinda watched him put them on and pick up his shears.

"All right."

He looked at her, standing there contritely.

"All right, then." He reached for her hand. "Let's go."

Neither Alfred nor Melinda said much in the truck.

Twenty minutes later, they drove down a long lane to an unpretentious ranch house with stone and natural wood siding and a green metal roof.

Melinda followed Alfred down the walk. It was still winter, but a few hyacinths were nosing out from the soil.

Alfred unlocked the door to his house and stood aside. "Ladies first."

She entered a spare yet tastefully decorated room with a slate-tile floor. The opposite wall was composed entirely of windows, allowing for a lot of light. She wanted to curl up on the masculine beige couch beneath one of those globe lights and never get up.

In all the years she had known Alfred, after all the

times he'd hinted at bringing her here, this was the first time she had come.

"Want to see the rest?"

She nodded.

Everything was as tidy as if he'd known he'd be bringing home a guest, though, of course, he hadn't.

When they circled back to the living room, he grabbed two apples from a wooden trencher on the dining table and said, "I'll take you to meet Dave and Petey."

Outside, Alfred's half-dozen fruit trees had been meticulously pruned. Up against one stable wall was a neat stack of firewood.

A horse, hearing them coming, clopped over and hung his head over the opening in the half door. "This is Dave," said Alfred. Producing a pocketknife, he cut the apples into slices, gave Melinda some, and fed Dave a piece.

"Hee haw."

Melinda looked at Alfred wide-eyed, a smile growing on her face.

"I didn't forget you," Alfred said, reaching through the opening.

"It's a donkey," she said, peering around him.

"Dave and Petey were brought up in the same stable. I didn't have to buy Petey when I bought Dave, but horses are herd animals. I didn't want Dave to be lonesome while I was at work."

Melinda thought of Alfred's long, long workdays. "Sometimes I forget you have a life outside work." A very peaceful, satisfying life, from the looks of it.

"I'm a simple man. I never wanted for much. Not much I need."

The apples gone, he offered Melinda first dibs to wipe her hands with his bandanna.

"Though it'd be nice if Dave and Petey'd hold up their end of the conversation a little better."

"I've been a fool, Alfred," she said stoically, blotting the corner of her eye.

Alfred tossed an arm around her shoulder companionably and they began to walk slowly back to the cabin. "Heh-heh. Show me the man—or woman—who hasn't made a mistake and I'll show you a man who's done nothing with his life."

"I thought I was doing the right thing, protecting my son. But in doing it, I wronged him. And I don't know how I can ever make it right."

Chapter Forty-six

"Careful! Don't get too close!" Jack tried to be cool about standing atop a thousand-foot sandstone monolith, but he couldn't help startling when Frankie and Freddie, holding hands, wandered toward the sheer drop-off to look out at the three hundred sixty-degree view of the desert.

Harley didn't appear a bit worried. She shielded her eyes as she peered into the sky, her long skirt blowing sideways as if there was a string tied to her hem and an invisible force was pulling on it.

"What are we waiting for?" Jack yelled nervously. The orange helicopter had set them and the officiant down ten minutes before.

"Just a little longer," said Harley.

And then Jack heard the sound of another chopper.

"That's them!" said Harley.

"Who?"

"You'll see."

A few minutes later, the chopper landed, and a couple emerged from beneath the rotors.

"Mom! Dad!" Harley ran across the butte in her cowgirl boots, holding up her kimono.

Cindy threw out her arms. "We made it, baby girl!"

Jack jogged over and caught up with Harley. "You invited your parents to our wedding?" he asked, incredulous.

"We're not guests—we're getting hitched right alongside of you," said Tucker.

"When I told Mom we were getting married overlooking the Navajo Nation, she thought she and Dad should get married, too."

"It was a sign," said Cindy, showing Jack her turquoise ring.

"How was Spain?" asked Harley.

But before she could answer, the officiant came up to them. "Are we all here now?"

"I'll tell you all about it later," replied her mother.

Jack lifted an inquiring brow at Harley. "Any more surprises?"

"Always," she laughed, brushing an untamed lock of hair from her eyes.

Chapter Forty-seven

Six months later

Jack walked through the vineyards, Alfred at his side, nibbling grapes picked here and there as he had been doing for weeks.

"Something I wanted to run past you. What's in that little barn next to the goat pen?"

"A mower and some odds and ends of tools. That's about it."

"I'm not ready to sell my bottomland yet, but because I've been spending more time with your mother, I'm looking for a closer place to keep my horse and donkey."

"The twins would go nuts. I can talk to Harley."

"That Freddie's something else on the soccer field," said Alfred. Now that he and Mother had become an acknowledged couple, he was getting to really know the twins for the first time. Alfred's easy chair and lamp had come out of the supply closet and into what had once been Don Friestatt's den.

"You got plans for Thanksgiving?" asked Alfred offhandedly.

"Not yet."

Jack didn't want to think about the upcoming holidays.

When Mother had realized the twins were able to choose where they wanted to spend their time, she had made some adjustments. She quietly researched other locations for the tourist center, finding space to lease in an existing building that would be more economically feasible in the long run.

And she had quit the country club.

But despite all the adults behaving cordially for the sake of the girls, relations between Jack and his mother were far from healed.

"It's still early," said Alfred.

"Why?" asked Jack, not meeting his eyes. "Did Mother say something?"

"Not in so many words. But I can read her mind. I can tell she's already fretting over it."

Jack held the refractometer up to his eye like a spyglass. "I think this is it. I think we've got Brix."

But when it came to deciding when to pick, Alfred had always had the last say. Jack handed Alfred a grape to try. "What do you think?"

Alfred crushed the grape in his mouth. "Don't go by what the book says. What's your gut tell you?"

Jack thought. "I feel this anticipation in the pit of my stomach. Like I'm ready to skydive."

"Or jump off the Berryessa Bridge?" asked Alfred.

"What?"

"Never mind. You've waited for this. The time has come. It's your decision."

"Let's do it," said Jack.

Alfred nodded his approval, making it official.

In October, Jack and Harley took Frankie to a modern dance performance in Portland and bought her a costume she wore for Halloween. Freddie was Wonder Woman.

In early November, Harley and the twins sat on the floor in her studio, the old comics Harley had given Freddie scattered around them.

"The whole philosophy behind altered books is to take something that already exists and change it into something new," said Harley, cutting a shape into a book.

"I can't find the one I want to use," Freddie complained. "Hey. What's this?"

Harley reached for the creased and yellowed paper printed with childish lettering. "Where did you find that?"

"Here, tucked inside this *Wonder Woman* comic."

A smile split Harley's face. "Wait till your dad sees this!"

"What is it?"

"I know where to find him," said Harley. "Let's go."

She rose and, extending one hand to each of the twins, pulled them up.

Jack and Alfred were checking the lot of grapes left unpicked during the crush. Jack saw Harley and the girls wading through the tall grass long before they reached him.

"Thought you guys were working on an art project."

"We found something," Freddie panted, handing Jack the paper.

"It's a buried treasure map!" exclaimed Frankie.

Jack's eyes met Harley's. "Where on earth'd you—"

"Stuck in one of Harley's old comics," said Freddie.

"That explains the spades," said Alfred, nodding to the shovels the girls carried.

"We're going to try to find the treasure," said Freddie. "Want to help?"

Jack looked at the map and then at their surroundings.

"If I remember right, this tree, here," he said, pointing at the map, "could be that old sycamore, over there."

He set out for a row of virgin woods that had been left standing a hundred years before, when the land had been cleared for planting filbert orchards, followed closely by the girls and, farther back, Harley and Alfred.

When they got to the tangle of trees choked with vines and thorny shrubbery, Jack scratched his head. He kicked at the newly fallen leaves, revealing layer upon layer of rich duff. "There's more than twenty years' worth of detritus here. It's going to be hard to find anything."

"Just read the map," cried Frankie. "See? Right here, where this *X* is."

"It's not that easy," said Harley. "But there's something about this spot that calls to me." She got down on her hands and knees, sunlight shining through the half-bare tree branches dappling her shoulders, and brushed away the litter until she reached bare soil. Then she stood, and with her boot, pushed her spade into the ground. Everyone watched as she dug spadeful after spadeful of dirt.

"That's not it," said Jack. "It can't be deeper than that."

"Let us try," said the girls, digging randomly.

They dug experimental, shallow holes until the ground was pockmarked. Meantime, Jack kept studying the map, turning this way and that, trying to find his bearings.

"Freddie," he called. "Try here."

Everyone gathered round as Freddie dug until she was grunting with effort.

"Here. Let me try," said Frankie. With fresh energy she shoved in her spade. Immediately, they heard a dull, metallic clink.

"Hear that? I hit something!"

"Keep digging!" shouted Freddie, joining in.

"Careful, now," said Jack. "Whatever it is, you don't want to damage it."

"I see something!" shouted Frankie.

When the curved shapes became apparent in the dark soil, the girls threw their tools aside and dug faster, using their bare hands.

"I found the treasure!" Freddie cried, holding up a spoon covered with tarnish.

"Well I'll be," said Alfred. He frowned. "Where have I seen that before?"

"I found another one!" shouted Frankie, brushing dirt off hers.

They found two more.

"You can stop now," said Jack, throwing his arm around Harley. "There were only four."

"How do you know?"

"Let me see one," said Harley. She rubbed the handle with her thumb. The dirt embedded in the engraving revealed the scrolled initial, F.

But the girls were on a roll. If they could find one treasure, maybe they could find another.

Their search took them farther and farther from the grown-ups.

"The jig is up, you two." Alfred grinned. "I remember where I've seen that pattern before. Just this morning, sticking out of my cereal bowl. Your mother must've given up getting those spoons back years ago. Can't wait to see her face when you hand 'em to her."

"Who says I'm going to give them back?" asked Jack.

"It's going on a year now," said Alfred, referring to their rift. "You can afford to meet her halfway."

"She might have made some conciliatory gestures." He and Mother still worked together, but they hadn't all sat down to a meal together since the elopement. "But there's no sign she's willing to take a step back and let me take my rightful place in the company."

He felt a light touch on his sleeve.

"Jack," said Harley, with a nod toward where the girls sat in the dirt. "Not so loud."

But though he'd managed to tamp it down, deep inside his anger still smoldered. His head whipped around to her. "How can I forgive my mother for coming *this close* to ruining my life?"

"Nothing's all bad," said Alfred. "You got your twins, don't you?"

"That doesn't fix Mother's need to control everyone and everything around her."

"How much do you know about your mother's childhood?"

Jack shrugged. "She never talked much about it. Mother was always more about looking ahead than behind."

"Did you know her parents?"

He shook his head impatiently. "She didn't have anything to do with her father. She said he abandoned the family. Her mom died right after she and Dad got married."

"They were your grandparents. Didn't you ever wonder about them?"

"That was a long time ago. What do two people I never knew have to do with what's going on now?"

"I'm about to tell you if you'll just give me a chance."

"Go ahead. I'm listening."

"Your mother grew up scrimping and scraping for everything she ever had, while all the time hearing stories of how well-off her grandparents had been."

Jack looked at Alfred blankly.

"By the look on your face, she never burdened you with that information."

"Mother has always thought she was better than everyone else."

"The truth is, it's just the opposite. Your mother grew up feeling *inferior*, not *superior*."

Alfred explained what Mother had told him about living without knowing if she would have enough food to eat from day to day. "She never told you that?"

Jack shook his head. "I still find it hard to believe."

"She developed an obsession about never being poor again, and especially, never letting what happened to her happen to you."

"That explains so much," said Harley. "The music lessons to make you well-rounded, the golf to forge connections. A business degree on top of your apprenticeship under Alfred and her."

"Don't forget her idea of the right kind of woman," said Jack.

"I know what it feels like to be an outlier," said Harley. "Here come the girls. They must have fizzled out. I'll take them home now. See you two later."

Chapter Forty-eight

Two of the twins' chores included bringing the mail up from the mailbox down on the road and taking care of the animals.

"Here you are," said Frankie before running back outside to the goat pen.

"Anything interesting?" asked Jack from where he stood on a ladder, screwing a light bulb into the ceiling.

Harley ripped open an envelope made of heavy white card stock. "Your sister-in-law's getting married in June in Portland," she read, leaning against the counter. "We're invited."

"Cait." Jack looked down from his ladder. "Good for her."

"And . . ." She slit open the next envelope and pulled out the enclosed card. "We are cordially invited to the home of Mrs. Melinda Friestatt and Mr. Alfred Ricasoli for Thanksgiving dinner. Répondez s'il vous plaît."

"I think we should go," said Harley.

"I still don't know how you managed to just brush off everything Mother did to you."

"Melinda has no power to hurt me anymore."

"As long as she holds the reins of the company, she still controls me."

"She's your mother, Jack."

When Jack and his family arrived at the estate on Thanksgiving Day, their coats were taken by a member of the catering staff.

The girls went immediately to Alfred, watching football on TV.

"I'd almost forgotten how stuffy this place is," Jack said under his breath.

"Shh," replied Harley. "It's just one dinner."

Harley glanced across the room at where the twins were talking animatedly to Alfred and smiled contentedly.

"Jack. Harley. I'm so glad you came." Melinda leaned into Harley and gave her an air kiss.

Then it was Jack's turn.

Harley's elbow poked him in the ribs.

"I brought you something." He handed his mother the simple white box tied with twine.

"How lovely." She passed it to a servant standing behind her. "I'll open it later."

"No—open it now."

Melinda raised an eyebrow. "If you insist." Taking the box back, she pulled on the twine and lifted the lid. In the light of the hall chandelier, the newly polished silver shone. She gasped as her hand flew to her pearls. She picked up a spoon and examined the monogram. "Jack! My spoons. Where did you ever—"

"Don't ask. Just take them and be happy."

"I've been searching for those spoons for years! Now I have a full set again."

"Anyone up for throwing the pigskin around?" asked Alfred, tossing a football in his hands.

"Ew. Is that what footballs are made of—pigskin?" asked Frankie.

"Just an old turn of phrase," said Tuck, setting his hand on Frankie's shoulder and nudging her toward the door.

A half hour later, Harley stumbled away from the action, clutching her side. "You guys keep playing," she puffed. "I need a break."

"Side stitch," yelled Jack, as confident of his diagnosis as if he had an MD behind his name.

"I'm out, too," panted Mom, following Harley across the close-cropped lawn.

"You okay, honey?"

"Fine. Never could run."

"You can thank your dad's genes for that," said Mom.

They fell into cushioned lawn chairs, trying to catch their breath.

Harley couldn't help but notice Griffin galloping around the yard, pretending to be part of the game. He was going on two now.

Angelique would be almost one, thought Harley. She wondered where she was today . . . what she looked like. After all this time, she had begun to let go of the hope that she would ever have a baby of her own.

As always when that sinking feeling threatened to

swamp her, Harley reminded herself of her many blessings. "I got another nice royalty check yesterday," she said proudly.

She hadn't gone back to the club after losing the baby. And as for the B and B, the twins had claimed two of her guest rooms after they had turned twelve and decided they wanted rooms of their own, and she'd converted the nursery into a place for them to study—though she couldn't bring her self to repaint the blue walls.

"Good for you. That's wonderful."

"I was thinking. If you get tired of cleaning houses, maybe I could help you out a little, so you don't have to."

"That's awful sweet of you. It's not much, but as long as I still have the energy, I kinda like making my own money." She sighed, and gazed around at the manicured grounds. "Feels weird not cooking on Thanksgiving. I asked Melinda if I could help, but the whole meal's catered."

"I'm just hoping Jack will be able to relax enough to eat without getting indigestion," chuckled Harley.

"Hey. You got him to show up, didn't you? Baby steps."

"Is this *real* silver?" Cindy whispered to Harley as they scooted into their chairs.

"How are your dance lessons going?" Mother asked Frankie.

Under the table, Jack kicked Harley and grinned. She had been the one to scout them out.

"Good! We have a recital in the spring. Maybe you can come."

"I wouldn't miss it."

"Please pass the turkey," Frankie asked Jack.

He arched a brow as he handed her the platter.

"Don't worry. Mimi promised me this turkey lived a happy life eating grass and bugs and crickets."

"Mmm." Jack looked around the table, daring anyone to disagree.

"Freddie tell you she was picked for the all-star team?" Tucker asked Alfred. Those two had hit it off like gangbusters.

"Don't you miss playing piano?" Mother interjected.

"Hm-mm," she said, shaking her head, her mouth full of mashed potatoes.

The entire meal was like that—the adults making forced conversation over the kids' heads. Somehow they made it through the main course.

Melinda tapped her water glass with her spoon. "Could I have everyone's attention? Before dessert is served, there's something I'd like to say."

Jack sighed and shifted his weight. All that was left was coffee and pie, and then they could hightail it out of there until the next holiday rolled around.

"Thirty years ago, I married Don Friestatt believing we would both live forever. Isn't that what we all think, starting out? But only thirteen years later, I found myself faced with parenting a teenage son and running a burgeoning wine business, alone."

Freddie yawned.

"I've made my share of mistakes throughout the years. If I took the time to list them all, we would be eating our pumpkin pie at midnight."

Cindy gazed around at the well-appointed dining

room, Tuck coughed behind his hand, and Alfred twiddled his dessert spoon.

"Suffice it to say that there are two people—" She nodded at Jack. "Two *men*—who never left my side.

"Alfred. Your loyalty has been obvious in everything you do. Your commitment to excellence has propelled our company forward by leaps and bounds. Without you, I don't know where we'd—where *I'd* be today."

Alfred bowed his head humbly.

"And my dear son, Jack."

What was this? Jack braced himself for more empty platitudes.

"We've been through a lot together, haven't we—"

To Jack's surprise, he saw tears spring to his mother's eyes.

"—the good, the bad and everything in between? It's taken me a while, but I've come to recognize and value your unique perspective in business and in life. This was your first year in deciding when to harvest, and your timing couldn't have been better. All signs point to this vintage being our best ever.

"And so, I'd like to announce that starting today, I am promoting you to CEO of Arabella Cellars. Not that I'm going anywhere." She held up a finger. "No such luck. But you've proved that it's time for me to step aside and let you take the lead." She raised her wineglass. "I wish you every success."

Murmurs of "hear, hear," were heard around the table as glasses clinked. Harley started the applause, the others joining in.

When they got back to Honeymoon Haven, the girls ran ahead of them.

Jack slung his arm around Harley and gave her a companionable squeeze. He tilted his head, and into her ear, he said, "I give ye fair warning . . . Captain Jack is bound to plunder ye tonight."

She was in a sentimental mood. She laid her head on his shoulder as they walked. "It hasn't been easy for us, has it?"

"Aye, lass, but it's been worth it. You know how 'tis with us. The rougher the seas, the smoother we sail. Ye make me feel like I'm seventeen again. Ahoy!" With a grunt, he swept her off her feet to a squeal. Then he carried her over the threshold where he set her on her feet, tossed his coat across the back of the couch, and headed toward his favorite chair.

"I think I'll go upstairs and rest for a little while," she said.

He frowned. "You look a little pale. Are you okay?"

She smiled softly. "Just tired."

Sometime later, he was startled awake from his post-feast nap by the soft pad of footsteps. He blinked to see Harley come into the room. Frankie was still curled up on the couch, and Freddie lay on the floor, reading a comic.

"Must have dozed off for a minute." He stretched and yawned. "Feeling any better?"

Silver glinted in her palm. Suddenly he was wide-awake. "What's that?" he asked, fingers of dread creeping over him. Had the holidays triggered a bout of grief? They'd already had enough heartache to last a lifetime.

Frankie glanced up from her book. "That's the rattle we got her for Christmas."

Her hand on her flat stomach, Harley flashed a

Mona Lisa smile. "There's a chance it might come in handy after all."

Jack sprang to his feet. He took her by the arms, every fiber of his being on alert. "Cramps," he said, chills shooting down his spine. "You have cramps."

Freddie and Frankie turned as crimson as the chair Mrs. Grimsky had left behind.

"I just remembered I have homework." Freddie scrambled to her feet and hurried past them.

"Er, time to feed the goats," said Frankie, and she was gone, too.

Harley floated into Jack's embrace. For a moment he rocked her gently from side to side. Then he pulled back and gazed downward, his eyes melting into hers. "I love you, Harley." He swallowed, tasting salt water. "Always have, always will."

Love Heather Heyford?

Then be sure to check out the other books in

The Willamette Valley series

THE SWEET SPOT

And

FIRST COMES LOVE

And read her other series

The Napa Wine Valley Heiresses

and

The Oregon Wine Country Romances!

Available now wherever books are sold